* * * * * * *

"First of all, I want to assure you that what I want you to do is nothing illegal. It is in the realm of what an investigator usually does. It will not jeopardize your investigator's license. I believe that is something that concerns you?"

"Yes, it does, and I'm glad to know that," I said, then waited for him to continue.

"It is very important that your investigation is kept quiet. If the wrong people should find out before the investigation is completed, it could be a problem for a certain individual who holds a high office in government. It could also be a big problem for me. I need someone who can investigate an individual without his knowing it. That is why I need someone like you, someone who doesn't have any connection to government."

"Are you going to tell me who it is you want me to investigate, or do I have to guess?"

* * * * * * *

Other titles by J.E. Terrall

Western Short Stories
  The Old West
  The Frontier
  Untamed Land
  Tales from the Territory

Western Novels
  Conflict in Elkhorn Valley
  Lazy A Ranch (A Modern
    Western)
  The Story of Joshua Higgins

Romance Novels
  Balboa Rendezvous
  Sing for Me
  Return to Me
  Forever Yours

Mystery/Suspense/Thriller
  I Can See Clearly
  The Return Home
  The Inheritance

Nick McCord Mysteries
  Vol – 1 Murder at Gill's Point
  Vol – 2 Death of a Flower
  Vol – 3 A Dead Man's Treasure
  Vol – 4 Blackjack, A Game to Die For
  Vol – 5 Death on the Lakes
  Vol – 6 Secrets Can Get You Killed

Peter Blackstone Mysteries
  Murder in the Foothills
  Murder on the Crystal Blue
  Murder of My Love

Frank Tidsdale Mysteries
  Death by Design

DEATH BY ASSASSINATION

A Frank Tidsdale Mystery

by

J.E. Terrall

ISBN: 978-0-9916232-5-9

This is a work of fiction. Names, characters, and incidents are either a product of the author's imagination or are used fictitiously, and any resemblance to actual persons, living or dead, is purely coincidental.

Printed in the United States of America
First Printing / 2014 – wwwcreatspace.com

Cover: by J.E. Terrall

Book Layout/
Formatting: J.E. Terrall
               Custer, South Dakota

DEATH BY ASSASSINATION

A Frank Tidsdale Mystery

To
Jene Campbell,
Thank you for your support.

CHAPTER ONE

It was getting on toward noon when I got up from my desk and walked over to the window. I leaned against the window frame and looked out for no particular reason. There was nothing going on outside of any real interest. It was a bright and sunny day, the kind of day that should make a person want to be outside. Yet, there were only a few people walking along the sidewalk enjoying the nice weather.

I had just finished writing checks to pay my bills and had them ready to mail. I was thinking about my expenses and hoping I would find a new client pretty soon – a paying client, that is.

My thoughts were suddenly disturbed by someone knocking on my door. I turned around and found a good-looking man leaning against my doorjamb. He was wearing a nice dark blue business suit and a red striped tie. His arms were folded in front of him and he was smiling at me. It was none other than Robert Patrick Greene, the state's Attorney General.

"What brings you to my humble office?"

"Oh, I just thought you might like to take on a job for me," he said casually.

"Really?"

"Really. I need a good investigator who can keep his mouth shut. I happen to know that you are both good, and you can keep your mouth shut."

"I'm glad I have that kind of a reputation, I think," I said with a grin. "Grab yourself a cup of coffee, then sit down and tell me why the Attorney General needs a private investigator when he has several rather good ones in his office?"

AG Greene walked over to the small table in the corner of my office where I have the coffee machine. I watched him as he picked up a cup and filled it with coffee. He seemed hesitant to say anything, or maybe he was simply trying to think of what he should say. I wasn't sure which, so I decided to give him as much time as he needed to get his thoughts together.

"First of all, I want to assure you that what I want you to do is nothing illegal. It is within the realm of what an investigator usually does and will not jeopardize your investigator's license. I believe that is something that concerns you?"

"Yes, it does, and I'm glad to know that," I said, then waited for him to continue.

"It is very important that your investigation is kept quiet. If the wrong people should find out before the investigation is completed, it could be a problem for a certain individual who holds a high office in government. It could also be a big problem for me. I need someone who can investigate an individual without his knowing it. That is why I need someone like you, someone who doesn't have any connection to government."

"Are you going to tell me who it is you want me to investigate, or do I have to guess?"

"I want you to investigate Judge Marcus Eugene Weatherby."

"You weren't kidding when you said it was someone holding a high office in government. He's the senior judge on the bench in criminal court, and he has a lot of influence in this state."

"You are right about that. Maybe now you can see why it's important that your investigation be done with the greatest discretion."

"Yes, but why him? What is it you think I will find?"

"I'm hoping you don't find anything because I have a great deal of respect for him. That having been said, I'm afraid you will. Right now, it's just some of the things I've heard, or I should say, have overheard. Rumors, if you will. But the rumors appear to have some merit."

"Can you give me more to go on?" I asked.

"Not at the moment. I want you to look into his practices as a judge. I don't want any connection between us to become public. I don't want anything you find to leak out just in case what I've heard is not true."

"Do you think he's dirty?" I asked.

"I don't know, but that is what I want you to find out."

"Come on. You have to give me a little something to go on," I said. "You're not here because of a few rumors. You have to have more than rumors to go to the trouble of hiring me to look into it."

"Just do an in-depth investigation into him and his finances. Find the truth about him."

"The truth always interests me. Okay, I'll give it my best shot," I assured him.

"I'll give you my secure phone number where you can contact me at any time. Never call me on my home or office phones."

"Why all the cloak-and-dagger stuff? Do you have a mole in your office?"

"Yes, at least I think so. Unfortunately, I think this whole thing will spill over into my office. During your investigation, you may find others in the criminal court system who are involved. I want to know who they are as well. I'll send you more information in the morning by courier."

"Okay. Since I might find I'm being watched, we'll use cell phones to keep in touch. Don't come to my office again or call here," I suggested.

"Good idea. By the way, I have an envelope for you. If you need more, let me know," he said as he stood up.

He reached into his inside coat pocket, and took out a large white business envelope. I stood up and reached across my desk. He handed the envelope to me. I took the envelope, then watched him as he turned and walked out of my office.

As soon as he walked out of the door, I sat back down and opened the envelope. Inside was five thousand dollars in cash. I looked at the money, then looked toward the door. I wondered what I had gotten myself into. That kind of money usually meant I was going to have to work hard to earn it.

It was mid-afternoon when a large black sedan drove up in front of a small café in the downtown district of Denver. There were three men in the car. Two of the men got out of the car and walked toward the door of the café, while the third man remained in the car with the engine running. All the men were wearing black clothing from head to foot, and had full black beards and dark sunglasses.

The first man to go inside the café was carrying a black attaché case. He went to a table just to the left of the door, sat down, then carefully slid the attaché case under the table. He did it while looking around the room to make sure no one was watching him.

The second man entered the café only a moment or so after the first. After stepping inside the café, he stopped and began looking around the room. There were not very many people in the café at that hour. There were several tables scattered around the middle of the room. Only three tables had anyone sitting at them. There were four people sitting at one, three at another and one woman sitting at a table by herself. There was a row of old-fashion high-backed booths along one wall with only one of them occupied. It was occupied by a man wearing a suit.

The second bearded man to enter the café was clearly looking for someone. It wasn't until he looked at the booths that he saw anyone of interest to him.

The man in a booth had his back to the front door and had not seen either of the two men enter the café. He was busy looking over several papers spread out on the table in front of him. He seemed to be studying them very carefully.

The second man to enter the cafe slowly walked toward the man sitting in the booth. As he approached the booth, he drew a pistol from his coat pocket and held it close to his side. When he was only a few feet from the man in the booth, he pointed his gun at the man's head.

The man in the booth turned around and looked up. The man in black shot the man in the head before he could even react. When the man slumped over the table, the man in black took a step closer and shot his victim again in the back of the head at very close range. He then turned and fired several shots into the ceiling.

"Everyone down on the floor, face down," he yelled.

He fired a couple more shots into the ceiling of the café as a way to hurry those he thought were moving too slowly. As soon as everyone was on the floor, he reached inside the dead man's suit coat and removed his wallet. He then turned and headed for the door.

The man with the attaché case reached down and hooked his finger in a small ring attached to a short string. He pulled the ring on the side of the attaché case, then stood up. Both of the men in black hurried out of the building and jumped into the car, which immediately sped away. The car had no more than turned the corner at the end of the block when the attaché case exploded, leaving most of the café in shambles. The explosion started a fire.

It was only a matter of five minutes before the first police car arrived on the scene. The fire department arrived shortly after the police. It took the fire department only about fifteen minutes to put the fire out and clear out the smoke. When the smoke had cleared, they check the café to make sure it was safe to enter the building.

Several ambulances had arrived on the scene by the time the fire was out. The firemen where carrying the victims out of the building. The dead were laid out on the ground and covered with sheets, except one.

There were four who had survived the explosion and the shooting. They were placed on stretchers and rushed to a local hospital for treatment.

CHAPTER TWO

It was just shortly after noon when Green left my office. I was feeling a bit hungry so I went to a small café located on the ground floor of the building. I picked out a booth in a corner and sat down.

While I waited for the waitress, I took a small notebook out of my coat pocket. I didn't write any names in it, but I did write down a few things I thought would be good to know about the person I was to investigate.

After looking at the list, I decided the best place to start was at the public library. The public library would provide me with some basic information about state judges.

I finished my lunch, then drove to the library. I arrived at the library about ten minutes later. There were not many people in the library at that time of day. There was a small group of about nine or ten children and a few adults sitting on large pillows on the floor. A middle aged woman in the costume of a queen or fairy princess was sitting on a chair reading a story to the children. I smiled as I walked by. It was nice to see that the kids were being introduced to the joy of reading and to the library.

I went to the research section of the library and sat down at one of the computers. I typed in "state government". Not being a computer whiz, I was sure it would take me awhile to find what I was looking for. With much searching and mentally wondering what the hell I was doing there, I finally discovered the file labeled "employment information". I clicked on it and waited. It came up with a bunch of categories. I clicked on the one that said "salaries". It brought up a list of all the different positions of state employees over the entire state. It did not give the salaries of the individual employees, but listed the salary ranges for each position in state government.

I must have spent close to fifteen minutes running through the different categories of state employees before I got to judges. When I highlighted the category of state judges, I found a fairly wide range of wages for the different classifications of judges. Since the judge I was interested in was a senior judge with a lot of years on the bench, I took the highest amount of income a judge in that category would make. I wrote it down in my notebook and put it in my pocket.

The next thing was to find out what he owed and to whom. I looked around to see if anyone was watching me. I didn't see anyone. I thought for a moment as I stared at the computer monitor. I wasn't sure it was a good idea to run a credit check on the judge from a computer that might not be very secure, especially a computer that was part of the state system.

The more I thought about it, the more I thought that if I was to find out if any of the other judges under him might be involved, I would have to run a number of credit reports. If I ran too many of them at once, someone might get the idea I was just a little too interested in the local judges, and would want to know why I was going to need some help with this, and I knew just the guy to help. It was time to go back to my office and call my friend.

I cleared off the computer of any information that would let anyone know what site I had visited. I left the library and walked out to my car. A quick look at my watch told me it was getting on toward dinner time. I could see no reason to go back to my office. I could go home and place my call from there.

Don Wright, a Denver Police Department Detective with the Homicide Division, was the first detective on the scene of the explosion in the café. He arrived shortly after the fire had been put out. He took a minute to talk to the fire chief in an effort to find out what had happened.

"We have five dead and four injured," Chief Miller said. "One of the dead was shot in the head."

"Shot in the head?" Don said surprised to hear it.

"Yeah. One of the survivors told us a man came in the café and shot the man sitting in a booth twice in the head. Since it was obviously murder, and we had the fire under control rather quickly, and there was no more danger of something happening to the body, we didn't move it. We were sure you would want to see it before we took it out and sent it to the morgue."

"Thanks. Was your witness able to give any idea as to why the man was shot?"

"No. He was in pretty bad shape. We were lucky to get as much out of him as we did."

"Were you able to get a description of the shooter?" Don asked hopefully.

"No. Like I said, he was in pretty bad shape. I hope he makes it, but I have my doubts."

"I hope he makes it, too. Where were the injured taken?"

"Denver General. I think all of the survivors were taken there. It's the closest hospital," Chief Miller said.

"Thanks. Is it safe to go in?"

"Yeah. Just be careful where you walk. There's a lot of rubble on the floor. One other thing, if the explosion was supposed to cover up the shooting, it didn't work very well. The booths in this old café helped keep the force of the

explosion to the front of the café. Except for the man who was murdered, the rest of them were pretty close to the explosion."

Don looked at the chief for a moment, nodded, then turned and went into the café. Once inside, he stopped and looked around at the destruction. It didn't take him but a couple of seconds to find the murder victim's body. It was still slumped over the table in the booth.

On the table were several pieces of paper. A few of them were burned, but there were several small pieces with writing on them that survived the blast and the fire. They had not been completely destroyed in the fire, or by the water used to put the fire out. He would have to wait until the forensic people got finished and the lab had a chance to look at them before he would know what was written on the paper. He only hoped the lab would be able to get something from them.

Don Wright was looking at the shooting victim when the forensic team arrived on the scene. It was clear the victim had been assassinated. Two shots to the head at close range with what appeared to have been a large caliber gun was a sure sign of it. There was no way he could identify the man by looking at him.

Don not only wondered who the victim was, but he wondered why the victim had been shot twice, either shot would have killed him instantly. The only reason he could think of was to send a message to someone, someone who would have known the dead man.

"What do you have, Don?"

The man who had just walked up behind Don was Melvin Street, the lead forensic investigator. He had a large black case in his hand.

Don glanced over his shoulder before he spoke. "Hi, Mel. It looks like a hit. This guy took two to the head at close range. You'll need fingerprints to figure out who he was."

"At least we can get fingerprints from him. You think the explosion was to cover it up?"

"That would be my guess, but it didn't do a very good job of it. These old hardwood booths took up a lot of the force of the explosion. That and the fact the bomb was some distance away from the booth. It looks like the explosion was centered near the door," Don said as he pointed toward the door. "It was probably set off there to keep anyone who survived the blast from getting out."

"You're probably right," Mel said as he looked toward the door.

"I don't know if all this paper stuff on the table has anything to do with why he was killed, but gather up all you can and see if you can make anything out of it. It would be nice to know who this guy was and why he was assassinated."

"You'll know everything we can find out about him and this place. If there's anything here that can help, we'll find it," Mel said confidently.

"How about some fingerprints on a cartridge casing or two? That would help a lot."

"I'm sure it would. If it's there, we'll find it," Mel said with a slight nod of his head.

"Good. I'm going over to the hospital and see what I can find out from the four survivors of the explosion."

Mel just nodded, then began to look around. He was giving instructions to his forensic investigators as Don left the café.

CHAPTER THREE

As I headed for home for the evening, my mind was filled with thoughts of my conversation with Greene. Maybe better put, my mind was filled with speculations on what I might have gotten myself into. By the time I got home, I had decided how I was going to proceed with my investigation.

When I drove into the parking lot of my apartment building, I noticed the lights were on in my apartment. I smiled. I was sure Jackie had come over. I wasn't sure if she had come to stay the night or just to fix me one of her special meals. Either way, it would be nice to see her.

Jackie and I had been friends for a very long time, but we had been dating seriously only for the past year or so. She had a body that was as nice as any of the Victoria Secret models. She was one of the sexist women I had ever known, and she was smart, too.

I parked my car and went into my apartment. She greeted me at the door wearing a flowered apron over dark colored slacks and a light colored blouse. Jackie looked very good, and very domestic.

"Hi," she said as she leaned close to me and gave me a kiss on the cheek.

"Hi. What brings you here?"

"The manager of my apartment is having my carpet cleaned so I thought I would come over and make you dinner."

"Is that all?" I asked.

"No. I thought I would stay the night, if you don't mind," she replied with a sexy grin.

"I don't mind, but aren't you glad I didn't bring home some sexy gal to spend the night with me?"

"Now, why would you do that when you can have me anytime you want me?" she asked with a slight chuckle in her voice and a big grin on her face.

"You have a point there. When do we eat?"

"In about ten minutes. Why don't you relax?"

I kissed her lightly on the lips, then went into the bedroom while she went back to the kitchen. I hung my sport coat in the closet and put my gun on the top shelf before returning to the living room. I walked over to the door to the kitchen and leaned against the doorjamb. Watching her as she did her thing in the kitchen was always a pleasure. Just watching her was a pleasure.

We spent the next little while talking about her day and what she had been doing while she finished getting dinner ready. When dinner was ready, she put it on the table. We sat down to enjoy a very good meal. One thing about Jackie was that with all her other assets, she was also a darn good cook.

After dinner, we went into the living room to watch a movie on television. Jackie curled up against me during the movie. When it was over, I turned to the news. It came on with the news anchor talking about a local café that apparently had had a fire. He was using the café as his backdrop.

"We are told that the café had an explosion this afternoon. Five people died and four were seriously injured in the explosion. It was first believed to have been a gas explosion, but one of our sources told us it was not a gas explosion, but an explosion caused by some kind of explosive device that went off inside the café. It was most likely a pipe bomb," he said with an air of authority.

"We talked to a man who would not agree to appear on camera. He said he saw two men all dressed in black run out of the café and jump into a big black car just before the bomb went off. We have not been able to confirm his story with the police. The police are keeping very quiet about what happened here," the news anchor reported.

The anchor stood looking into the camera for a moment before it went to a commercial. It was apparent there was nothing else for him to report on the explosion. Probably because there was not much known by the time he went on air.

My mind turned to thoughts of what I would be getting from Greene in the morning. Since I had no idea what it would be, I was hoping that whatever it was, it would give me some sense of direction.

"What's the matter?" Jackie asked as she looked at me.

"Ah, nothing. I was just thinking about something. It's not important. I guess I'm a little tired."

"Does that mean you are ready to go to bed?" she asked with a smile.

"Yes, but I would like a shower first."

"I'll take one with you, if you don't mind."

"I never mind showering with you."

I stood up, took her hand and led her to the bathroom. It didn't take us long to get out of our clothes and into the shower. After a warm shower along with some serious necking, we dried off and climbed into bed.

Jackie was a very passionate woman. It was a long time before our need for each other dwindled and we drifted off to sleep. I have to admit, I did enjoy the time from when we took a shower until we fell asleep in each others' arms.

Don got in his car and headed to Denver General Hospital. It wasn't a very long drive, but it gave Don time to think about what had happened at the café. For someone to cause an explosion in a café where there were innocent people was one way to send a clear message to someone. The one thing that was clear, whoever set off the bomb didn't care one bit about collateral damage.

When Don got to the hospital, he went directly to the emergency ward. It was very quiet. He wondered if any of the victims were still there or if they had been taken to some other ward. He walked to the admission desk and asked the woman where the victims had been taken.

"I'm Detective Wright with the police department. Can you tell me where I might find someone who can tell me the condition of the four survivors of the bombing at a downtown café?"

"They have been taken to ICU, except one. One of them was taken directly to surgery. He is in surgery now, but I don't know which one of the survivors it was."

"Who can tell me their condition?"

"The doctor in ICU. That would be on the second floor."

"Thank you," Don said, then headed for the second floor.

When Don got to the ICU, he was stopped by a nurse just outside the ward. Don identified himself and showed his badge and ID.

"Can you tell me how the victims from the café bombing are doing?" he asked.

"One of them is currently in surgery. I've been told he is not likely to survive the surgery, but it was their only chance to save him. The others are in no condition to talk to anyone. Their condition is listed as "Grave".

"All four of them?"

"I'm afraid so," the nurse said.

Don thanked the nurse for her report. It was obvious that there was nothing he could do tonight. The forensic team wouldn't have anything for him until morning. All the witnesses he knew about apparently had little chance of living long enough to tell him anything.

All he could do at the moment was to hope that at least one of them would live long enough to tell him something that would be helpful. It was time to go home and try to get some rest and hit it again in the morning. Don left the hospital and drove home.

CHAPTER FOUR

I woke much earlier than I had planned. The clock on the nightstand showed it was six-fifteen. Jackie was still sleeping. Although I had my back to her, I could hear her slow steady breathing. I thought about getting up, but decided I would not disturb her just yet. I rolled over on my back as quietly as I could and laid there looking up at the ceiling.

My mind was cluttered with thoughts of yesterday. I knew that investigating someone like Judge Weatherby would not be easy. It would be difficult to find anything on him. He seemed to be a rather smart man, not one who could easily be fooled. I would have to be very careful who I talked to about him. There was nothing I could do until I received the information from Greene.

My mind turned to thoughts of the bombing of the downtown café. It briefly crossed my mind that it might have had something to do with my investigation, but I couldn't see how. How would a bombing of a café be connected to a man like Judge Weatherby?

I knew the café was within a few blocks of the courthouse, and some of the people working in the courthouse would probably visit the café from time to time. There were also several other buildings near the café where government agencies had offices.

Although the bombing of businesses was not something that happens every day in Denver, I could only think of two possibilities. It was either a terrorist attack, which didn't seem impossible. Yet, bombing a small café at a time when there were very few people in it didn't seem to make much sense if it was a terrorist attack.

With the rather vague description of the two men who ran out of the café just before the explosion, it was certainly a possibility. If it was a terrorist attack, then why that small café? What was it about that café that would make someone want to blow it up?

It was possible that it was gang related. Maybe the owner of the café pissed off some lowlife who was simply getting his revenge. We have some pretty nasty gangs in the Denver area, some capable of killing innocent people just to make a point.

Then there was the possibility it was one of the crime families trying to make a point or send a message. It was certainly not unheard of for a crime family to be into extortion. It was also possible that one crime family was attacking another and used the bombing to make it clear they didn't care who got hurt or killed in the process.

I knew I was running a lot of different scenarios through my head with nothing much to go on, but it had always been something I did when I had so little information. It often helped me to think ahead. As a result, I was not often surprised when I finally discovered what was really going on, or what I was up against.

Just as I was turning my attention to the investigation Greene had hired me to do, my thoughts were suddenly interrupted by movement next to me. I turned my head and looked over to find Jackie looking at me. I smiled at her and she smiled back.

"You ready to get up?"

"No," she said softly. "I thought maybe you would like to spend a little time with me."

Now that was an offer I had no desire to turn down. I smiled as I rolled over next to her. I took her in my arms and pulled her gently up against me while she wrapped her arms around my neck. I don't know how long we spent kissing and touching each other, or how much time we spent making love to each other. I do know it didn't seem like it was long enough.

Jackie was the most loving woman I had ever known. After we had made love to each other, she curled up against me with her head on my shoulder. We lay in each other's arms for several minutes enjoying our closeness before either of us spoke.

"I would love to spend the entire day right here with you, but I really have to go to work," Jackie said with a hint of disappointment in her voice.

I slid my hand down her side to her hip. She was so soft and warm, yet her body seemed firm. I could certainly understand her desire to want to spend the day in bed together. It was not a very practical idea, but one that brought thoughts of much pleasure to mind.

"I would like that, too, but I have things to do today as well. Besides, I need to get something to eat. I'm starving after last night and this morning."

"I am, too," she admitted with a grin.

"I'm going to take a shower, then I'll make breakfast while you shower."

"Don't you want me to shower with you?" she asked softly.

"Yes, but if we do, we might very well find ourselves back in bed."

"I see your point," she said with a grin.

After a rather passionate kiss, I got up and headed for the bathroom. After a short but warm shower, I dressed while Jackie was in the bathroom. Jackie joined me in the kitchen just as I finished putting breakfast on the table.

After breakfast, I walked Jackie out to her car and saw her off to work. I then got in my car and drove to the office.

Don Wright walked into his office at five minutes after seven. He knew there was little chance he would have anything more than the preliminary report of the forensic team's findings, if that. He was hoping he would have something, anything that would give him a place to start his investigation. He had not been in his office for more than about fifteen minutes when someone knocked on his door.

"Come in," Don said, then sat back to see who had knocked.

A young officer stepped into his office and handed Don an envelope. Don took the envelope and opened it while the officer stood by waiting to see if Don wanted to reply. Don found a preliminary report on the forensic team's findings at the café in the envelope. He turned and looked at the officer.

"Thank you. You may go."

"Excuse me, sir, but did you see the news last night?"

"No. As a matter of fact, I didn't."

"Well, sir, I watched the news. The news anchor was talking about the café bombing downtown. He said there was a witness who saw two men all dressed in black leaving the café just before the explosion."

"You're kidding?"

"No, sir. That's what the reporter said."

"What station?"

"I believe it was channel three, sir."

"Thank you."

Don looked at his watch. It was still early. He decided he would call the hospital to see if he could find out the condition of the survivors of the bombing. He picked up the phone and placed a call to Denver General Hospital. Don was able to find out that the person who had been in surgery died on the operating table. He was also told that the other *three survivors were still comatose, and it was not looking good for any of them.*

That was a big disappointment. Don had been hoping that the one who had gone to surgery would survive. As far as Don knew, he was the only survivor who had apparently seen the shooter up close. He could only hope one of the other three survivors would be able to tell him something that would help him find those who had bombed the café, and who shot the one shooting victim.

At this time, he had but one other witness who might be able to shed some light on who was responsible for the bombing. It was time to head out to the television station to find the reporter who had interviewed a witness that may have seen the bombers.

Don knew there was a good chance that the so called "witness" was a fake, or it was some story made up by the reporter to help with their ratings. There was always the possibility it was some jerk who was trying to get his fifteen minutes of fame, but that didn't seem likely because he would not allow his face to be seen on television. No matter what it was, he still had to check it out.

Don glanced at the preliminary forensic report, but it could wait. He wanted to interview the person who talked to the news reporter, but not the police, about what he saw just before the bomb went off. Don left his office, went to his car and headed to the television station. He only hoped he didn't get some run around from the television station or its legal department.

CHAPTER FIVE

I arrived at my office just a little after eight in the morning. I sat down at my desk and started planning out my day. The first thing I had to do was to take a look at the information I had gotten at the library. I began examining the information, but I had no idea what its value was to my investigation.

My thoughts were interrupted by a knock on the door. I stood up and went to the door. When I opened the door there was a courier with a big yellow envelope with a string tied around it in his hands.

"I have an envelope for Mr. Frank Tidsdale," the young man said.

"I'm Frank Tidsdale," I replied, then reached for the envelope.

"I'm sorry, sir," he said as he pulled back. "I was told to get some kind of identification before I hand it over. I'm sure you understand."

"Certainly."

He stood there watching me as I took my driver's license out of my wallet and showed it to him. He looked at it, then smiled before he handed me the envelope. I took a couple of bucks out of my wallet and gave them to him. He thanked me, then turned and walked away.

I went back into my office, locking the door behind me. I had no desire to be interrupted while looking over what had been sent to me.

I placed the envelope on the desk, and examined it to make sure that the seal had not been tampered with. It didn't appear to have been opened.

I cut off the end of the envelope with a very sharp knife. Once I had it opened, I looked inside. All I could see was a stack of standard typing paper and a large business envelope that was shaped as if it might have money in it. That surprised me a little since Greene had already given me a retainer.

I dumped the contents of the yellow envelope out on the desk. I opened the business envelope and found another five thousand dollars in cash. On the band around the bills was a note that simply read, "Balance of retainer".

Now, ten thousand dollars for a retainer was nothing to sneeze at. It was a good size retainer by any stretch of the imagination. I began to wonder what I was going to have to do to earn that kind of money. Few of my cases brought anywhere near that amount of money.

I picked up the stack of papers and began to read. The information had more details about what Greene wanted me to do. The papers stated he was looking into Judge Weatherby because he had information from an unknown source that Weatherby was taking bribes from one of the city's crime bosses. The information stated Greene had no idea who the crime boss might be. There were some indications, according to the letter, that there might be other court employees involved as well, but they were currently unknown.

The letter laid out what Greene was hoping I could find out, namely who the others involved were, if any, and to what extent the criminal activity went within the criminal court system. He wanted names, dates and what was done; who was getting payoffs and what those involved had to do to get the payoffs.

I had no idea how I was going to get all the information Greene wanted, but I had some ways of finding out things about people. In this case, it looked as if I needed to follow the money. That would be the money the judge received and how he spent it. That information would tell me if he was spending more than he was paid as a judge. It might also tell me where the money came from, but I didn't think that was likely.

The interesting thing about it was the Attorney General's Office would be able to do it, too, at least most of it without my help. It soon became clear in the letter why he wanted me to do it. The letter indicated there was someone in the AG's office who was involved, but Greene didn't know who.

Greene had already told me he thought there might be a mole in his office. With this additional information, it made good sense to have someone outside the government do the investigating. A mole in his office would make it difficult to keep any information found quiet. A mole could leak out all sorts of information which could blow the whole case, and end up leaving the AG with egg on his face.

Since I knew who the primary individual was they wanted me to look into, I had already started looking into his finances. What I really needed to know was something about the man. I knew who he was, though I had not had any direct dealings with him. Judge Weatherby was the senior judge on the bench in Denver's criminal court. He handled most, if not all, the cases dealing with white collar crimes, among other crimes that dealt with racketeering and the mob, which included assaults and murders by mob members.

As the senior judge, Weatherby would also assign cases to the different judges within the criminal court system. That would give him at least some control over who got which cases. That was a lot of power for one man, especially if he abused it.

I pushed back my chair and stared at the letter. I once again thought about what I might be getting into. The letter had been signed by Attorney General, Robert Patrick

Greene. It was not hard for me to recognize his signature, it was very unusual and I had seen it many times.

It was time for me to get started. Since I already knew what Judge Weatherby made as a judge, another trip to the library was in order to see what else I could find out about him. There had to be some information about his political and private life. I would be able to find some information from the newspaper archives. The library would have a computer hooked up to the local newspapers that would have most of the information I would want.

I put the letter in my safe along with the money, except for a couple of hundred dollars. I then went to the elevator and took it to the parking garage. I got in my car and headed for the library.

Don walked into the television station of channel three. He saw a nice looking blonde sitting at the reception desk. She smiled up at him as he approached her.

"May I help you?"

"Yes. I'm Detective Donald Wright with the Denver Police Department," he said as he showed her his ID and badge. "I would like to talk to the reporter who reported on the bombing of the café downtown on last evening's news broadcast."

The smile faded from the blonde's face as soon as he said he was a detective. It was not a good sign that there was going be any real cooperation from the station.

"He isn't in right now."

"Could you at least tell me who covered the bombing yesterday afternoon?"

"I wouldn't have that information," the blonde said nervously.

"Then who would?" Don asked.

"I don't know."

"Listen, six people died as a result of that bombing. Would you be kind enough to get someone out here who can answer my questions?"

"Is there something I can help you with, officer?" a man said from behind Wright.

Don turned around and saw a man wearing what looked like an expensive suit. The man had a stupid grin of superiority on his face.

"That depends on who you are and what you know about the bombing of the café downtown yesterday," Wright said.

"I'm the reporter who talked to the man who said he saw two men dressed all in black run out of the café shortly *before the explosion. What took you so long to come and see me?" he asked with a stupid grin.*

"What is your name?" Don said ignoring his question.

"You don't recognize me?" the man asked, seeming a bit surprised.

"Just answer the question."

"I'm Joe Sanders, the senior reporter and news anchor for this station. I get all the important assignments," he said with a tone of superiority.

"I want to know the name of the man who claims to have seen two men run out of the cafe." Wright said.

"I'm sorry, but I can't tell you that."

"Six people died because of that explosion and you can't tell me the name of the man that saw them run out of the building just before it blew up? What the hell kind of a human being are you?"

"I'm the kind that knows what his rights are as a journalist. If you're any kind of a police officer, you know I don't have to reveal my sources of information."

"I take it you are still in touch with your 'source?'"

"I am, but I won't tell you who he is," Sanders said, looking very sure of himself.

"Then tell your witness that I would like to talk to him."

"I will tell him, but I wouldn't expect any help from him," Sanders said with a grin.

"You might want to advise him that withholding information from the police is also a crime."

"I'll tell him, but I will also advise him not to talk to you," Sanders said with a grin. "He's a valuable witness to me."

Don looked at him with distain. Sanders had someone who could possibly give him important information on who bombed the café, but would not tell the police. Don was sure that Sanders was keeping the witness hidden from the police so he could use him to further his career and increase his ratings.

There was also the possibility there was no witness, that it was a scam. Don knew he could arrest the reporter for impeding a murder investigation, but a judge would release him before he could get the paperwork completed.

"Do me a favor. Tell your source that if I find out who he is, and I will find out, I will have him arrested for withholding information from the police and will hold him as a material witness unless he contacts me very soon. And I mean very soon. If I find out there is no witness, I'll see to it that every radio and TV station in the country will know what a fake you are."

Don looked at Sanders for a moment, then turned and started to leave the building. Don glanced back as he crossed the parking lot.

Sanders watched him leave. Sanders didn't look so confident now.

By the time Don got to his car, he was fuming. He was just about ready to go back and arrest the reporter just to make his life miserable, but thought better of it. The one thing he could do that would do more good was spread the word throughout the precinct that no one in the department was to talk to anyone from channel three about anything. They were not even to give them the time of day.

Don decided he would go back to the office and cool down. He would then take a serious look at the preliminary forensic report in the hope of finding a lead in among all the technical stuff. Maybe he would get lucky and find something in there that might help.

Don left the television station parking lot and drove back to the precinct. As soon as he got back, he told the desk sergeant to spread the word that no one was to talk to anyone from channel three about anything, period. He then went to his office and sat down to look at the report.

CHAPTER SIX

I arrived at the library about at nine-fifteen. As I walked through the door, I saw a group of kids from the local Boys Club. They were walking across the entry way toward a classroom where I was sure they would spend most of the morning enjoying some activity designed just for them. It seemed the library had a number of activities for the younger set these days.

I went to the research section of the library and sat down at one of the computers. I typed in the name of the local newspaper. Once I got it, I typed in Judge Weatherby's full name in the search tab. Within a couple of seconds, it came up with a number of articles that had something to do with him.

I spent the next couple of hours reading through each article. I printed off the ones I believed might prove interesting and possibly provide some information about him. The more I read about him, the more I began to think that he handled an exceptional large number of cases involving mob leaders or people closely associated with the mob bosses.

I also found out that his wife had died about three years ago. He had apparently taken it very hard. They had been married for a long time, which made it easy to understand. I found an article that showed me that he went back to work after what I would consider a relatively short time after his wife's death. I got the impression he had thrown himself into his work, however, I was not sure that was the case.

One article showed me that a judge by the name of Colton, James Colton, had stepped in and took over for

Weatherby while he was out due to the death of his wife. I looked up Colton in the papers. I found Colton was taking on more of the type of cases that Judge Weatherby had handled in the past even after Weatherby returned to work. I wondered if Colton might be someone I should look into as well.

I took a moment to look up the income made by judges. I found the category of wages that fit Colton's position and years of service. I wrote down the high figure for his wage bracket. I would add his name to the list of those I wanted to know how much they earned and how much they were spending. I decided it might be a good idea to write down all the wage brackets in case I had to find the income of some of the other judges who didn't have a lot of years on the bench. The next thing was to get credit reports on all of the judges I might have to investigate, but I didn't want to get that information from such a public computer.

As soon as I had all the information I thought I would need for now, or could safely get from the computer, I cleared the computer of all the websites I had visited. I didn't want anyone to know what I was doing.

I left the library and walked out to my car. It was time to contact my friend and see what information he could get on the spending habits of Judge Weatherby as well as the judges under his supervision. The one thing I knew for sure was my friend would be very, very discreet.

A quick look at my watch told me it was getting on toward lunch. I decided to stop and have lunch somewhere on my way back to the office. Since I was going right past the office building where Jackie worked, I decided to stop in and see if she would like to go to lunch. My call to my friend could wait until I got something to eat. It didn't take me very long to get to Jackie's office.

Detective Wright began looking over the preliminary forensic report. The first thing he noticed was the name of the shooting victim. It was listed as a "John Doe". He wasn't all that surprised. The fact the man had been shot twice in the head, once in the front and once in the back, left the man with little facial features that would help identify him. The report showed that the report of his fingerprints had not come back from the FBI, or the state crime lab.

The report did indicate the victim had no identification on his person. The only reason Don could think of for the victim not having any identification was that it had been taken by the shooter after he was shot.

Don leaned back in his chair and thought about it. Had the victim's wallet been taken to make it harder to identify him, or was there some other reason? He put that thought aside while he went over the rest of the preliminary forensic report.

The report indicated most of the pieces of papers found on the table in the booth had been damaged enough that it would be difficult to retrieve anything useable from them. However, it did state they had not given up on testing them in the hope of finding something that might help identify the victim, help figure out why the victim was there, and what he was working on.

Don's thoughts were disturbed by the ringing of his phone. He reached over and picked it up.

"Detective Wright."

"Detective Wright, this is Doctor Armstrong at Denver General Hospital."

"Yes, Doctor. I certainly hope you have some good news for me."

"*I hope its good news. One of the women who survived the bombing of the downtown café has come around.*"

"*Can I talk to her?*"

"*Yes, at least at this time. She is still in critical condition, and it is still touch and go, but you can try.*"

"*I'm on my way,*" *he said, then hung up the phone.*

Don did not wait for a response from the doctor. The woman could relapse into unconsciousness at anytime. He needed to know what she might have seen.

He literally ran out of his office to his car. He jumped into the car and headed for the hospital with flashing lights and blaring siren.

CHAPTER SEVEN

I arrived at the state office building where Jackie worked and found her at her desk. She smiled when she saw me walking toward her.

"Hi. What brings you here?"

"I thought you might like to go to lunch with me."

"I would like to," she said, then stood up.

I reached over to the coat rake near the door and took her coat off it. She walked to me, then turned around so I could help her with her coat. As soon as she had her coat on, she took my arm and walked with me to the entrance of the building.

Jackie and I walked around the corner to a little diner located across the street. Once inside, we found an empty booth. After hanging Jackie's coat up on a hook at the end of the booth, I slipped into the booth across from her.

"How has your day been going?" she asked.

"Not all that bad. I spent a good part of the morning at the library looking up information on what a few of our state employees make at their jobs, and some articles from the newspaper."

"What were you doing that for? Are you looking for a job with the state?" she asked with a hint of hopefulness in her voice.

It was obvious that she was hoping I was looking for a job. She had expressed several times that she didn't like what I do for a living.

"No. I have a job. I can't really tell you what my job is, at least not now. I do have something to ask you, though."

"What's that?" the tone of her voice showing her disappointment.

"How do I find out how a person spends his money?"

"Why would you want to know that?"

"I'm trying to find out if someone is spending a lot more than he is making at the only job he apparently has."

"Well, a credit check would tell you where he spends some of his money. A credit check would only tell you what he owes, who it is owed to and how much the payments on the loans are, but only to his creditors. It would not include any private loans he might have, or what he pays for with cash. Now, if the payments on what he owes to creditors are greater than the amount of his reported income, then you would know he is either in serious financial trouble, or he is not reporting some of his income."

"Well, that's a start," I said.

"Do you have access to getting a credit check on someone?" Jackie asked.

"No, but I know someone who does."

The waitress showed up and we ordered our lunch. It was a good lunch. Our talk turned to things other than the case I was working on.

After we finished our lunch, I walked Jackie back to her office. I gave her a kiss and told her I would call her later to let her know how things were going, and if we could get together in the evening. I then left and headed back to my office.

When I arrived at my office, I placed a call to a man whom I considered to be a longtime friend. He makes his living on the edge of the law, and knows a lot of what the police would like to know about some of those who make their living outside the law. He is able to move inside the underworld of the mobs, and knows most of the lowlifes who live in the cities along the Front Range. The phone rang only three times before it was answered.

"Hello," a friendly female voice said.

The fact that a female answered the phone surprised me. It had never been answered by a woman before.

"Yes, this is Tidsdale."

"Oh. Hi, Franky. I'll get him for you."

"Thank you."

It didn't take long for my friend to answer the phone.

"Franky, what's up?"

"Who was the woman that answered the phone?"

"Just a friend, a very good friend," he said with a hint of humor in his voice.

It was obvious that he wasn't going to tell me anything about the woman, so I got back to why I called.

"I could use a little of your help."

"Sure. What can I do for you?"

"I need to know if a couple of state judges are spending more than they are making."

"You think they're crooked?"

"They might be, but I'm not sure. Can you help me?"

"Sure. No problem. I'll look into it. You want to know which judges are spending more than they make, right?"

"Generally. If you can come up with where and how they are getting the, shall we call it, "extra money", that would help. My main interest is in the judges in the criminal court system."

"No problem. If I hit on anything else that might help, I'll get that, too."

"That would be great. Thanks."

"I'll have it for you in a couple of days. Is that all you need?

"I think so."

"Okay. Take care of yourself."

"Will do. And you take care, too," I said, then hung up the phone.

I sat back in my chair with my hands behind my head and smiled. I knew I would have the information within a couple of days. He had never let me down. The only question I had at the moment was who was the woman that answered the phone? I wondered if he might have found himself a woman he felt he could trust. I would ask him next time I talked to him, but right now I needed to think about my case.

I sat up and began to look at the information I had gotten at the library. I wondered what I was going to find out about the judges. I took a minute to revisit the information I had gotten from the attorney general. I guess I was hoping there was something that would jump out at me and give me a clue as to who was really involved in the investigation, besides the one judge I already knew about. There was nothing in the newspaper stories that seemed to help very much.

I began to think about what my next move should be. It crossed my mind that it might be a good idea if I got a computer for my office and learned how to use it in my investigative work. It would save me a lot of time going to the library, and I could do it in the privacy of my office. I certainly had the money from the retainer I had received. I should discuss it with Jackie.

It only took Don about fifteen minutes to get to the hospital. He parked his car in a space reserved for official vehicles, then pulled the sun visor down making the Police Department sticker visible from outside the car. He hurried into the hospital to the Admission Desk. The woman behind the desk knew who he was and smiled.

"Good afternoon, Detective Wright. How might I help you today?"

"I need to find Doctor Armstrong as soon as possible."

"He is on the second floor in ICU."

"Thank you," Don said, then quickly turned and headed for the elevator.

As soon as he got to the elevator, he pressed the call button and impatiently waited for it. When it got there, he had to wait for several people to get off. As soon as it was empty, he got in and pressed the button for the second floor, then pressed the button to close the door.

It seemed to Don that it was the slowest elevator he had ever been on. When it arrived at the second floor, he got off and almost ran to the nurse's station. He was about to ask the nurse where Doctor Armstrong was when he stepped out of the Intensive Care Unit.

"Doc, how is she doing?"

"It has been touch and go. She was conscious for a little while, but she has slipped back, I'm afraid."

"Was she able to tell you anything?"

"No. I'm afraid not."

"Damn," Don said in frustration.

"I'm sorry," Doctor Armstrong said, not knowing what else he could say.

"Doc, would it be all right with you if I hung around for a little while?"

"I don't know what good it will do, but it's all right with me."

Don looked around and saw several chairs just outside the doors to the ICU. He walked over to the chairs and dropped down in one. The doctor sat down beside him.

"How are the other survivors doing? I believe it was an old man and another woman?"

"Yes, the man is in his seventies. He's not any better, I'm afraid. I would say that his chances of surviving are even less than the women's. The women are holding their own at the moment."

"Do you have a name for any of them?" Don asked.

"The man's name is Carl Hammer. It doesn't look like he will make it. If he does, I seriously doubt he will be able to tell you anything. He has had a lot of brain damage."

"What about the women?"

"The younger of the two women has not been identified yet. We don't have any idea who she is or where she is from. What we do know is she is in pretty bad shape. She has come around, but it was only for a short time. It was encouraging, but she is still critical.

"The older woman is Lynn Freeman. She is sixty years old and lives in Englewood."

"How did you find out who she is?"

"She was wearing a medical alert bracelet. She's a diabetic."

"Do you think she will be able to tell us anything?"

"At this point, it's hard to say."

"I'm going to have an officer placed outside your unit. I want the officer to be notified immediately if either of the women comes around. He will be here to get a dying declaration, if at all possible. One of them may have the only lead we have to who set off the bomb and who shot one of the victims."

"I guess that's about all you can do for now. I've got to go check on them," the doctor said as he stood up.

"One more thing, can I have an officer take the young woman's fingerprints? It might help identify her."

"Sure. Have the nurse call me when your officer gets here."

"I will. I'm going to wait for the officer," Don said as the doctor walked toward the Intensive Care Unit.

Don took his cell phone out of his pocket as he watched the doctor disappear behind the frosted glass door to the Intensive Care Unit. Don talked to his watch captain about having an officer stationed outside the Intensive Care Unit in the hope of getting some kind of statement from one of the women, should one of them come around. His watch captain agreed that it was about all they could do at the moment and would send someone over.

He also told the watch captain he wanted to take the unknown woman's fingerprints in the hope of finding out who she was. He agreed with Don. There was nothing else Don could do for now but wait for his relief to come.

CHAPTER EIGHT

At the moment, I could think of nothing that I could do to move my investigation along. I felt as if I was at a point where it was wait and see what might turn up. It was still in my mind that the bombing of the downtown café had something to do with what I was investigating.

My thoughts were disturbed by the ringing of my cell phone. I sat up and reached for my cell phone. The caller ID did not show who was calling. I answered the call.

"Frank - - "I said before I was interrupted."

"No names please," the voice on the other end of the line said.

I immediately recognized the voice. It was the AG.

"All right. I hope you have a little more information for me."

"I want you to know there has been a problem. I would like to meet with you as soon as possible."

"Okay, but how do you plan to do that without the possibility of someone seeing us?"

"Take the elevator down to the ground floor and get in your car. I want you to go over to Colfax, then drive east to the airport. When you get to the airport, park your car in the parking structure and go to the waiting area for Concourse Three and wait. I want you to leave now."

"Okay," I said, then hung up the phone.

I took a minute to check my gun before I got up to leave my office. I had no idea what I was getting into, but I wanted a little help just in case I needed it.

As I stepped out into the hall, I looked around. I didn't see anyone who looked suspicious so I locked the office door and headed for the elevator.

Once on the elevator, I took it to the underground parking garage where I got off and walked over to my car. I looked around to see if anyone was watching me as I unlocked the car. I slipped in behind the wheel, put the key in the ignition and started the car.

I could smell something that was not normal in my car. It was some kind of aftershave lotion. I didn't say anything. I backed the car out of my parking space and left the building. As I drove toward Colfax, I watched to see if anyone was following me. I didn't see anyone.

"You probably shouldn't wear aftershave lotion if you're trying to sneak around," I said without turning around.

"I'll remember that," the voice said from behind my seat.

"What's so important you needed to talk to me?"

"I figured I should let you know that the bombing of the downtown café is connected to our investigation."

"I had a feeling it was," I replied.

"How did you figure that out?"

"It was just a guess on my part. Just how does it affect the investigation?" I asked.

"I'm not sure. One of my investigators was killed in it. Actually, he was murdered before the café blew up. The bombing was a rather lousy attempt to cover up my investigator's assassination. It didn't do as much damage as was expected because of the heavy wooden booths in that old café."

"How does that affect me?"

"The police have a lot of the papers that my investigator had with him. Some of it will not be of any value, but some of it might. I understand you have worked with a certain detective in the police department in the past."

"You wouldn't happen to be referring to Detective Donald Wright?" I asked.

"Yes. He is leading up the investigation of the bombing and the death of my investigator. He probably doesn't know the man shot in the head in the café is one of my men, yet. I'm sure it won't be long before he will know."

"What is it you want me to do about it?"

"First of all, would I be able to trust Wright?"

"He is as honest a cop as I have ever met. We have known each other for years," I said.

"Do you think you can trust him to keep his mouth shut?"

"That depends. As long as it is legal, yes. But he won't break the law for you or anyone else."

"Okay. I want you to have a talk with him. I don't want you to tell him any more than you have to about what you are investigating."

"Okay, but it would go a long ways with him if I could tell him the name of your agent."

There was silence from the back seat. It was clear he was thinking about what I said.

"Okay. His name was Robert Martin and he was shot twice in the head. He had worked for me for the past four years."

"Thanks. That will help."

"Since we are done for now, I want you to park your car as I told you on the phone and go to Concourse Three. Find a nice comfortable chair and sit down. After an hour and a half, go back to your car and drive back to your office."

I didn't talk to the man in the back seat of my car the rest of the way to the airport. Once I parked the car and got out without looking in the back. I went into the airport, got a magazine and found a place to sit down near Concourse

Three. I sat down and read the magazine. After an hour and a half, I returned to my car and drove back to my office. My rear seat passenger was gone.

It took about an hour before an officer arrived at the hospital to relieve Don. It didn't take very long for Don to give the officer instructions on what he was to do and a list of questions to ask either of the two women. The main thing Don wanted was a dying declaration from at least one of the women if at all possible. It wasn't that Don knew the women were going to die as it was his need for something to go on. Something that would help him find the men who had caused the explosion at the downtown café.

As soon as Don had given his instructions to the officer and took fingerprints of the unknown victim, he left the hospital and returned to his office. He had no more than entered his office and sat down at his desk when the phone rang. He reached over and picked up the phone.

"Detective Wright."

"Detective Wright, this is Mel Street. I have something that might be of interest to you. We have been working on the papers that were on the table where the man was shot. We haven't finished, but we found the name of Frank Tidsdale on one of the pieces of paper. Does that mean anything to you?"

"Yeah. That's great. At least I can call him and see what he can tell me. Maybe he will come up with a name for the guy. So far we've got nothing on him."

"We have not gotten anything back from the FBI, either," Mel said.

"I have a set of fingerprints of one of the victims in the hope we can at least identify her."

"I'll send someone over for them," Mel said.

"Was there anything in the papers that might give us an idea why this guy had a paper with Frank's name on it?"

"Not so far. Actually, all we have is the last two letters of his first name and s-d-a-l-e of his last name. I know it's not much to go on."

"Then you are not sure it's Frank Tidsdale's name, am I right?"

"That's true. However, the spacing on the paper would fill in nicely with the missing letters of his name."

"I sure hope you can come up with more than that," Don said with a note of frustration.

"We are working hard on this," Mel assured him. *"We're not giving up. Between the blood, tissue matter and everything else on the paper, it isn't going to be easy."*

"I know. I also know I'm asking for the impossible."

"We'll try to give it to you. I'll call you back when I have something more. By the way, we found a total of eight spent casings from a forty-five on the floor near the booth. They were newly fired. We are checking them for possible fingerprints. It's not looking good, but we might get lucky. We also have a few of the spent bullets. We will run them to see if we can come up with a matching gun."

"Let me know what you find out. And thanks," Don said, then hung up the phone.

CHAPTER NINE

As soon as I got back to my office, I sat down at my desk, picked up the phone and placed a call to Don Wright. It didn't take but a few seconds before the phone was answered by the duty officer. He quickly transferred my call to Don's office.

"Detective Wright."

"Don, Tidsdale here. Are you working on the bombing of the downtown café?"

"Yeah. I was just about to call you. What's your interest in it?"

"I can't reveal my source, but I was wondering if you have found out the name of the man that took a double tap to the head in the café before the place went up?"

"How did you know there was a shooting victim in the cafe? We never let that piece of information out."

"Like I said, I can't reveal my source."

"You're the second person I talked to today that told me that," he said with a hint of anger in his voice.

"Relax, Don. I can assure you that my source didn't have anything to do with the shooting or the bombing. I can't tell you why I know this, but the dead man's name is Robert Martin."

"Do you know who he worked for and why he had a piece of paper with your name on it?

"He had a paper with my name on it?"

"Yeah. At least we think it is your name. We don't have all the letters, but what we have sure would fit your name."

"I guess it's possible. I think we need to get together. I need to talk to you in private. It might prove to be best if we meet somewhere we will not be seen together. I have no idea who might be involved."

"I think that's a good idea."

"I'll call you back in a few minutes."

"Okay."

As I hung up, I remembered I had left my cell phone in my car. I went directly to my car in the parking garage, got in, picked up my cell phone and placed a call to Don. My call was immediately transferred to him.

"Detective Wright."

"Go to your car and drive to Washington Park. Park on the east side of the park and walk over to the pavilion next to the duck pond and wait for me there," I said, then hung up.

I knew it wouldn't take him very long to get there, so I had to hurry. I left the parking garage for Washington Park.

It didn't take me very long to get to the park. I parked on the west side of the park and walked toward the pavilion. I found a place next to a couple of big old trees close to the pavilion. I hid behind one of the large trees and waited for Don.

In the judge's chamber of the courthouse in downtown Denver, Judge Marcus Weatherby was sitting at his desk reading the local morning newspaper that he had not had a chance to read earlier. He was taking a very special interest in an article about the bombing of the café downtown yesterday afternoon. His interest increased as he read that there had been five people killed in the bombing, and that four people had survived the blast. The article did not say anything about the condition of the four survivors, or the fact that one of them had died after he was taken to the hospital.

Judge Weatherby leaned back in his chair to think about what had happened. There had been nothing to tell him the names of the survivors or the names of those killed. It worried him not knowing any of the names, but what worried him the most was the report that four had survived the blast.

Just then his secretary buzzed him. He reached over and pressed the button on the intercom.

"What is it, Martha?"

"There is a man on the phone who would like to talk to you. He wouldn't give me his name, but he said it was very important. I told him you were busy, but he insists on talking to you, now," she said apologetically

"I'll talk to him and straighten him out about calling me. Would you be kind enough to go down to the snack shop and get me some milk?"

"Yes, sir. I'll put him through."

Judge Weatherby listened as the call was put through.

"What do you mean talking to my secretary like that?" the judge said with a harsh tone in his voice.

"I need to - - -." the male voice said before he was quickly and sharply interrupted.

"I don't care who you are, or what you need. You don't give my secretary a hard time."

He then heard a faint click on the line.

"Okay. You can talk. I thought I told you never to call me at my office."

"You did, but I thought you should know that things didn't go well yesterday."

"I already know what happened. What I don't know is did you complete our primary goal?"

"Yes, sir."

"Good."

"We have a couple of loose ends to clean up, but they shouldn't be a problem. One of them has already been cleaned up."

"See to it they aren't a problem, and don't call me here again."

"Yes, sir." the male voice said, then the phone went dead.

The judge tipped back in his high back chair and smiled. A major problem had been eliminated. However, there were a couple of loose ends still hanging out there, and he didn't like loose ends. He was sure the other problems would be taken care of before they became serious, so all was well.

The more he thought about it, the more he realized that there was a strong possibility there would be more problems ahead. The only thing he could do was to deal with them when they became apparent.

His secretary returned with the milk he had requested. He thanked her and told her that she would not be hearing from the guy again. He also told her it was getting late and she was free to go home. She said goodnight, then left.

The judge leaned back in his chair again and thought about what was happening. The bombing of the café to cover the killing of one person had not gone well. It was beginning to look like things might be starting to fall apart.

He thought it might be time for him to retire and disappear to the Cayman Islands before the police got interested in him. He had already deposited enough money in the Caymans to be able to live comfortably on the islands for a good many years. It was also a place where he could not be extradited back to the U.S. to stand trial if they found out what he had been doing.

He decided he would submit his letter of resignation at the end of the week along with his retirement papers. It wouldn't take long to get retired. He could use his vacation time to move before the mob boss found out he was gone. He had been planning for this day for some time. He knew it was only a matter of time before everything would fall apart. He didn't want to be around when it did.

CHAPTER TEN

It wasn't very long before Don showed up at the pavilion in Washington Park. He walked into it and sat down on one of the concrete benches. I waited until he looked like he was settling in before I spoke to him.

"I've been here for a few minutes and haven't seen anyone hanging around," I said.

I didn't leave my hiding place as I didn't want anyone who might walk by to see us together. I noticed Don didn't turn to look toward me. He sat there on the bench just looking out over the duck pond as if he were thinking, which I was sure he was doing.

"What's with all the cloak-and-dagger stuff?" Don asked.

"I need your assurance that what I tell you will not go any further than between us."

"I can't do that," he said.

"I guess that takes care of it. I'll see you around."

I didn't leave immediately. Instead, I gave him a minute or so to change his mind. He was not a stupid man, and he knew me well. He knew that I would at least give him a chance to think about what I said, and to change his mind. When it looked like he wasn't going to cooperate with me, I started to leave.

"Wait. You know who the guy in the café was, and you know something about it."

"All true," I said, then waited for him to decide if he was going to take my terms."

"Okay. Fill me in. I will not say anything to anyone without your permission. I'm probably going to regret it," Don said with a hint of frustration in his voice.

"The man who was shot in the café was Robert Martin."

"Can you tell me who he worked for?"

"Yes. He was an investigator for the Attorney General, Robert Patrick Greene."

"I had a feeling I had heard that name before. Do you know what he was investigating?"

"Yes. He was investigating corruption in the criminal court system here in Denver."

I didn't want to say much more about it. The last thing I wanted was to put Don out on a limb. If someone found out that he knew about the investigation and who was being investigated, he could end up in a world of hurt if he didn't tell his superiors. He could even lose his job and his career as a cop. I didn't want that to happen.

If he did tell his superiors, it could blow the lid off the whole thing and end the investigation by the AG before he could prove anything. And that was to say nothing of whose life might be put in jeopardy as a result.

"Are you saying that the attorney general believes we have a judge that's corrupt?"

"At this point, we have no idea who is involved, how many are involved, or how far the corruption goes. It could go to several people working in the courts and several judges. At this point we just don't know."

"How come you're involved?"

"I've been pulled into it because Greene thinks there might be a mole in his office. Since he doesn't know who the mole is, he is looking to me to find out as much as I can and, hopefully, get some proof. Something that will prove there is corruption in the court system."

"In other words, he's not one hundred percent sure there is any corruption."

"Greene has no doubt that there is corruption in the system. The problem he is having is getting the proof needed to start making arrests. When he starts making those arrests, he wants to be absolutely sure he arrests the right people the first time," I said. "It could be a real big problem for him if he arrests the wrong people. He also wants to arrest all of them at the same time."

"No doubt. So he thinks there might be more than one corrupt judge?"

"It's possible. Right now we don't have a whole lot to go on. I've just started and don't have anything concrete so far. I only asked Greene if I could give you a heads-up and let you know the name of the man who was shot in the café. I figured it would help you a little."

"It will do that, and thanks. I'll try to keep a lid on anything I find out for as long as I can. Did the AG think that Martin might be his mole?"

"I don't know. He hasn't said. The fact that he had my name on a piece of paper leads me to believe he might have been. As far as I know, the AG is supposed to be the only one that knows I'm working for him."

"I'll do my best to keep a lid on it."

"Thanks. I'm hoping you will fill me in on anything you come up with that might help Greene and me," I said. "But whatever you do, don't call Greene. He might still have a mole in his office."

"I'll do what I can. If I find anything, I'll pass it on to you. You can relay it to Greene."

"Good. I'll fill you in on what I can as I can," I said. "I'll leave now. Wait a few minutes before you leave."

I didn't wait for a response from Don. I walked away from my hiding place by the trees and walked back to my car. I got in it and headed for home. It had been a long day and I needed to get some rest. Tomorrow would be another hard day. I had a lot of research ahead of me.

Two men wearing dark clothes and long black coats walked into Judge Weatherby's chamber shortly after eight o'clock in the evening. The courthouse was almost empty of people and most of the offices were closed. The judge was getting his coat from the coat rack when he heard the men enter his office. His secretary had left almost three hours earlier. The judge turned to see who had the nerve to walk into his chamber without knocking.

"What do you think you're doing? You can't just come barging into my office without knocking," the judge said angrily.

"Hang the coat back up and sit down, Judge," the taller of the two men said sharply.

Judge Weatherby noticed that the man had a strong note of authority in his voice, and his right hand was deep inside the pocket of his coat. Reluctantly, the judge hung his coat back on the rack, then returned to his desk and sat down. The shorter of the two men casually walked around behind him. Judge Weatherby watched him, but quickly turned his attention to the taller man standing in front of his desk.

"It seems that you are drawing a lot of attention in the Attorney General's Office. The boss is not happy about that. He's also not very happy about how things turned out at the café."

"That wasn't my fault. You guys messed that one up."

"Maybe, but it wouldn't have happened if you had done what you were supposed to do. You drew too much attention to yourself. The boss can't have that."

"Listen, I've kept your boss and several of his henchmen out of jail at great risk to myself. Your boss owes me plenty," the judge said, but his voice couldn't hide the fact he was afraid.

"That may be so, but you have become a liability. A liability the boss can't afford."

Judge Weatherby let out a sigh. The tall man's last statement made it perfectly clear why they were in his chamber. He also knew he would never get to the Cayman Islands to enjoy all the money he had waiting there. The building was almost empty of people so there would be no one to help him. The night watchman would not be making his rounds of the building for some time. His time had come, and he knew it.

Judge Weatherby began to think about when he had stepped over the line, when he had become indebted to the mob. It was right after his wife of forty years had died. The judge had become so depressed that he started drinking, then began to gamble. He got so far into debt with the mob that in order to get himself out of debt he started doing favors for them. He continued even after he had "paid them off". Once he started helping the mob, there was no stopping if he wanted to continue to be a judge. There was no way for him to get out of their control without going to jail. The thought of jail was more than he could bear.

Being the senior judge, he was able to get cases assigned to the judges in his group. He would get cases involving the mob assigned to his calendar so he could keep some evidence out of the trial and control what was presented in his courtroom. There were two other judges that made a little extra money by handling some of the cases so no one would get suspicious.

The demands of the mob were getting greater all the time. It would not be long before someone would get suspicious and start investigating. It would not take an investigator long to figure out what was going on.

Judge Weatherby knew the day would come when what he did would come back to haunt him. He had prepared for it, but not for this. The day came, and today was the day it would end for him.

Judge Weatherby looked up at the man standing in front of him. There was no doubt in his mind why they were there. They were there to kill him, to make sure he could not talk to anyone about what he had done or what he knew. He also knew there was nothing he could do about it. He let out a sigh as he accepted his fate.

"May I ask you something?" the judge asked as he looked up at the taller man.

"Sure."

"Would you be so kind as to make it quick? Please?" the judge asked as he looked into the tall man's eyes.

"Sure. Just close your eyes and it will be all over in a moment."

"Thank you."

Judge Weatherby looked at the man for a moment, then slowly closed his eyes. He twitched a little when he felt the cold steel of a gun barrel on the side of his head.

"I'm sorry," he whispered.

There was the sound of a gun going off, but the judge never heard it. The shorter man had placed the gun to the judge's head and pulled the trigger. The judge slumped over his desk and his hands slid off the desk and fell to his sides.

The shorter man lifted the judge's left hand up close to the side of the judge's head. He placed the gun firmly in the Judge's hand pressing his fingers tightly around the gun. He then let go of the judge's hand allowing his hand with the gun to fall down beside him.

The taller man looked around the judge's chamber, then motioned for the shorter man to leave. The taller man followed him out of the chamber, locking the door behind them. They left the building without being seen.

CHAPTER ELEVEN

After I arrived home, I fixed myself something to eat, then sat down to watch the news. It seemed that it was the same old thing, just different names and different locations around the city. A robbery here and a murder there seemed to be the usual news of the day.

There was nothing new about the bombing of the downtown café on the news. The death of Robert Martin was not even mentioned, which didn't surprise me. I was sure the attorney general would not want his name released to the public, at least, not yet. The only comment on the story was a repeat of what had been on the news last night with the exception that it reported one of the four survivors had died, and it was almost a footnote to the story.

I did notice the names of those killed in the bombing, and of the survivors, were not mentioned. It was obvious that the police were keeping a tight lid on what they had on the bombing.

When the news was over, I started watching a movie. It was an old black and white movie I had seen some years ago. I wasn't very much into the movie when my phone began to ring. I was hoping it was Jackie calling to say goodnight.

"Hello, Honey. Did you call to say goodnight?"

"No," a male voice on the line said. "I called you because there has been another murder."

"Don?" I asked with surprise.

"Yeah. I take it you were expecting someone else," Don said with a slight chuckle in his voice.

"Yes, I guess I was. What's this about another murder?"

"Was Judge Marcus Weatherby one of the judges you were investigating?"

"I can't answer that at this time," I said, but I had a feeling Don suspected he was one of the judges.

"The judge is dead."

"Are you where you can talk freely?"

"Yeah."

"Are you talking about Judge Weatherby?"

"Yeah."

"How did you know he was the one I was looking into?

"A good guess," Don said.

"What happened?"

"He committed suicide. He shot himself in the head."

"Are you sure?"

"To be honest, no. Frankly, I don't think it was suicide. I think he was assassinated, but someone tried very hard to make it look like suicide."

"What makes you think that?"

"The judge was right handed, but he was shot just above his left ear. The angle of the bullet doesn't look right, either. I know it's not much to go on, but its enough to make me want to take a closer look at it," Don said.

"Would it do any good for me to come over there and look around?"

"No. There's too many people here already. There are some people here that I don't think you would want to see you. It might blow your investigation. I'll get all the forensics reports and pictures I can to you as soon as possible. I have to go. I'll get in touch with you as soon as possible."

"Thanks, Don."

"The attorney general just walked in the door. I've got to go."

The phone suddenly went dead. As I hung it up, I wondered what was going on. With Weatherby dead, where was my investigation headed? I remembered it was hinted that there might be more people involved, which was very likely. All I had to do was find out who they were and what they were really involved in. Simple.

After shutting off the television, I went into my bedroom and laid down on the bed. Going to sleep was not a part of my immediate plans. I needed to think. There was little doubt that I would be contacted by the attorney general with new instructions. I could only hope he had another name of someone who he felt was involved. I needed someone who might get me on the right track to finding out what was going on.

My thoughts turned to Judge Weatherby. The first question that came to mind was why he was killed. Had he screwed up something that would cause someone else a problem? Did someone know he was being investigated by the AG's Office and felt he might fold under the pressure of an investigation? Had he become a liability in some way? Had the mole in the AG's office found out that Judge Weatherby was the one being investigated and told the person he was really working for about the investigation? The last question that came to mind seemed like a real good possibility.

They were all good questions, but I had no good answers. The best I could do was to speculate. I knew I was not likely to get any answers tonight. I had a feeling I would hear from the attorney general in the morning. There was nothing else for me to do but turn in for the night.

I got ready for bed, then slipped in under the covers. I found it difficult to shut down my mind so I could sleep, but managed after awhile.

Detective Don Wright saw the attorney general get off the elevator and start walking down the hall toward the judge's chamber. Don quickly terminated his call and slipped his cell phone into his pocket. He then returned to the judge's chamber from the hall. As Greene entered the judge's chamber, he walked past Don without commenting.

Don stood by the door and watched Greene as he walked toward Mel Street, the head forensic investigator. The rest of the forensic team continued to do what they do best, find, gather and log all possible evidence.

Don turned his attention to one member of the forensic team who was taking pictures of the crime scene. He had taken them of the judge's head, then took a good number of pictures of the judge and the entire area around him. He took pictures that would show everything on the desk, on the floor around the desk, of the gun and its position in relationship to the body, and several of the entire room. When the forensic photographer was done, Don walked up to him.

"I want a copy of every picture you took tonight," Don said quietly.

"Sure enough. Detective. I'll have a set of them for you in the morning."

"Thanks."

After Mel Street finished talking to Greene, he walked over to Don. He stood there looking at his team members while they gathered and logged every minute piece of evidence they could find.

"I've seen a lot of suicides, Don, but there's something about this one that just doesn't add up," Mel said.

"What are you getting at?"

"I don't think this was a suicide. I think he was assassinated. Whoever did it tried to make it look like a suicide," Mel said as he turned and looked at Don.

"What makes you think so?"

"Just a hunch more than anything right now. I've got no proof, yet."

"The guy at the café was assassinated, too. Do you think there is a connection to that one?" Don asked, hoping Mel might have found some kind of a connection.

"Maybe, but I don't have anything pointing in that direction so far. Everything about this one is different. The victim in the café was just plan shot at close range with a .45 caliber automatic. Either one of the shots would have killed him instantly. That being the case, he was differently assassinated. It was almost as if they where sending a message to someone, or making a point.

"In this case, the victim was shot once in the side of the head with the muzzle of the gun pressed against his head. A .38 caliber revolver was used. Whoever shot the judge just wanted him dead and wanted it to look like suicide."

"Why?" Don asked.

"Probably to avoid an investigation into Judge Weatherby's death?"

"Possibly, but why?"

"Sorry, Don, but that's your department," Mel said. "I tell you how, your job is to figure out who and why."

Don just nodded his head as he thought about what Mel had said.

"I've seen a lot of suicides, too," Don said. "Rarely do you see a right-handed man shoot himself on the left side of his head, and especially where the shot was placed."

"I didn't know the judge was right-handed, but that helps support my belief it was not suicide. It was the position of the gun to the side of his head that made me wonder if he actually killed himself. It is possible to hold a *gun at that angle, but it wouldn't be natural or comfortable. The problem is there's not enough to rule out suicide. I'll have to do more tests. I'll let you know what I come up with as soon as I can."*

"Thanks. The only people we know of that were in the building at the time of his death have been interviewed. I guess there's nothing else I can do here tonight. I think I'll get out of your way and let you do your job," Don said.

"One of us might as well get some sleep," Mel said with a grin. "It doesn't look like it will be me. I'll talk to you tomorrow."

Don turned around and walked out of the judge's chamber and on down the hall. He returned to his car and drove back to his office. He wrote out a brief report and made a few notes of things he wanted to look into, then went home to get a few hours of sleep.

CHAPTER TWELVE

Morning came early for me. I woke up a good hour before my alarm clock was to go off. My mind was busy thinking about Judge Weatherby. First of all, I wondered if the judge had actually committed suicide. If he had, was it because he found out that he was being investigated by the AG's office? From what little I knew about the judge, he struck me as the kind of man who would not want to have to go through a trial and all the press stories about him. It seemed logical to me that he might kill himself, but only if he was guilty of some serious wrong doing. Otherwise, he would fight tooth and nail to disprove the charges against him.

However, Don didn't think it was suicide. I knew Don pretty well. If he thought it was not suicide, he was more than likely right. He had seen enough cases that he could see the little things that would tell him what really happened.

I knew I was not going back to sleep so I decided I might as well get up. I went directly to the shower. It felt good and it seemed to wake me up and clear my head. After my shower, I dressed, then went into the kitchen for breakfast. I had no more than sat down to eat when my phone began to ring.

"Hello," I said.

"Have you heard?"

I immediately recognized the voice. It was Attorney General Greene.

"Yes. I heard about it last night."

"I figured you had since your friend, Detective Wright was at Judge Weatherby's chamber when I got there. Do you have any details?"

"No, but I might have something later this morning," I said.

"Keep me posted. You can call me on my private line."

"Right. I'll keep my cell phone on all the time."

"Good," he said, then the phone went dead.

I hung up, then sat back down at the table to finish my breakfast of toast, orange juice and coffee. If nothing else, the phone call let me know that I still had a case. He was expecting me to continue my search for anyone else who might be involved in the corruption, or alleged corruption. I was sure that he was hoping I would find out who had the judge murdered, too.

After I finished my breakfast, I headed for my office. Since my breakfast had not been as filling as I had hoped, I made a quick stop at a doughnut shop on my way. I went inside and noticed a television on the wall behind the counter. It had a local news reporter standing in front of the courthouse with a mike in his hand.

"Say, could you turn that up a little?" I asked the clerk.

She turned it up, then looked at me. The news reporter was talking about the suicide of Judge Weatherby.

"Judge Marcus Weatherby shot himself in the head last night shortly after his secretary had left his office. It is not known why, but an undisclosed source said that the loss of his wife almost three years ago had caused him to be depressed, and he was still having a hard time dealing with it. It was felt that he was depressed and had never sought help for his depression."

"Are you going to buy something," the young clerk asked, interrupting me.

"Oh, ah, yes. I would like a filled long john, please."

She put a long john in a bag and I gave her the money for it. I then turned and left for my office.

It was early in the morning when two men walked into a local bar and grill on East Colfax. They didn't even stop at the bar, but walked to the back of the bar and entered a room in the rear of the building. There was a rather large man sitting at a table with his breakfast setting in front of him. The large man was wearing a fancy suit with the coat open. He had a rather large stomach that overhung the gold buckle on his belt. He looked up at the two men as he took another mouthful of food.

"Well, what do I tell the boss," the big man said while still chewing his food.

"You can tell him that everything went well. He no longer has a problem."

"Are you sure? You know how he don't like loose ends."

"There aren't any loose ends," the taller of the two men said. "The judge killed himself. We put the word out to the press that he was depressed because of his wife's death."

"Sounds good. It seems the press will buy into almost anything these days. What about the three survivors from the café?"

"They don't know anything. There is no way for them to identify us. They saw two men dressed all in black with black hair and beards. As you can see neither of us are dressed in black, nor do we have black hair or beards."

"Okay. Here, this should take care of it," the fat man said as he handed the taller man an envelope full of cash. "The boss wants you to take a little trip."

"Where are we going?"

"He wants you to go to Las Vegas. He wants you to call me and tell me how I can get in touch with you, just in case

he wants you back sooner. Plan to stay there for two weeks. If everything is quiet here, I'll call you back."

"And if it's not?"

"I'll be calling you back sooner. Consider it a vacation. You will be staying at the Palazzo. Here's the tickets for your flight to Las Vegas and a little spending money. He thinks you need a vacation, now," the fat man said with a grin as he handed the tall man another envelope.

"Okay. See you around," the taller man said as he slipped the envelope of money and the tickets into his jacket pocket.

He then turned and left the bar with the smaller man right behind him.

* * * *

Don arrived at his office at his usual time, a little after seven in the morning. He sat down at his desk and placed a call to the police lab to find out what Mel might have found out. Mel was not in, but he was told that Mel would be in within the hour and would call.

Don was a little disappointed, but he knew how hard Mel and his forensic investigators had worked last night. He had hoped to have at least a preliminary forensic report or some of the pictures of the crime scene. It had not been established that it was a crime scene and not a suicide, yet. However, there was little doubt in Don's mind that Judge Weatherby had not committed suicide.

Leaning back in his chair, Don began to think about the death of Judge Weatherby. Both Mel and he thought it was not a case of suicide. If it was not suicide, why was Judge Weatherby killed? Who would want him dead? That was the question Don needed answered. A look at some of the judge's cases might produce an answer. After all, he had sent a lot of men to jail over the years. It might be a good idea to find out where those who had gotten out of jail might be now.

Don had not had time to think about it for more than a few minutes when there was a knock on his door. He sat up and looked at the door.

"Come in," he said.

A tall, slender, young female police officer entered Don's office. She was carrying a fairly large yellow envelope in her hand.

"I have an envelope for you from the crime lab," the young female officer said.

She handed the envelope to Don, then turned to leave.

"Wait," Don said. "I would like to talk to you."

The young officer turned around and stood in front of his desk. She wasn't sure what he wanted to talk to her about.

"Please, have a seat," he said, then waited for her to sit down. "It's Officer Williams, isn't it?"

"Yes, sir."

"If I remember correctly, I heard you worked for Judge Weatherby at one time. Is that correct?"

"Yes, sir. I worked as a translator for the hearing impaired in his court a couple of times."

"You sign, then?"

"Yes, sir."

"What can you tell me about Judge Weatherby?"

"Not much, I'm afraid. I didn't work all that closely with him. I really worked for several of the judges before I took the police exam. He seemed like a nice enough man. He was always nice to me."

"Did he seem to have any trouble with any of the other judges?"

"Not that I can recall. I haven't worked with him for maybe six months or so."

"Okay. If you should think of anything unusual or out of character for him, would you please let me know?"

"Yes, sir."

"Thank you," Don said as he smiled at her.

Officer Sharon Williams stood up and started to leave Don's office. He thought of something else.

"Wait, please. Do you happen to know the name of Judge Weatherby's secretary?"

"Yes. It's Martha Hanson. She's been his personal secretary for at least twenty years."

"Thank you. Could you get me her home phone number and address?"

"Sure," she said with a smile, then left Don's office.

He leaned back to think while he waited for Officer Williams to get Martha Hanson's phone number. He had not visited with her, yet. He had no idea what she might know about the judge's activities, but she might have seen something or heard something that was not normal for the judge. It crossed his mind that she probably knew him better than just about anyone, as was often the case when two people work closely together for so many years.

CHAPTER THIRTEEN

As soon as I arrived at my office, I put the coffee pot on. While I waited for the coffee, I stood at the window and looked out over the street below. I wasn't looking at anything special, just looking while I thought about what had happened last night.

While I was thinking, I came up with a couple of things that might help me get a handle on the case. The first was I wanted to see Judge Weatherby's court assignment calendar. I would like to see his court calendar for at least the past two or three years. It would show which judges handled which cases. I had no idea what it would tell me other than to show me if there was a good distribution of all kinds of cases among all the judges in the criminal court system. If it showed certain kinds of cases always, or most often, were going to a specific judge; it might give me a clue to who the judge might have favored. The information might also give me an idea of who might be involved in any corruption.

The second thing I thought about was who was likely to be the next judge in line to become the senior judge. Who would be the next judge to schedule the court cases and decide who was going to get which cases seemed important to me. That judge could be the one I needed to investigate to see if he was doing something that was not in the best interest of justice.

The third thought that came to mind was to have a talk with Judge Weatherby's secretary. The secretary of a busy man often knew more about him than his wife. In this case there was no wife, but I needed to find out everything I could about Marcus Weatherby. I needed to know everything I could about both his professional life and his private life. His secretary seemed to be the one who could provide me with the best information on the judge. Don would most likely be the one who would know where she could be located. He certainly would have talked to her by now and would know where she lived.

I sat down at my desk after pouring a cup of coffee. I had just opened the bag containing the long john when my phone began to ring. I put my long john down on the bag and reached for the receiver.

"Tidsdale Investigative Agency. How can I help you?"

"Mr. Tidsdale, my name is Martha Hanson. Do you know who I am?"

"No, I don't believe I do," I said as I tried to recall the name.

"I was Judge Marcus Weatherby's secretary."

"Oh. What is it I can do for you?"

"I would like to talk to you about the judge."

"Okay. Is there something important you would like to talk to me about?"

"Yes, but I don't want to talk about him on the phone. Is there some place private where we could meet?" she asked.

I got the impression from the sound of her voice that what she had to say to me was very important. I had a few things to talk to her about as well, but I didn't want to mention them now.

"Sure. How about if I come to your home? Would that be private enough?"

"No. I think it might be better if we talk someplace else. My home might be bugged."

"What makes you think that?"

"I don't know. I'm sure you think I'm imaging things, but I don't think that Marcus, Judge Weatherby, killed himself. He wouldn't do something like that. I'm sure of it."

I thought I could hear a catch in her voice. It sounded as if she had been crying, or maybe she was afraid. It caused me to believe that the relationship between the judge and Ms Hanson might be more than just business.

"Martha, where are you now?"

"I'm calling from my cellphone in a restaurant just a couple of blocks from my apartment."

"Whatever you do, don't go back to your apartment. If the press hasn't been banging on your door, they soon will. Did you drive to the restaurant?"

"No, I walked."

"That's even better. Don't go back home to get your car. Are there many people in the restaurant?"

"It's not full, but there are – ah – maybe – seventeen or eighteen customers here," she said.

"Good. Stay inside the restaurant, and don't leave there for any reason. I'll be there as soon as possible. Where is the restaurant?"

I waited for her to give me the name of the restaurant and where it was located. I told her again to stay there until I got there. She said she would.

I hung up and grabbed my coat, then quickly went to my car and left for the restaurant. It was only about a twenty-five minute drive. I was hoping to get to her before the press could find her. If the press got to her first, it would make it more difficult for me to talk to her without the whole world knowing, and that could jeopardize my investigation for the AG.

Officer Sharon Williams returned to Detective Wright's office and knocked on the door. She was immediately told to enter.

"Did you find her phone number?" Don asked.

"Yes. I also have her address," she replied with a smile.

"Good," he said as she handed a slip of paper to him. "Would you mind waiting for a minute?"

"No, sir," she said with a smile, then sat down in front of Don's desk.

Don reached over and picked up his phone. He dialed the number. The phone rang only three times, then suddenly the line went dead. Don looked at the phone. He had been disconnected just as the receiver was picked up. He wasn't sure if Ms Hanson had picked up the phone then quickly hung it up to avoid talking to someone, or if something else had caused the phone to disconnect. It happened so quickly that it caught Don a little off guard.

It was obvious to Officer Williams that there was something wrong. She could see on Don's face that he was thinking very hard.

"I want you to come with me," Don said suddenly, as he stood up.

Officer Williams had no idea what was going on, but she stood and followed him. She followed him to the police garage where Don pointed at a car.

Don went around to the driver's side and got in while Officer Williams got in on the passenger's side. He started the car and pulled out of the parking space, then headed out onto the street.

"Call in and have a car sent to Martha Hanson's address," Don said as he hit the siren.

"Lincoln 24 to dispatch," she said, then waited for a response.

As soon as dispatch replied, Sharon gave dispatch the address of Martha Hanson's apartment and requested a black-and-white unit be sent to that address as quickly as possible. She also told dispatch they were headed there now.

It didn't take them very long to get to the block where Ms Hanson's apartment was located. As they rounded a corner, they could see smoke coming from the third story of the apartment building. The first thing on Don's mind was that they were too late.

Don pulled out of the way to make room for a fire truck that was coming up behind him. He jumped out of the car and headed for the building. From what he could see there didn't seem to be very much damage, at least to the outside of the building, but there was smoke coming from only one set of windows on the third floor.

Don and Officer Williams began directing people out of the building. It was only a couple of minutes before two firemen ran by them and headed up the stairs. A ladder truck was already starting to run a ladder up to the window.

Since there was nothing Don could do but wait for the firemen to put out the fire, he instructed Officer Williams to begin interviewing as many of the spectators as possible to find out what they saw and what they heard.

It wasn't long before one of the firemen came out of the building. He looked around and saw Don, then walked up to him.

"Are you Detective Wright?" the fireman asked.

"Yeah. Can you tell me what happened?"

"There was a fire in apartment 302. The fire was completely contained in the living room. It was a good thing you called and sent a patrol car. The quick response saved most of the apartment and kept it from spreading to other apartments.

"It looks like there was an explosion at a small table at the end of the sofa. There were some small pieces of what looked like a phone."

"Explosion?"

"Yeah. It wasn't a very big explosion. It looks like it was set to kill whoever answered the phone, but I'm sure your forensic team can tell you what happened. I'm just guessing based on the pieces of table and other material scattered around the room," the fireman said.

"In the living room?"

"Yeah."

"Was there anyone in the apartment?" Don asked, afraid that Martha Hanson had been in her apartment.

"Yes. It looks like the maid was killed in the explosion."

"You said the maid was killed. What makes you think it was the maid?"

"From what we could tell, she was wearing the uniform of the staff of a cleaning service that several of the tenants use."

"You don't think it was the woman who lives there?"

"No. The fire's out. You can go up and look around. This is a case for you and the Fire Marshal now, anyway."

"Okay."

Don looked around for Officer Williams. He could see she was busy interviewing those who had come out of the building immediately after the explosion. He also noticed several other police officers had showed up to help her.

Don went to his car and called for an ambulance and a forensic team. He would have to wait to find out if the female body found in the building really was the maid. He couldn't help but think that by making the call to Ms Hanson, he had helped kill the woman in the apartment. It angered him to think someone would use such a way to kill someone. Right now there was nothing else for him to do, but wait for the forensic team.

CHAPTER FOURTEEN

Fortunately, traffic had been light and I arrived at the restaurant in about twenty minutes from when I had hung up my phone. I was hoping that Ms Hanson had done as I told her. The last thing I wanted was for her to be on the street or in her apartment. I had nothing except the bodies in the café and the judge to make me think she might be in danger. That, and the fact she had worked very closely with a man who had probably been assassinated.

As I was walking to the front door of the restaurant, I could hear the sounds of sirens just a few blocks away. Once inside the restaurant, I stood there looking around. I had no idea what Ms Hanson looked like, but from what little I knew about her, she had to be in her mid-fifties.

There was a woman in her mid-to-late-fifties sitting in a booth away from the door. She was alone and had a cup of coffee on the table in front of her, but she was not drinking it. She was just holding it in both hands as if to warm her hands while looking into the cup.

I walked over to her table and looked down at her. She looked up at me with fear in her eyes. I had seen women before who had that same look. She was scared.

"Are you Martha Hanson?" I asked as I looked down at her. "I'm Frank Tidsdale."

"Yes," she said, a look of relief seemed to come over her face.

"Are you known at this restaurant?" I asked as I slipped into the booth across from her.

"I think there are a couple of the waitresses who might know me by sight, but I don't think they know my name. Why?"

"I think we should get out of here. It's too open, and there is a chance that someone might recognize at least one of us."

"I don't know," she said as she looked around the restaurant. "I don't really know you."

"That's fair enough," I said as I reached inside my coat and pulled out my PI license and showed it to her.

"Now, can we get out of here before someone sees us together? I think I know just the place where you will be safe," I said as I stood up.

"Where's that?"

"It's a quiet little motel in Aurora. I will get you a room there."

She looked like she was still scared and maybe afraid to go with me. I guess I couldn't blame her. After all, she didn't know me.

"Martha, we can't stay here," I said trying to emphasize the importance of getting somewhere she would be safe.

"Yes. I'm sure you're right," she finally conceded.

Slowly, she stood up as I reached over and picked up her coat. She slipped her arms into the coat as I held it for her.

"Stay close to me," I said, as I dropped enough money on the table to pay for her coffee.

I took her by the arm and walked her to the front door of the restaurant. We stopped while I looked out. I couldn't see anything that might present a danger to either of us. We walked briskly to my car. I opened the door for her then looked around while she got in. As soon as I closed her door, I hurried around to the other side and got in. I started the car and drove out onto the street and headed for a little motel in Aurora.

A small man in work clothes stood by a trash can at the street corner about a half a block from the front entrance to the apartment building where Martha Hanson lived. He watched as the police and the fire department arrived on the scene.

He waited patiently while the police began interviewing the onlookers. All the man could think about was that he had done his job, and had done it well. He watched with interest when the ambulance arrived. He had to know if he had been successful. If he had, he was to receive a good deal of money.

It was almost more than he could stand not knowing if he had accomplished the task. If all went well, he was to be paid enough money to go someplace where the weather was warmer all year around, and where he could enjoy himself. If not, he could be in a lot of trouble.

It had taken the ambulance crew what seemed like a very long time to return from inside the apartment building with their stretcher. A feeling of satisfaction washed over the little man when he saw the black body bag on the stretcher. He smiled to himself, satisfied that he had completed his job. He was sure that he was going to get his money, and then he would be able to get out of town.

The little man turned and began walking away. He headed down the street toward where he had parked his car. As he walked, he took his cell phone from his pocket and dialed a number. The phone rang just twice before it was answered.

"Yeah," a male voice said.

"Mission completed," was all the little man said, then hung up his phone.

The little man got in his car and started it. Before he could leave the area, he had to drive by the apartment one last time to see the confusion he had caused. There was no smoke coming from the windows of the apartment, but the explosion had blown out the windows. He smiled to himself until he saw an old man walking toward a car.

The old man had seen him come out of the parking garage earlier, and had even greeted him in passing. The thought that he had been seen got him to thinking. The police had been questioning everyone they came across. If they had questioned him, he could end up being a problem. The little man decided he would follow the old man in the hope of making sure he didn't get a chance to talk to the police again.

CHAPTER FIFTEEN

I drove down the block toward the apartment where Martha Hanson lived. There was a police officer standing at the corner. He motioned for me not to turn. When I got to the corner, I glanced down the street and slowed as I drove straight through the intersection. I could see fire trucks and police cars at the front of the apartment building. I wasn't sure what had happened.

Martha was looking out the window at what was going on. I was too busy with traffic to be looking at her. I heard a gasp come from her. When I quickly glanced over at her, she had her hands over her face.

"What's the matter?" I asked.

Martha began to cry hysterically. She had obviously seen something at the intersection that disturbed her deeply.

I looked for a place where I could pull over to the curb and stop. It took me a couple of blocks before I found a place to park. I pulled into a parking space and stopped. It seemed as if Martha was having difficulty breathing.

"What's the matter?" I asked as I reached over and put my hand on her shoulder.

She turned and looked at me. Her eyes were filled with tears, but she didn't say anything for a moment. She just looked at me as if something had scared her half to death.

"My – my – my apartment," was all she could manage to say.

"What about your apartment?

"It was – on – fire," she said between gasps of air.

"Your apartment was on fire?"

"Yes."

I was a little surprised someone had made an attempt on her life so quickly, even though I knew I shouldn't have been. It had become apparent that someone didn't want anyone to talk to Martha. What was it they thought she might know? I wondered if it was the same thing I hoped that she knew, and hoped she would tell me.

"Martha, I think it is more important than ever that I get you somewhere you will be safe."

"The maid from the cleaning service was in my apartment when I left," she said as she looked at me.

"Do you think she might have had something to do with the fire?"

"Oh, no. I have known Alice for years. She is a very nice person."

"I think we will get you settled in a safe place, then I'll have a talk with a friend of mine on the police force. He might be able to give me some information on what happened in your apartment."

I checked for any oncoming cars, then pulled out into the street again. I headed out toward Aurora. The guy who owned the motel was my cousin from my mother's side of the family. He would make sure no one knew she was there.

Don waited for the forensic team to show up. When they arrived there were two investigators and the lead investigator, Mel Street. Don walked over to the van just as Mel was getting out.

"Seeing you at all these crime scenes is getting to be a habit. Is this something of interest to you?" Mel asked.

"Yeah. We were on our way over to see the woman who lives in the apartment that had the fire. It looks like the phone exploded and killed the cleaning woman. At least that is who it appears to be. We don't think the woman who lives in the apartment was even there when the phone exploded. I'm hoping you can confirm that for me."

"I'll let you know what we find out," Mel said. "You said the phone exploded?"

"Yeah, and I think I set it off," Don said.

Mel looked at Don. The expression on his face showed that he didn't understand Don's comment.

"I called her from my office. The phone rang three times then as soon as it was picked up, the line went dead."

"What is the woman to you?"

"She was Judge Weatherby's secretary."

"I see. Well, we'll see what we can find out for you."

"Good. Give me a call when you have something," Don said.

Mel nodded, then turned and started into the apartment building.

Don turned and looked for Officer Williams. As soon as he saw her, he walked toward her. She had just finished questioning one of the tenants of the apartment building.

"Thank you for your cooperation," she said to the lady, then turned and saw Don coming toward her.

"Hi," Officer Williams said with a smile.

"Are you about done here?"

"Yes. All I have left is to get all the interviews that were done by the other officers."

"Okay. Collect them and meet me at the car."

"Yes, sir."

Don turned and left Officer Williams to collect the interview reports done by the other officers. He then called dispatch and requested the license number, the make and model of Martha Hanson's car. As soon as the dispatcher gave him the information he wanted, he went into the underground parking garage and began looking for her car. He wasn't sure it would be there, but it was the best place to start looking for it.

It didn't take him but a few minutes to find it. He quickly looked it over, but found nothing to make him think there was anything unusual about the car. Seeing her car parked in the garage told him that she had left the building either with someone else, or she had walked to someplace close by.

As Don stood looking at Ms Hanson's car, he wondered if her car might have also been rigged to explode in case the phone bomb didn't work. Not wanting to take a chance, he called dispatch and requested a bomb squad come and check out the car.

Don waited until the bomb squad arrived. He told them what he suspected, then watched from a distance while the bomb squad went over the car. It didn't take them long to find another explosive under the dash of the car. They disarmed it and showed it to Don.

"Any idea who might have planted it?" Don asked the lead officer.

"No, but we might be able to tell you after we look it over. Most of these guys have a signature way of hooking up such a bomb. I'll let you know what we come up with. The car is safe to drive now."

"Thanks," Don said, then turned and left the parking garage.

Don went back to his car and waited for Officer Williams. It wasn't long before she showed up and got in the car. Don told her about the bomb in Ms Hanson's car while driving back to the office. Once in the office, they sat down and went over the interview reports looking for something unusual.

CHAPTER SIXTEEN

We arrived at the small motel in Aurora around mid-morning. Martha waited in the car while I visited with my cousin and explained the situation, and what I wanted him to do. I took a few minutes to register Martha in a room with an adjoining room. I had him register Martha as Mrs. William Hubble. I had the adjoining room registered to a William Hubble.

Once I had the room keys, I returned to the car and got Martha. I quickly guided her into her room, then sat down on the bed. She sat in a chair by a table in the corner while I placed a call to my friend.

"Yeah," the male voice on the other end of the line said.

"Frank Tidsdale here."

"I'll get him," the voice said.

It was only a matter of a couple of minutes before my friend came on the phone.

"Franky, what can I do for you? I don't have all the information you wanted, yet. I'll need another day or so."

"No problem. I need something else."

"Okay. What do you need?"

"I need a muscle who can keep his mouth shut."

"No problem. When?"

"Now."

"Where?"

I gave him the address of the motel and told him the room number.

"He'll be there in thirty minutes."

"Tell him to come prepared to stay here for several days at least."

"Sure. Will you be there till he can get there?"

"Yes. He is registered as William Hubble."

"Okay."

"When he comes to the door, he is to identify himself as William Hubble."

"Got it."

"Thanks," I said.

"You're welcome, Franky," he said then the phone went dead.

I looked over at Martha. She was sitting with her arms wrapped around herself. It was obvious she was scared, but then she had every right to be.

"Martha, there will be a man coming to stay with you. He will stay in the adjoining room. He will be here to protect you. If anyone should come to your door, you get him to answer it. Don't answer the door yourself."

"Are you leaving?"

"Not until he gets here. Do you feel like talking about Judge Weatherby?"

"Would you mind it I lay down for a little while?"

"No, of course not. I'll go into the other room and wait for your bodyguard."

"Thank you," she said.

I got up and secured the door to her room and closed the drapes. I went into the adjoining room, but left the door between the rooms ajar. I sat down in the chair at the small table and waited for her bodyguard. While I waited I wondered what Ms Hanson would tell me about the judge and what she would keep from me.

Don and Officer Williams sat at a table in Don's office and went over the interview reports. They separated them into people who lived in the building, and people who didn't. Don took the interview reports from those who didn't live in the building.

As he went through the reports, he found one consistent thing they all seemed to agree on. All the witnesses said there was a loud explosion that blew out the windows before the fire. When asked if they saw anyone leaving the building or acting strangely, only one person said he saw a short man with a heavy coat and dark work pants leave the parking garage several minutes before he heard the explosion. He had been carrying a small black tool chest. Unfortunately, he couldn't give any better description of the man to the officer.

Don stopped, leaned back in his chair and closed his eyes. He was thinking about what the witness had told the officer. If the man the witness saw was the one who placed the bomb in the phone, how did he get in? Was he posing as a telephone repairman? His thoughts were disturbed by Officer Williams.

"I talked to one of the residents of the apartment building who said she saw Ms Hanson leave the building shortly before the explosion."

"Did she say where she was going?"

"She didn't know for sure, but she thought she might be going down the street to a restaurant for breakfast."

"Was that something she usually did?" Don asked.

"She indicated Ms Hanson usually went to the restaurant on Friday with a couple of the other single or widowed women from the building."

"*Since this is not Friday, there had to be another reason for her to go to the restaurant. It was probably a place where she felt safe. Did she go with anyone?*"

"*No. She said she was alone, but she could have been going to meet someone.*"

"*I think it would be a good idea if we have another talk with her. What was her name?*"

"*Mrs. Jill Hartman,*" *Officer Williams said.*

"*Check with her and see if you can get the name of anyone in the apartment building who might be Hanson's friend.*"

"*Okay. Did you find anything?*" *Officer Williams asked.*

"*Yeah. Someone saw a short man wearing dark work pants, large coat, and carrying a small black tool box leave the parking garage. He could have been a repairman, or he could have been our bomber.*"

"*I would like you to go have another talk with Mrs. Hartman. See if she can give you any more information.*"

"*Right now?*" *Officer Williams asked.*

"*Yes. I'll meet you back here. I'm going to have another talk with - - ah - - Mr. Joseph Miller,*" *Don said as I looked at his name. "I hope he can tell me more about this 'repairman'. I'll meet you back here.*"

"*Yes, sir,*" *she said as she stood up and left Don's office.*

Don leaned back as soon as Officer Williams left. A call to the Bomb Squad's precinct was in order. He wanted to see if they had anything on the bomb they found in Ms Hanson's car. He reached over, picked up the phone and dialed the number. The phone was answered on the second ring.

"*Bomb Squad, Sergeant Walker.*"

"*Sergeant Walker, this is Detective Don Wright. A couple of your guys took a bomb out of a car this morning. I* was hoping they might have found something that would give me an idea who made it or who planted it in the car."

"We've been discussing that. We haven't decided who made the bomb, but we are leaning hard toward two individuals. One is Charley Goodman. He's from out of town. Colorado Springs, the last we heard. The other is Max "The Bomber" Carlson. The last known address we have on him is in the Las Vegas area. We're trying to pin it down to one of them."

"What compelled you to look at those two?"

"They both have used the type of detonators that were used in both the car bomb and the pieces of the bomb that was used in the telephone at Ms Hanson's apartment."

"Do you know if either of them is in town?"

"Not for sure, but we will get an APB out on both of them, just in case they're here."

"Good. By chance does one of them happen to be a little guy?"

"Yeah. Max "The Bomber" Carlson. Why? You got a witness?"

"I have a guy who was near the apartment building who said he saw a little man leave the parking garage shortly before the explosion. He was wearing dark work pants, a large coat and carrying a small black tool box."

"That sounds like Max. I'll get an APB out on him right away. My guess is he is headed for home as fast as he can get there."

"Thanks. Let me know what you find."

"Will do."

Don was thinking about the bomber as he hung up the phone. It would cost a good deal of money to get someone from out of town to kill someone with a bomb. For now there was nothing Don could do except follow the leads he had. That meant paying a visit to Mr. Miller.

Don went to the Police Garage and got a car. He then headed for Mr. Miller's home.

CHAPTER SEVENTEEN

Ms Hanson slept until almost noon. It was probably the first time she felt safe and secure since the death of the Judge. I was in the next room softly talking to Jake Simpson, one of my friend's bodyguards. He was a nice looking man, and except for his size no one would guess that he was a bodyguard. He was clean cut and very polite. I was quietly giving him his instructions with regard to protecting Ms Hanson when she called me.

"Mr. Tidsdale?" she called out softly.

"Yes, Ms Hanson. Are you presentable?"

"Yes."

"I have someone I would like you to meet," I said as I got up and walked into the adjoining room.

I couldn't help but notice the look on her face when she saw Jake. Actually, Jake was a rather handsome man and looked like any nice little old lady's adult grandson.

"Ms Hanson, this is Jake Simpson."

"Jake, this is Martha Hanson."

"It is nice to meet you, Ms Hanson," Jake said with a very pleasant smile.

"Jake is going to protect you from anyone who might want to harm you or disclose your location so others can find you. He will be with you at all times. Should you need something, all you have to do is tell Jake what it is and he will make sure you get it.

"However, I want you to do whatever he says. He cannot protect you if you don't. Do you understand?"

"Yes. He doesn't look like a thug. Oh, excuse me for my choice of words," Martha said as she glanced at Jake.

"I'm not really a thug," Jake said with a smile. "I'm a bodyguard. I wouldn't hurt anyone unless they try to hurt you."

"Are you ready to talk to me about Judge Weatherby?" I asked.

She looked over at me for a moment, then looked down at the floor. I waited until she looked up again.

"Yes," she said softly.

"Judge Weatherby was the senior judge. It was his responsibility to schedule cases, or at least assign cases to the other judges, is that correct?"

"Yes, except he didn't really schedule the cases. He did assign some cases to the judges in his area, which was the criminal court. However, the judges schedule the court dates and any hearing dates that were required to fit their calendar. The only cases he actually did the scheduling on were the cases he assigned to himself."

"But he did assign the cases to the other judges?"

"Yes."

"Did he assign the same kind of cases to the same judge? What I mean by that is he would assign divorce cases to the same judge, for example?"

"He didn't handle divorce cases in criminal court, but not really. He tried to spread them around, but like in any organization, there were some who were better at a particular type of case then others."

"For example?"

"Murder cases he often gave to Judge Colton. Robbery cases, especially those involving weapons, he would often give them to Judge Samuelson. He was really good with those cases, especially when there were young people involved."

"What about cases that involved the mob or mob enforcers? These would be cases like extortion, murder and racketeering."

"He handled most of them himself. Sometimes he would assign one to Judge Wilkinson, especially if it didn't involve the mob boss."

"Did Judge Weatherby handle all the cases involving a mob boss?"

"Yes. Well, most of the time."

"Do you know why Judge Weatherby took so many of the cases that involved the mob boss?"

"I'm not sure, but he indicated that he felt since he was the senior judge he should take the 'tougher cases', as he liked to call them. He felt there would be less chance of an appeal if he handled them himself."

I looked at Jake and noticed that he was looking at me. The expression on his face made me wonder if he was thinking the same thing I was. I got the feeling that Judge Weatherby was taking most of the big cases so he could control them. It was not a new thought on my part. It had crossed my mind before.

"Martha, do you know of anything that might have been bothering the judge, say for the past few months?"

She sat there looking at me for several minutes. I wasn't sure if she was trying to decide if she should say something, or if she was trying to think of something.

"Marcus lost his wife about three years ago. He took it very hard. They were very close. It took a long time before he seemed to pull himself together. The past few months he seemed to be doing very well. No. I don't think there was anything bothering him lately."

"Do you happen to know who will be the judge to take Weatherby's place as the senior judge?"

"I wouldn't know that."

"If you had to guess, who do you think it is likely to be?" I asked.

"It will probably be Judge John Wilkinson or Judge J. Barlow Smith."

"Not Judge Colton?"

"No. I think it would be Judge Wilkinson or Judge Smith.

"Why not Colton? It seems that he took a lot of Weatherby's cases while he was out immediately after his wife died."

"Judge Colton didn't take any of Judge Weatherby's cases. He covered for Judge Wilkinson while Judge Wilkinson covered for Judge Weatherby. I overheard Judge Weatherby tell one of the other judges that Judge Colton didn't have enough experience to be senior judge."

"So you're saying that Wilkinson and Smith had more experience?"

"Yes."

"So Wilkinson is likely to be Judge Weatherby's replacement?"

"I would think so. Judge Weatherby mentioned once that he thought Judge Wilkinson would be best suited for the position."

"Why's that?"

"Judge Wilkinson has more experience in the tougher cases, and Judge Smith is getting close to retirement."

"One more questions. Why did you call me?"

"I overheard Marcus recommend you to a friend of his awhile back," she said

"Thank you, Martha. We'll talk again later, but for now I have a couple of things I need to check on. Jake will keep you company. If you think of anything that might help, please tell Jake that you want to talk to me."

"I will."

I left the motel and drove back to my office. I was a little short on ideas at the moment, but the one thing I wanted to find out was what cases had Judge Weatherby heard over the past few years.

Detective Wright pulled up in front of a small Cape Cod styled house in one of the older parts of Denver. The house was located several miles from Hanson's apartment. He wondered what Mr. Miller was doing at the apartment building.

As Don stepped up on the porch, he heard a dog barking inside the house. He reached out and pressed the doorbell. Don could hear it ring. He waited, but no one answered the door. He rang the bell again, but still no answer.

Don was getting a little worried about the man who had claimed to have seen the repairman at the apartment. He stepped over to a window near the end of the porch and looked in. He couldn't see anyone inside, but he could still hear the dog barking.

He stepped off the porch and walked around to the side of the house. There were several windows on the side of the house. The first one he could not see in because the drapes were closed. The second window had the drapes closed also, but there was a gap that allowed him to see part of the room. He could see a small dog that seemed very agitated about something. Don tried the window to see if he could get it open, but it wouldn't budge. His efforts to open the window were suddenly disturbed by a voice coming from behind him.

"Hey, you! What do you think you're doing? Get away from that house before I call the cops," the elderly man yelled from his window.

Don turned and looked at the man, then reached into his coat pocket and said, "I am the cops." Don held up his badge and ID for the man to see.

"Oh. What's going on? You lookin' for Joe?"

"Yes. Is Mr. Miller's dog usually so agitated?"

"No. He's usually pretty quiet."

"Are you on good terms with the dog?"

"Yes, sir. I take care of him when Joe goes to his daughter's place in Vale. His daughter doesn't like dogs."

"Something has got the dog upset and it isn't me. Would you happen to have a key to Mr. Miller's house?"

"Yes, sir. I'll get it," the man said then disappeared from the window.

It wasn't but a minute or so before the elderly man showed up in the driveway. He showed Don that he had a key in his hand.

"It's for the backdoor," the man said then started for the backdoor.

When they got to the backdoor, Don found that one of the small panes of glass in the door had been broken out near the latch. There was glass on the ground near the door, but it looked like most of the glass was inside, indicating the glass was broken from the outside.

"Will the dog come to you if you call him?"

"Sure."

"I want you to call the dog and take him to your house."

"Okay."

Don took a handkerchief from his pocket and slowly opened the door. He looked at the man to make sure he was ready.

"Don't touch anything but the dog."

The old man moved up close to the door and called the dog. It was only a matter of seconds before the dog came running to the man. The man grabbed the dog by the collar and took him in his arms.

"Thanks. Take the dog to your house and wait for me there."

"Yes, sir.

As the man turned and took the dog to his house, Don pushed the door open and stepped inside. He carefully moved from the kitchen into a small hallway. It was there that he found a man lying on the floor. He moved next to the man and checked to see if he was still alive. When he touched the man's neck for a pulse, the man groaned softly.

"Lay still, I'll get some help," Don said.

Don stood up and looked around. There was a phone on the wall just inside the kitchen. He dialed 9-1-1. As soon as it was answered, he identified himself and requested a black-and-white unit and an ambulance be dispatched to the house. He also requested a forensic team. He hung up the phone, sat down on the floor beside the man and waited. It didn't take very long before a black-and-white unit arrived on the scene. The ambulance arrived within a few minutes.

As soon as Mr. Miller was taken away in the ambulance, Don walked next door to talk to the man who had taken the dog. He knocked on the backdoor. It was answered within a couple of seconds.

"How is Joe?" the man asked. "I saw them take him away in the ambulance."

"I don't know, but he responded to me when I touched him. I didn't get your name."

"Fred, Fred Winkelman."

"Mr. Winkelman, did you see anyone around Mr. Miller's house today?"

"No," he said after thinking about it for a minute.

"No one walking down the street, or a car parked out in front you didn't recognize?"

"No. No, I don't think so."

"When did you first notice the dog was barking?"

"I was working in the basement on the other side of my house so I didn't hear anything until I saw you from my kitchen window," he said looking as if he should have heard something.

"Is your wife at home?"

"My Jenny died about two years ago. I live alone."

"I'm sorry. Mr. Winkelman, I would appreciate it if you would call me if you think of anything," Don said as he handed the man one of his cards.

"I will. I will think on it. If I remember anything, I'll give you a call. Tell Joe that I'll take good care of his dog."

"I will. Thank you," Don said, then turned and went to his car.

Don waited until the forensic team arrived and began going over the house looking for clues that might tell him who had been in the house. As soon as the forensic team was working, Don returned to his office.

CHAPTER EIGHTEEN

I took my cell phone and placed a call to the special number that Greene had given me. The phone ran only twice before it was answered.

"Yeah," he said.

"I need some information. I need to know what cases Judge Weatherby handled over the past two or three years."

"I can get that for you. Anything else?"

"Yes. I want to know the name of the judge that will take Weatherby's place as the senior judge of the criminal court. I would also like his court assignments for the past couple of years as well."

"I'm not sure who will be his replacement. I'll get reports on all the likely candidates for the job."

"That would be helpful," I said. "It looks like there was an attempt on Ms Hanson's life, but luckily she was not at home to answer the phone."

"I heard about that. Do you know where she is now?"

"Yes."

I thought it was interesting he didn't ask me where I was hiding Martha. I wasn't sure if it was because there was someone in his office. If that was the case, it would explain why he didn't ask me much of anything that could give away who he was talking to. The only other reason I could think of for him not asking was because he already knew I had her hidden away.

"I need to go," Greene said, then the phone went dead.

I sat at my desk thinking about Greene and what he didn't say. I wondered just how much of what I knew, he already knew. I knew he would have some contact with the forensic teams that had worked on both the bombing of the café and the death of Judge Weatherby.

I decided to take a couple of minutes to contact Don. I called Don on my cell phone. My call was answered quickly and immediately transferred to Don's office.

"Detective Wright. How may I help you?"

"Don, Tidsdale. How are things going for you?"

"Not well. But we do have a lead on the guy who bombed Ms Hanson's apartment."

"So that was what all the commotion was about at her apartment. From what I saw, it looked like a fire."

"You were there?"

"Not really. I drove by the place. With all the fire equipment, I thought it was probably a fire."

"You wouldn't happen to know where we can find Ms Hanson, would you."

"Yes. I can assure you she is in a very safe place with a well trained bodyguard."

"Have you talked to her?"

"Yes. She doesn't believe the judge killed himself any more than we do."

"I would like to talk to her," Don said.

"I'm sure you would, but I don't think it is a good idea until we have a better idea of what is going on here. I can't risk her life. She may be the only lead we have to why the judge was murdered."

"I don't like not having her available to question, but I can see your point."

"I have an idea. It's not great, but it would be safer for her. How about if I arrange for her to answer any questions you have over a cell phone where it can't be traced or bugged?"

"Like you said, it isn't perfect, but it is better than nothing," Don agreed.

"Give me a little time to get her a cell phone. When I have it arranged, I'll call you."

"Okay," Don said, then hung up.

I knew Don didn't like the idea of having to interview Ms Hanson over a phone. He would like to be able to see her face when she answered his questions, but he also understood it would be safer for her.

I leaned back in my chair to think. My thoughts turned to the bombing of Martha's apartment. I thought about calling Don back and asking him about it, but decided it could wait. Martha was safe for the moment.

Don hadn't been in his office very long when Officer Williams showed up. He looked up at her from behind his desk and waited for her to sit down.

"Was Mrs. Hartman able to give you any more information?"

"Yes. She said one of the other tenants in the apartment building saw Ms Hanson leave a restaurant only a couple of blocks from her apartment with a man. That was all the information she could give me.

"I talked to the other witness. She described the man as fairly tall and rather nice looking. She said she got into his car and left the parking lot before she could call out to her. She couldn't tell me what kind of car."

"That would be Tidsdale," Don said casually without thinking about it.

"I take it you know who this Tidsdale is?"

"Yes. I've known him for a long time. He's a private investigator."

"You trust him?" she asked as if she doubted he would trust any private investigator.

"Yes. I know that PIs are not thought very highly of by a lot of police officers, but he is one I would trust with my life. In fact, I have."

The look on her face told him that she wasn't sure trusting the private investigator was a good idea. But she would take his word for it.

"Have you heard any more about the bomber?" Officer Williams asked.

"No. I have an APB out on him. I also have the bus station and airport covered. We have as many roads covered as possible in case he is driving back to Las Vegas. His name is Max "The Bomber" Carlson.

Don looked at his watch, then looked at the female officer sitting across the desk from him. He thought about asking her to go to dinner with him, but decided it would be inappropriate since he was a superior officer.

"It's getting late. We should call it a night. I'm going home and get some rest. We'll hit it again in the morning."

"Okay. I'll talk to you tomorrow," she said, then got up and left the office.

As soon as she left, Don sat at his desk for a few minutes before he got up and left for home.

CHAPTER NINETEEN

I left my office and started for home. I hadn't gone very far when I noticed there was a black sedan that seemed to be following me. I decided I would not head straight for my apartment, but take the time to find out if it was actually following me.

As I turned off Colfax onto Downing, I watched in the rearview mirror to see if it followed me. It continued on Colfax. I quickly found a parking space and pulled into it, then sat and waited.

I waited, but didn't see the car again. I didn't see any other cars that looked like there was someone looking for me. After waiting for almost fifteen minutes, I pulled away from the curb and drove on home. I didn't see the black sedan again, and I didn't see anyone else who seemed to be following me.

When I arrived at my apartment, I parked in the garage then went inside. I had no more than entered the kitchen to make a cup of coffee when my phone rang. I picked it up.

"Hello."

"This is Mr. Hubble."

"How's everything?"

"Mrs. Hubble would like to talk to you. She said she didn't know if it was important, but she remembered something."

"Okay. I'll be there shortly," I said, then hung up.

I went to my car and headed to the motel in Aurora. I kept a very close watch for anyone following me, but didn't see anyone.

When I arrived at the motel, I knocked on the door to Ms Hanson's room. It took a minute or so before Jake looked out the window to see who was there. When he saw me, he smiled then opened the door. I went inside and found Ms Hanson hiding in the adjoining room.

"You have something important to tell me?"

"Yes. On the night Judge Weatherby was shot, a man called and insisted I let him talk to the judge. He was quite forceful."

"Did you put the call through?"

"Yes, but only after I told the judge about the man being so insistent."

"What did the judge say to you before he took the call?"

"He told me to put the call through, and he would teach the man not to be so rude to me."

"Do you remember what the judge said to you before you put the call through? I mean his exact words?"

"No, but it was something like, I'll straighten him out."

"That doesn't sound so bad," I said as I started to think about it. "Has anything like that happened before?"

"Yes, but not very often. The strange thing was, in the past he has always wanted me to be on the line as a witness to what was said."

"I take it he didn't want you on the line this time?"

"No. Another strange thing was before he had me transfer the call he asked me to go to the cafeteria to get him some milk."

I sat there and thought about what I had just been told. He had someone who was insisting on talking to him, but makes the caller wait while he orders a carton of milk. That, along with the fact it was the first time he had Ms Hanson not remain on the line to witness what was said, caused me to wonder who called him.

"Did he often ask you to get him milk?"

"Not that late in the evening. He rarely drank milk."

"Did he need it for his coffee?"

"He doesn't – ah – didn't drink coffee and he never took milk in his tea."

I had to admit that what she told me was strange. A check of phone records was in order. I would have to ask Don to see if he could get them.

"Thank you for the information. I'll have it checked out in the morning. Try to get some rest. If you think of anything else, let Jake know."

"I will."

"Goodnight," I said as I left the motel.

I drove back to my apartment. I had kept an eye out for anyone following me, but saw no one. By the time I got home it was getting pretty late. I grabbed a light dinner, then headed off to bed. It had been a busy day and I was tired. It didn't take any time at all for me to get to sleep.

Don arrived at his office the next morning to find Sharon Williams already there. She was going over some of the material from the forensic team. She looked up and smiled at Don as he entered his office.

"Good morning."

"Good morning. Are you trying to take over my job?" Don said with a grin.

"No, sir," she said. "I was just looking over what evidence we had hoping for a fresh look at it. I didn't mean anything by being in your office.

The smile on Officer Williams' face quickly changed to a very worried look when she suddenly realized that she might have overstepped her bounds. He may not like the fact that she was in his office.

"It's okay," he said with a smile. "It never hurts to give it a second look. Do you think you might have found something?"

"No. I'm afraid not."

"What have you looked over so far this morning?"

"I've been looking at the forensic evidence we have."

"Did you find anything?"

"Well, sir. I might have."

"What did you find?" Don asked.

"Ah – ah – I'm not sure, but I don't think Judge Weatherby committed suicide."

"You don't?"

"No, I don't. I think he was assassinated, murdered."

"Very good. Mel and I happen to agree with you."

"So we're looking for a murderer?"

"Yes, we are." Don said.

She looked at him and began to smile.

"You knew all the time, didn't you?" she said.

"We suspected it from the first time I saw the crime scene. It was good work on your part, just the same."

"Thank you. What do we do now?"

"We contact Mel at the state lab and find out if he has anything more for us. I think we should drive over there and see what he has firsthand."

Officer Williams nodded that she agreed. Don turned and held the door for Officer Williams then followed her to the police garage. They checked out a car and drove to the State Lab.

CHAPTER TWENTY

I was up before the alarm clock went off. After a quick shower and a cup of coffee, I was on my way to my office. I needed to get hold of Don and ask him if he could get the phone records for outside calls to Judge Weatherby's chamber for the past couple of days. I had no idea what it would tell me, but I was hoping it might give me a place to start looking for who might have killed Weatherby. If I could find that out, I might be one step closer to finding out why the judge was murdered.

After parking my car in the parking garage of the office building, I took the elevator to the floor were my office was located. As I stepped off the elevator, I noticed the door to my office was open. I drew my gun from under my coat and walked toward the door. Leaning up against the wall next to the door, I listened in the hope of hearing something that would tell me if there was someone in my office. I could hear two people talking, but there was only one I could understand.

"Do you think Franky will be upset that you picked the lock on his door," a female voice said.

The woman sounded a little worried that I might be upset. However, I immediately recognized the woman's voice. It was the woman who had answered the phone when I called my friend to ask him for help. The other voice was that of my friend, although I couldn't understand what he said. I slipped my gun back under my coat as I walked into my office.

"I'll never be upset when it's you who breaks into my office. How are you doing?" I said as I stuck out my hand to my friend.

"I'm doing great," he replied. "I would like you to meet a friend of mine. Betty, this is one of my best friends, Frank Tidsdale, or Franky to us.

"Hi, Franky. It's nice to put a face to the name. I've heard a lot about you."

"All good, I hope."

"Well, maybe not all, but most," she said with a grin.

"What brings you here?" I asked as I looked at my friend.

"I have a lot of information for you, but have a question for you first. Are you working on the murder of Judge Weatherby?"

"Yes, but what makes you think it was murder?"

"This is what I do know. Judge Weatherby was into the mob for a lot of money. He paid it back by helping keep certain people out of jail. He was also paid a lot of money to keep doing it after his debt was paid. He has a large bank account in the Cayman Islands. It was my guess he was planning on retiring there. There was apparently a screw up somewhere, but it got the AG looking into the judge. I think the judge was murdered to keep him quiet."

"What about Robert Martin? You know anything about that?" I asked.

"Yeah. He was murdered because he was in debt to the same crime boss that had the judge under his thumb. The word is he was planning on talking to the cops in the hope of saving his own skin. It seems that a mole in the AG's office figured out what Martin was planning on doing. As a result, he became a liability to the crime boss. You know what that means. How he was found out, I don't know."

"Any idea who the mole is?" I asked.

"Like I said, there's another mole in the AG's office. I don't know who it is, but if I find out I'll let you know. You be careful out there."

"Thanks for the warning," I said.

"No problem," my friend said with a grin.

"Are there any other judges involved in this?" I asked.

"I think so. Judge Wilkinson, and maybe Judge Smith. Rumor has it Judge Wilkinson will be taking over as the senior judge. If that happens, it will most likely be business as usual."

"Any proof?" I asked.

"Not yet, but Wilkinson seems to be spending more than he makes. At least Judge Weatherby was smart not to spend the money the mob paid him. He hid it in a numbered off shore account in the Caymans."

"I won't ask you how you know that."

"That's good, because I wouldn't tell you," he said with a smile.

"At least now I know why Robert Martin and Judge Weatherby were assassinated. Now all I have to do is figure out who did it and prove it."

"Sounds pretty simple to me," he said with a laugh. "Do you still need all the information you asked for?"

"You have it?"

"Yeah."

"Keep it in a safe place, just in case I need it later."

"Okay. We best be going. Call if you need anything."

"I will. It was nice to meet you, Betty."

"Nice to meet you, too," she said.

I watched as my friend and Betty left my office. As soon as they were gone, I thought it would be a good idea if I called Greene and let him know what I learned. The more I thought about it, the more I was sure he probably already knew. I got the feeling he was looking to me to find the proof.

I decided I would give Don a call and see if he found out anything that might help me. I still wanted the phone records. Given what I was told, I wondered how much I could tell Don. The one thing I didn't know was the name of the mob boss who was involved? I needed time to think.

I placed the call to the precinct where Don had his office. The desk sergeant told me Don was not in and asked if I wanted to leave a massage. I decided not to leave a message, then hung up.

Don and Sharon arrived at the State Lab about eight-thirty in the morning. They found Mel in the autopsy room. On the table was Judge Weatherby. Don knocked on the window next to the door to get Mel's attention.

Mel looked up and saw the two of them standing just outside the room. He was just finishing up his examination of the body. He held up a finger to indicate that it would be just a minute or so before he could talk to them.

Don watched as Mel finished. Don noticed that Sharon looked away, but he understood. His first autopsy was hard to look at, but he had seen a lot more gruesome scenes at several of the murder cases he had investigated over the years. At least on the Medical Examiner's table, the body had been cleaned up and it wasn't lying in a pool of blood.

Mel covered the body on the table, then took off his surgical gloves and clicked off the tape recorder. He walked around the table to the door and stepped out of the examining room. He glanced over at Sharon, but didn't say anything to her.

"Well, this much I can tell you. Judge Weatherby died of a single gunshot wound to the left side of his head just above the temple. The bullet entered the skull at an almost twenty degree downward angle. He had severe arthritis in his left shoulder that would have made it very difficult, if not impossible, for him to shoot himself in that manner. My conclusion is he was murdered."

"So, I officially have a murder case on my hands."

"Yes, you do."

"Anything else?"

"Yeah. The gun at the scene was a .38 caliber revolver. It was the gun used to kill him. The shell casings were wiped clean. The only fingerprints on the gun were Weatherby's.

There was no powder residue on his hands, meaning he did not fire the gun. Whoever thought he was making it look like a suicide doesn't know anything about forensic."

"Do you have anything more on the gun? Was it Judge Weatherby's gun?"

"We don't have anything on the gun. We are trying to find out where it was purchased and who purchased it. No luck so far."

"Were there any drugs in the judge's body?" Don asked.

"The only drugs we have been able to find was one used to control high cholesterol and one used for his arthritis. The judge had problems with those two conditions. There was nothing else."

"Okay. Thanks. If you come up with anything else, let me know."

"I will. By the way, who is your new partner?"

"Oh. Sorry. This is Officer Sharon Williams."

"I'm Mel Street," he said as he reached out and shook her hand.

"Nice to meet you," she replied with a pleasant smile.

"We best get going. We have a lot to do."

"Talk to you later," Mel said, then watched them leave.

Don and Sharon returned to the car, then drove back to the office. Neither of them said much as they were deep in thought.

CHAPTER TWENTY-ONE

Since Don was not in his office, I placed a call on my cell phone to the private phone of Attorney General Greene. It was answered almost immediately.

"Yeah."

"Can you talk?"

"Yeah. What's up?"

"I was wondering if you could get me the phone records for the past six months on the phones of Judge Weatherby, Judge Wilkinson, and Judge Smith. That's Judge J. Barlow Smith?"

"You think you have something?"

"Maybe. It seems Judge Weatherby got a phone call from someone that insisted on talking to him without giving his name. I'm hoping he called from a landline phone or an unsecured cell phone. It might lead me to where the call came from."

"You think the caller might have had something to do with the death of Weatherby?" Greene asked.

"I'm not sure, but it might have something to do with why he was murdered. It's a lead and I need to follow up on it."

"Why do you want that information on Wilkinson and Smith?"

"Rumor has it Judge Wilkinson is likely to be promoted to senior judge. I'm not sure if Judge Smith plays into this or not, but he could get the job of senior judge based on his long time on the bench. I want to know if either of them got any calls from the same number."

"I can get that for you."

"Thanks," I said then hung up.

I sat back and wondered what the phone records would show. If it showed both men received or made calls to that number, I might want to check out the rest of the judges to see if any other judges got or placed calls to that number.

Once Don and Sharon were in the car, Don reached out to start the car but hesitated. Sharon looked at him and wondered what he was thinking. She decided not to disturb his thoughts.

"Why was Judge Weatherby assassinated?" he asked, thinking out loud.

"Do you think he was into something crooked?"

"Apparently someone does."

"Do you know who?"

"I have an idea, but I'm not ready to say anything about it," Don said thoughtfully.

"What do we do next?"

"I think it is time to contact Tidsdale and get him to let me talk to Ms Hanson."

"Why do you have to ask him for permission to talk to her? She could provide us with information that would be hard to get from anyone else. She was the man's personal secretary. She probably knows more about him than anyone," Sharon said as if she thought Don was making a big mistake by placing his trust and being friends with Tidsdale.

"Because he has her hidden away to protect her."

"He is keeping a witness from giving the police information that may be helpful in finding the judge's killer. That's a crime by itself."

"You are fairly new to this kind of police work. There are a few things you need to understand. Not everything you learned at the academy is the way it is out on the street. There are things you have to learn on the job. One of those is learning who you can trust and who you can't."

"But he is keeping a witness from you."

"Not really. First of all, I already know he has her hidden away, and I have known it from shortly after he found her. In fact, he told me himself. He is hiding a possible witness in a safe place with a full-time bodyguard."

"We have safe houses where she can be protected."

"Maybe so. But there are a lot of people who know where the safe houses are. And I know for a fact the safe houses are not all that safe if some lowlife really wants to get at someone held there. The one thing about Tidsdale, he will have someone protecting her twenty-four hours a day. And more importantly, she will be the only one the bodyguard has to protect, and she will be secure."

"It sounds like you think our safe houses are not safe."

"I have lost a witness that was considered to be safe in one of our so-called 'safe houses'. As far as I'm concerned, Tidsdale can do a better job of keeping her safe then we can."

"How do you get in contact with Tidsdale?"

"I call him. When we get back to the office, I'll call him and arrange to talk to Ms Hanson."

Don reached over and turned the key to start the car. As the car started, he glanced at Sharon. He got the impression she still wasn't sure if it was a good idea to have a PI watching over a valuable witness.

Officer Sharon Williams sat straight up and looked out the windshield of the car as Don drove back to the office. She was deep in thought. Maybe he was right. Maybe he was trying to help her learn how it really was on the street, but then he wasn't protecting a witness according to the book.

It wasn't long and they were back in his office.

CHAPTER TWENTY-TWO

It was now mid-morning and I still hadn't called Don to see what he could tell me. I decided I would wait to see what Don had for me before I would tell him about my visit with Ms Hanson. I picked up the phone and placed a call to Don at the police department. Don had returned. My call was transferred to Don's office.

"Detective Wright, how may I help you?"

"Don, Tidsdale."

"How's it going?"

"Slow. Do you have anything that will help?" I asked.

"It's official. Judge Weatherby was murdered. The ME said it would have been very difficult, if not impossible, for the judge to shoot himself with the gun at the angle the bullet traveled. The judge had severe arthritis in his left shoulder, and there was no powder residue on the judge's hand so we know he didn't fire the gun."

"Was your forensic team able to find any evidence that might lead us to who pulled the trigger?" I asked.

"No, not so far. They are still working on the evidence from the café and from Judge Weatherby's chamber. I still don't have the crime scene photos from either scene. I should be getting them later today. I'll get a set over to you as soon as I can."

"Thanks."

"Have you got anything for me?" Don asked.

"Not yet, but I hope to have something by this afternoon or tomorrow morning at the latest. I'll call you as soon as I know for sure."

"When can I talk to Ms Hanson?"

"I've got a couple of things to check out first, but I'll try to get it set up for this afternoon."

"Okay. I really want to talk to her."

"I'll make it this afternoon."

"Good. Talk to you later," Don said, then hung up.

It was getting close to noon and I was hungry. I had time to get to Jackie's office before she would leave for lunch. I hadn't seen her for a couple of days, and having lunch with her would be a pleasant relief from the case.

Don looked across his desk at Officer Sharon Williams. She seemed really interested in what had been said on the other end of the phone line and hoped Don would tell her.

"It looks like I will get to talk to Ms Hanson this afternoon."

"You mean it's not for sure?"

"Tidsdale is going to arrange it. If he knows it will be safe, I'll talk to her. If he thinks it will not be, I won't."

"In other words, you don't know if he is going to let you talk to her or not," she said rather sharply.

"What's your problem, Officer?" Don snapped. "Don't you think I know what I'm doing?"

It was clear Don didn't like what she seemed to be implying. He had known Tidsdale for a long time, a lot longer than he had known Officer Williams. Tidsdale had saved his life, to say nothing of the times when Tidsdale had helped him solve a case or two during the years they had known each other. He sort of took offense at her questioning his methods, and who he saw fit to trust.

Officer Sharon Williams quickly realized that Don was not happy with her questioning his way of investigating, and his friendship with Tidsdale. She felt she may have stepped over the line in questioning the way he handled a case. After all, he was her superior and had a lot more experience.

"Officer Williams, since you have not been officially assigned to work with me on this case, it might be best if you return to your usual duties."

Sharon looked at him for a moment before she stood up. She wanted to say something to him, but thought it might be best if she just excused herself. She quickly became angry with him for dismissing her.

"Yes, sir," she replied sharply, then turned and stormed out of his office.

Don didn't like to see her storm out the door, but he didn't like having his methods questioned by a rookie officer who was just out of the Academy, especially one who was not qualified to be a detective.

She had no more than left his office when another officer knocked on his door.

"Come in."

"I have a package for you from the state lab," the officer said.

"Thank you."

Don took the package from the officer then dismissed him. The door to his office had no more than closed when Don opened the package and dumped out the stack of eight-by-ten crime scene photos of the café, and from Judge Weatherby's chamber on his desk.

The crime scene photos from the bombing of the café were on top of the pile. There were at least two dozen photos. Don took them over to a long table that was against one wall of his office and spread them out. He began looking at them.

CHAPTER TWENTY-THREE

I went to the parking garage, got in my car and headed for Jackie's office. I arrived at the building where Jackie worked just as she was coming out the front door. She was talking with several other women, one or two of them I knew worked in the same office. Jackie smiled when she saw me, then excused herself and walked toward me.

"Hi, I didn't expect to see you here," Jackie said as she looked in the window.

"I thought I would stop by and see if you would like to go to lunch with me. If you have other plans, I'll talk to you later."

"No. I'd love to have lunch with you."

Jackie reached down and opened the door. She got in the car and closed the door.

"Where are we going?"

"I thought we would have lunch at the steak house on Broadway."

"That sounds good."

"I would like a little help from you."

"Okay. What do you need help with?" Jackie asked.

"I want you to help me pick out a computer for my office, along with the kind of programs that would be helpful to me."

"Sure. I'd be glad to."

"Would you help me learn to use it?"

"Well, I don't know. It would mean I would have to spend a lot of time with you," she said.

"Very funny. I catch on pretty fast."

"That's good, because a lot of the time we could spend working on each other."

"Now that sounds like something I might enjoy," I said with a smile.

"You better enjoy it. You certainly have in the past," she said with a knowing smile.

"Yes, I have."

We pulled into the parking lot of the steak house. I took her arm and led her into the restaurant. We were seated in a booth.

"When do you want to go looking for a computer?"

"I was thinking that we could go today, maybe after work."

"Okay. I'll look up some places that might have the kind of computer that would work for you. It will save us some time. Are you going to put it in your office?"

"Yes," I said just as my phone began to ring. "Excuse me."

I opened my cell phone and discovered it was Don calling me.

"I need to take this," I said to Jackie.

"Hello, Don. What's up?"

"I need to talk to Hanson as soon as possible," Don said.

"How about this afternoon?"

"I really want to talk to her in person."

"I think you know how I feel about that at this time."

"You know I could have you arrested if you don't let me talk to her."

"I know you could, but if you choose to go that route, I'll make sure you don't find her. I'll tell you what," I said before he could respond. "If you come alone, I'll tell you where we can meet, then I will take you to her. But I insist that you come alone and make sure you are not followed."

"Fair enough. Where do you want to meet and when?"

I suggested we meet at a gas station that was located about three miles south of the motel. I told him that her bodyguard had instructions to protect her at all costs, and without me someone could get hurt.

"Okay. I'll do it your way. I will meet you at the gas station at two this afternoon."

"I'll be there. Wait for me if I'm not there right on time. I'll be making sure no one is following me. You do the same."

"Got it. See you then," Don said then hung up.

As I hung up my phone, I noticed Jackie was looking at me.

"That was Don. I have a meeting with him at two."

"I take it that it has something to do with the case you are working on?"

"Yes."

"Are you doing something illegal?" Jackie said as she looked at me.

"I might be, but just a little."

"How can it be 'just a little' illegal?"

"I have a material witness hidden away for her own protection. Someone has already tried to kill her. Don wants to talk to her in person."

"I take it you don't want him to talk to your witness."

"I don't have a problem with him talking to her. It's just that I think it is risky to talk to her in person because he might be followed. If he is, it could make it very hard for me to keep her alive," I explained.

"Oh. I see your point. What are you going to do about it?"

"I'm going to let him interview her, then move her to another location as quickly as possible."

Jackie and I ate our lunch without much conversation. I think she was a little worried about the woman I had hidden from everyone. She might have been a little worried about me, too. As soon as we were done, I took her back to her office then returned to my office where I placed a call to Don.

"Hello."

"Tidsdale here. Give me your cell phone number."

Don rattled it off to me and I wrote it down.

"Go to the gas station and wait. I'm going to check out the area to make sure neither of us is being followed. If all is clear, I'll take you to Ms Hanson."

"Okay. I've got some crime scene photos of the café to show you," Don said.

"Great. Anything in them that might give us a clue as to who bombed the place?"

"Not that I've seen."

"Okay. I'd like to see them anyway. I'd like you to leave as soon as possible."

"I'm leaving right now," Don said, then hung up.

I went to the parking garage, got in my car and headed for the area of the gas station.

Don started to leave his office when he was met at the door by Officer Sharon Williams. He looked at her, but didn't say anything.

"Have you got a minute, sir?" Sharon asked, her voice sounding apologetic.

"I'm in a bit of a hurry."

"It will take just a minute."

"Okay, what is it?"

"I'm sorry I didn't listen to you. I guess I was expecting you to be a go-by-the-book sort of man."

"I am 'a go-by-the-book' man, but sometimes the book doesn't cover the situation. When that happens, you have to use your best judgment and be a little creative. And sometimes that means you have to trust others, but you have to know who to trust and who not to trust."

"I understand that, b - but - - ."

"But too many officers don't trust PI's, right? You have to think for yourself. You have to figure out which ones you can trust."

"I think I understand."

"Remember, a PI can sometimes get away with things you as a police officer cannot."

"Why do you trust Tidsdale so much?"

"That's a long story and I don't have time to get into it right now. I have a very important appointment to keep. I'll be glad to discuss it with you later, if you like."

"I would like that, sir" she said, with a pleasant smile.

Don smiled, then nodded before he turned and left the police station. He went to his car and headed for the gas station where he was to meet Tidsdale.

During the drive to the gas station, Don kept an eye out for anyone who might be following him. He saw a dark colored luxury sedan he thought might be tailing him, but soon lost it on a side street. It took him twenty minutes to get to the gas station.

CHAPTER TWENTY-FOUR

The drive to the gas station proved to be uneventful. I didn't see anyone following me. When I got to the gas station, I pulled around back and found Don sitting in his car behind the station. I pulled up alongside him and rolled down the window.

"Any problems?" I asked.

"I saw a dark colored Lincoln that I thought was following me, but I lost him."

"Are you sure."

"Yes, I'm sure," Don said, his tone was a little sharp.

"Get in. I'll drive."

I watched as Don got out of his car, locked it up, then got into my car. He buckled up as I pulled away.

"Keep an eye for anyone following us," I said.

I drove the three miles to the motel. Neither of us saw anything we thought might be someone following us. I did notice that Don glanced over at me every once in awhile. He was probably wondering where we were going. He had apparently gotten the idea that the gas station was very close to where I was hiding Ms Hanson. I hadn't said anything to him that would lead him to believe the gas station was close.

After making several turns, I turned a corner then almost immediately pulled into the parking lot of a motel. I drove to the very back corner of the motel and into a parking space. If anyone had been following us, they would not have seen where we went. The only way they would be able to see the car was to come all the way into the motel's parking lot where I would be able to see them.

I motioned for Don to get out, then led him to one of the rooms. I knocked on the door and waited.

"Who is it?"

"It's me, Tidsdale. You can open the door Mr. Hubble."

There was the sound of the door being unlocked before it slowly began to open. Jake peeked out of the door and saw Don standing next to me.

"Are you all right, Mr. Tidsdale?"

"Yes. You can let us in. This is Detective Donald Wright. He's here to interview Ms Hanson."

Jake stepped back and opened the door. When I stepped in, I saw Jake had a gun in his hand. He had been prepared to protect Ms Hanson.

"Jake, keep an eye on the parking lot. I don't think we were followed, but just make sure."

"Okay. Ms Hanson is in her room. She's sitting on the bed."

"Martha, are you presentable?" I called out.

"Yes, Mr. Tidsdale."

Don followed me as I stepped into the room.

"I would like you to meet Detective Donald Wright. He is the detective investigating Judge Weatherby's murder. He has a few questions to ask you. Is that all right?"

"I guess so," she said as she looked at Don.

"Good afternoon, Ms Hanson. I know this is hard for you, so I'll get right to the point. What can you tell be about the judge's activities over the past few weeks? Was there anything out of the ordinary going on with him?"

"Not really. Like I told Mr. Tidsdale, he got a call from someone who wouldn't identify himself to me, but insisted on talking to the judge. The man on the phone was quite forceful and very rude."

"When was that?"

"It was on the day he was killed," Martha said with a slight quiver in her voice. "It couldn't have been more than a few hours before he was murdered."

"Did the judge take the call?"

"Yes."

"Did he say anything to you about the call?"

"He told me to put the call through to him, and he would set the guy straight."

"Was that all?"

"Well, he asked me to go down to the cafeteria to get him a carton of milk," she said with a strange look on her face.

"I take it he didn't often ask for a carton of milk?"

"Before that, he never did," she replied.

"Did he ask you to get the milk before or after he talked to the guy on the phone?"

"Before. It – ah – it was almost as if he wanted to make sure I was out of the office while he talked on the phone. I didn't think much of it at the time, but I have had a lot of time to think about it."

"I'm sure you have," Don said with a smile. "Would it be possible for you to give me a schedule of the judge's cases that he has heard over the past year and what he might have had scheduled for the next few weeks?"

"I don't often see his schedule."

"Why is that?" Don asked.

"He keeps it in his desk. He does his own scheduling. He would tell me when he would be in court, or when he had a motion hearing so I wouldn't schedule any meetings for him that would conflict with his case schedule."

"Did he talk about his cases with you?"

"No. He never talked about his cases with me. He said he didn't want to burden me with such messy things."

"How did he handle motion hearings and things like that?"

"He had a stenographer come in to take minutes of any hearings he held in his chamber."

"So you never saw the minutes of those hearings?"

"No. The stenographer typed them up and gave them personally to Judge Weatherby. I was just his personal secretary."

Don looked over at me as if he wasn't sure what was going on. It seemed Judge Weatherby handled his cases differently than most judges. He then turned back and looked at Martha.

"Where did the stenographer come from? Was it one of the court employees?"

"Yes. It was Sharon Williams until she went to the police academy. She was replaced by Janice Nash. She works for several of the judges. She also signs for the judges."

"Did he always use Ms Williams or Ms Nash when he needed a stenographer?"

"Oh, yes. He said they were the best. He always liked the best," she said with a smile.

"Can you tell me who the other judges were that Ms Williams or Ms Nash worked for?"

"I know they worked for Judge Wilkinson and Judge Smith. They might have done some work for Judge Stillwell, but I'm not sure," Ms Hanson said.

"Did they work with any other judges that you know of?"

"No, but I'm sure they did from time to time. They were the only stenographers that sign."

"Thank you very much. I think that will be all for now."

"Could you tell me what happened in my apartment?" she asked. "I saw smoke coming from the windows when Mr. Tidsdale and I left the restaurant. I'm worried about Alice. She was there when I left."

"I'm sorry, but she was murdered," Don said with a gentle tone in his voice.

"Oh," Martha said then began to cry.

Don looked at me, then stood up. He walked over to the adjoining door and stepped into the other room with Jake.

After making sure Martha was all right, I turned and left the room.

"Jake, see that she's okay."

"I will."

"I have to take Don back to his car. I'll call you later."

Jake just nodded and went into Martha's room. Don and I left the motel. I drove Don back to his car.

"I have a couple of things to do at the office. When I'm finished, I'll stop by your office and take a look at the crime scene photos," I said.

"Okay. I'll see you later."

I waited for Don to leave the area, then placed a call to Jake. He answered the phone immediately.

"Hello."

"Jake, I want you to get Ms Hanson out of that room and have her moved to another room in one of the other wings of the motel. Do it in a way that no one will know she has moved. Also register Ms Hanson and yourself under a different name. Call me and let me know what name you are using."

"Got it. I'll get it done."

"Thanks," I said then hung up.

I headed back to my office. It didn't take me long before I was sitting behind my desk. I remembered I was to go to Don's office to look at some crime scene photos taken of the café. I was about to leave my office when my cell phone rang.

"Tidsdale Investigation, Frank Tidsdale, how may I help you?"

"This is Mr. Hubble. Are you free to talk?"

"Yes."

"I have our party of interest registered in room 242. Mr. and Mrs. Campbell are looking forward to visiting with you."

"Thank you. Tell them I will call for an appointment," I said.

"I will tell them," Jake said then hung up.

As soon as I hung up, I got up and left for Don's office.

Don returned to his office. He had no more than sat down at his desk when the phone began to ring. He reached over and answered it.

"Detective Wright."

"Don this is Sergeant Walker of the bomb squad."

"Yes. Do you have something for me?"

"I do. I have Max "The Bomber" Carlson."

"Where did you find him?" Don asked.

"He was at the bus station waiting for the bus to Las Vegas."

"I would really like to talk to him. Where are you holding him?"

"We have him here," Sergeant Walker said.

"Is he talking?"

"Not a word so far."

"Has he got a lawyer?"

"No. I get the impression that he's afraid to get a lawyer," Walker said.

"I can understand that. He doesn't want anyone to know the police have him. If he gets a local lawyer, whoever he's working for would know it in a minute. He probably knows his life wouldn't be worth a nickel."

"What do I do with him? You want me to send him over to you?"

"No. Keep him there and away from everybody. Don't put him in a holding tank with anyone else. We lose him, we may never find a witness that might be helpful in finding out more about the bombing of the café, or the death of Judge Weatherby."

"You think they are connected?" Sergeant Walker asked.

"More and more every day. The more I look at them, the more I'm convinced."

"We'll keep him for you. Talk to you later."

"Yeah," Don said then hung up.

Don looked over at the table with the pictures of the bombed café. He wondered if the bombing of the café and of Ms Hanson's apartment really were connected. At this point, he had no proof.

Don needed to find out if there was a connection. The best way to do that was to have the bomb experts go over the evidence from the café.

Don quickly placed a call to Sergeant Walker. He asked him to contact Mel Street in the State Lab for all the evidence on the bombing of the café. He explained what he wanted, that was to find out if there was a connection. Sergeant Walker said he would get on it, then hung up.

Don had no more then hung up when there was a knock on his door.

CHAPTER TWENTY-FIVE

"Come in," I heard Don say.

As I entered Don's office, I saw the table with a lot of photographs spread out on it. I also saw Don sitting at his desk.

"Are these the crime scene photos taken at the café," I asked as I walked up to the table.

"Yeah. Take a good look and tell me what you see."

I took my time looking over the crime scene photos. The photos of Martin told me that someone wanted him very dead. No one uses that big a gun and shoots a man twice at close range without letting someone know they were mad as hell.

There were several pieces of paper on the table that Martin was slumped over. If I recalled correctly, one of those papers had my name on it, according to Don. From the photos, I couldn't tell what was on the papers.

"I don't see anything that would help me decide who had bombed the place," I said.

"I didn't either, but I have a suspect. He's a little guy from Las Vegas that likes to go around blowing up things, people among them. He was the one who set off the bomb in Ms Hanson's apartment. He was also the one who put a pipe bomb in her car."

"Her car was rigged to explode?"

"Yeah. We think he was the one who bombed the café as well. He may not have actually been there, but we think he might have prepared the explosives. I have the bomb squad checking with the State Lab on how the bomb was made. If it has the signature of Max "The Bomber" Carlson written all over it, then we have him. Sergeant Walker's guys caught him just as he was trying to get aboard a bus to Las Vegas.

"I also have the crime scene photos from Judge Weatherby's chamber. Would you like to see them?" Don asked.

"Yes."

Don got out the photos and spread them out on the table. I carefully started looking at the photos. In the first five or six photos, there was nothing that I didn't expect to see if the judge had committed suicide. From the photos alone, there was no way to tell if it was suicide or not.

It wasn't until I got to the seventh or eighth photo that I noticed something in the background. It almost looked like a reflection off a piece of glass or shiny metal. It appeared as if it was on the end of a book. I looked at several other pictures of the same area in the judge's chamber, but didn't see anything that would help me figure out what it was I had seen. I decided it would be best if I could get into Judge Weatherby's chamber and look around. I examined the location of the reflection so that I could hopefully find it, if I could figure out a way to get into Weatherby's chamber.

"You see anything?" Don asked.

"No. Is the judge's chamber still a crime scene?"

"Yeah. You want a take a look at it?"

"Yes."

"I have to go talk to Sergeant Walker of the bomb squad and question Max Carlson. You want to come along?"

"No. Is Judge Weatherby's chamber still guarded?" I asked.

"Yeah. The AG has it closed off to everyone."

"I've got a couple of things I have to do. I'll talk to you later. Let me know what Carlson has to say."

"Will do."

I nodded at Don, then turned and left his office. I went directly to my car and placed a call to the AG before leaving the parking lot. It was answered on the second ring.

"Yes."

"I want to visit Judge Weatherby's chamber. Is there some way I can get into his chamber without being seen?"

"Yes. Do you think you have something?"

"I might, but I have to get into his chamber to find out for sure."

"There's a back way up to his chamber. I'll make sure no one is in the area. Where are you now?"

"I'm in front of the police station, Precinct One."

"Meet me in the basement of the courthouse. Give me a ten minute head start."

"Okay," I said then hung up.

I waited for ten minutes then started my car. I drove over to the courthouse. Not wanting anyone to see my car close to the courthouse, I parked a couple of blocks away on a side street and began walking toward the courthouse.

Don arrived at the Second Precinct where the Bomb Squad was located. He immediately went to Sergeant Walker's office and knocked on the door.

"Come in," Walker said, then looked up from the papers on his desk to see who was there.

"Hi, Sergeant."

"Don, good to see you, again. How's the investigation going?"

"Slow."

"Well, I won't waste your time. I know you've got a lot on your plate right now. I take it you are here to talk to Max?" Sergeant Walker asked as he stood up.

"Yes."

"He's down the hall."

Walker led Don down the hall to a small interrogation room. As he stepped into the room, Don saw a short little man who looked like any man you might see on the street in a middle income neighborhood. He was wearing dark blue slacks, a pale blue shirt and a dark blue blazer, no tie. There was nothing outstanding about him except his size.

"Max, this is Detective Don Wright. He has a few questions he would like to ask you."

"I don't want to talk to him any more than I want to talk to you," Max said defiantly.

"I can understand that," Don said. "If I was in your shoes, I wouldn't want to talk to the police either."

"What do you mean by that?" Max asked, not sure what was going on.

"I understand you don't want a lawyer, either. Is that right?"

"Yeah. I didn't do nothin', so what do I need with a lawyer?"

"Could it be that if you asked for a lawyer, the people who hired you would almost immediately know that you missed your bus to Las Vegas? It wouldn't be very healthy for you if they knew the cops got hold of you."

Don noticed that Max looked a little pale and he was breathing a little harder. Don had hit the nail on the head and he knew it.

"Sergeant Walker, how difficult would it be to leak to the press that we have the person who tried to kill Ms Hanson with a bomb, and made the bomb that was used in the café bombing?"

Don knew he was bluffing about the bombing of the café. He didn't have any proof that Max had anything to do with it. The State Lab had not had time to send the bomb fragments to Sergeant Walker for his analysis to determine who might have put the bomb together.

"No, problem. It could be in the morning paper."

"You can't prove I had anything to do with it," Max said, looking a bit scared.

Don immediately noticed Max had not denied his involvement in the bombing of the café. He had simply stated they couldn't prove he had anything to do with it.

"You know those newspaper people. They will print anything that even sounds like it might sell a few more papers. They don't care if it's true or not."

Don could see the sweat start to form on Max's forehead and his upper lip. He was scared to death. Don was convinced that he was on the right track. However, if he did leak it to the paper and Max didn't do it, he would be risking Max's life. But on the other hand, if Max did do it, it would be very difficult for Don to protect him.

Don turned and looked at Walker. He could see that Walker was wondering if Don had thought through what he was suggesting.

"Can I talk to you for a minute, Sergeant?"

"Sure."

Don turned and walked out of the interrogation room into the hall. Don looked around to make sure the hall was empty before speaking to Walker.

"Do you have a safe place where you can keep Max? It has to be someplace where no one, and I mean no one, can get at him."

"Yeah. We have a single cell in the basement we can put him."

"Can you put a guard on him 24/7? It has to be someone you trust."

"Sure."

"I don't know if this guy did the café bombing or not. I do know he did the bombing in Ms Hanson's apartment and rigged her car to explode if she started it. That's enough to charge him, but I don't want him charged, yet. I don't want anyone to even know we have him. Understand?"

"Yeah. I'll tell my men to keep quiet."

"Good. I'm hoping a couple of days in a private cell where he can't talk to anyone will loosen his tongue. That, along with the fear that someone will find out he is here,"
Don said.

Sergeant Walker began to smile and nod his head in agreement.

"It is most important that no one outside of here knows he's here."

"I'll see to it," Walker said with an air of confidence.

"I'll talk to you later."

Walker nodded, then watched as Don left the precinct. Don returned to his car and headed back to his office.

CHAPTER TWENTY-SIX

I walked to the back of the courthouse. After making sure there was no one watching, I entered the backdoor. I quickly turned to my left and stepped through the narrow door that led to the basement. When I got to the bottom of the stairs, I was greeted by AG Greene.

"We have to be very careful. I don't want anyone to see us together," Greene said. "How is your investigation going?"

"Slow, I'm afraid. The police may have caught the man who made the bomb that was supposed to kill Ms Hanson, and probably made the bomb that was used in the bombing of the café. At this point I'm not sure. The State Lab is examining the bomb evidence hoping it will connect their suspect to both bombings."

"Good. Have they found anything in the papers Martin had in his possession?"

"They found one piece of paper they think had my name on it. According to Detective Wright, it only has a few letters of my name, but the spacing of the letters would have fit my name. Other than that, I don't think they have much, yet."

"What is it you are expecting to find in Judge Weatherby's chamber?"

"I'm not sure. I saw the crime scene photos, but it didn't help much. I would like to see his chamber. I don't know if it will help, but it might help me get a better idea of what happened there. We do know he did not commit suicide. He was murdered."

"I was pretty sure of that the night he died." Greene said. "Follow me."

I followed him through the basement along dimly lit hallways. It seemed musty and all I was able to see were pipes and conduit all along the walls and ceiling. It was very quiet.

We had not gone very far when Greene stopped. He put his finger over his mouth.

"This stairway leads up three flights," he whispered. "At the second flight, turn left and go to the third door on the left. The third door on the left is to Judge Weatherby's chamber."

"I saw all the crime scene photos of his chamber and I didn't see any doors in his chamber except for the private door into the hall and the one into the front office."

"There are several hidden passageways in this old courthouse," Greene explained. "They were built so that the judges could get out of the building safely if there was a possible danger to them if they left by the front door."

"Do all the judges' chambers have a secret way out?"

"Yes," Greene said.

"That would mean that the judges could move from one chamber to another without anyone knowing."

"I hadn't thought about that, but you're right," Greene replied.

I could see by the look on his face he wondered why I found that interesting, but he didn't comment on it. Instead, he stepped back so I could go up the stairs.

As I started up the stairs, I could hear the sound of his street shoes as he headed back the way we had come.

I followed his instructions. I went up the stairs to the second floor, then turned left. I walked down the narrow hallway to the third door on the left. I took a pair of rubber gloves from my pocket and put them on. I had no desire to leave any evidence that I had been in Weatherby's chamber.

Not knowing what to expect, I reached out and turned the handle very slowly. I wanted a chance to escape before I was seen in case someone was in Weatherby's chamber so I opened the door very slowly. There was no one in his chamber.

A quick look around the room showed that it had been gone over by the forensic team. There was carbon black dust on the furniture from where they had dusted for prints, pieces of carpet that had blood on them had been cut out near the judge's desk, and there were drawers still hanging open that had been closed when the crime scene photos had been taken. I had no idea what the police or forensic team might have found in the drawers, but it showed me they had been very thorough in their search of the judge's chamber.

The thing I was most interested in was finding the book on the large bookshelves that had a shiny spot on it that I had seen in one of the photos. I looked toward the bookshelves, but didn't see anything shiny. Since the shiny spot had only shown up in one photo, I figured it was a reflection from the flash of the photographer's camera. It took me a couple of minutes to find the approximate place where the photographer had stood to take the picture, but I still didn't see anything. However, I was able to find the book that had the shiny spot on it, but it was not shiny now.

It wasn't until I moved closer to the book that I found something very interesting. There was an area smaller than a dime that almost matched the binding of the book, which was red. I took my small flashlight and shined it directly on that area of the book. I discovered my light reflected back. I reached up and tapped the area on the book and found it to be glass or a hard clear plastic.

I slowly pulled the book forward on the shelf, and quickly discovered there was a small cable of some kind hooked to the book. I carefully pulled the book off the shelf and opened it. The book contained what looked like a small camera. I set the camera down and pulled books off the shelf so that I could follow the cable from the camera. It led me to a small decorative box that looked like it might be a cigar box.

I opened the box and found it almost full of cigars. When I pulled up the cloth tabs on each end to lift out the top tray of cigars, I found another digital camera under the tray. The camera was hooked to the cable and a battery powered electronic switch that could be triggered from a remote place within the room. As I looked at it, I realized there had to be another remote switch somewhere that would trigger the one connected to the cameras in order to take pictures.

I looked for it but didn't find it. I didn't figure I had enough time to do a thorough search. If I stayed too long, I might get caught in the judge's chamber. That would not be good for me, to say nothing about how would I explain my presence.

The one thing I had to know was there anything on the cameras' digital cards that might be of some help. Was it possible the judge took pictures of the person or persons who killed him? The only way to find out was to take the digital cards out of the cameras.

I took the digital cards out of both cameras then put everything back where I found it. After checking around to make sure I had left no sign I had been there, I left the same way I had come in. I returned to my car and quickly returned to my office.

I hid the cameras' digital cards in the safe in my office. Being so small, it was easy to hide them where they could not be found easily. Once I was sure the digital cards were secure, I returned to my car, got in and drove home.

Just as I walked in the door, I heard my phone ringing. I rushed over and picked up the receiver.

"Hello."

"Hi, Honey," Jackie said.

"I didn't expect you to call. Are you ready to go looking at computers?"

"I'm sorry. Can we make it tomorrow? We've got some problems here and it doesn't look like I'm going to be getting out of here anytime soon," Jackie said.

"No. It's okay. Maybe we can make it tomorrow after work."

"Thanks, Honey. I've got to go. Goodnight. I love you," she said.

"I love you, too," I said then hung up the phone.

There was little doubt that I was disappointed, but there was not much else I could do tonight. I decided to get something to eat, maybe watch a movie and turn in. A good night's sleep might help me think a little clearer tomorrow.

After getting something to eat, I sat down and watched a little television. There wasn't much on, but it didn't really matter. I found it hard to concentrate on anything. Even the news of the day didn't interest me that much.

As soon as the news was over, I got ready for bed. I must have spent an hour or more thinking about what might be on the cameras' digital cards before I finally dozed off.

When Don arrived back in his office, he found a large yellow envelope on his desk. It was from the State Lab. Don dumped the contents of the envelope on his desk and began looking through it. In it was the results of most of the things that were found in the café that might have a bearing on the bombing, and reports on what were found.

Included were the autopsy reports on all the victims of the bombing, and the one victim of the shooting. The report on the shooting victim showed nothing that Don didn't already know. Cause of death was listed as gunshots to the head, the one in front first, the one to the back of the head was second. It showed the victim as Robert Martin, an investigator for the AG's Office. As for the other victims, the cause of death was listed as the result of fragments and pieces of debris from an explosive device that had apparently been in a briefcase that had been located near the front door of the café.

There was a report describing the papers that had been on the table where Martin had been sitting when he was shot. Several pieces of paper suggested the AG was investigating a prominent individual, but the State Lab was unable to bring up the name of the individual. There was a report on one sheet of paper with letters on it that when placed in line indicated the name was possibly Frank Tidsdale, but they were unable to be one hundred percent sure. With all the secrecy Frank had insisted on, it made some sense to Don that Frank's name might show up on something dealing with the AG's investigation.

There was also a report on bomb fragments that were found at the scene. Based on the trigger mechanism and other components of the bomb, the bomb had been set off by a timer that was started by pulling a small cord on the

*outside of a briefcase. The report stated the information on
the bomb had been sent to the bomb squad office in the hope
they could connect it to a known bomber. In general, there
was nothing new, just a few more details.*

*Don took a look at his watch and found it was getting
late. He was sure Sergeant Walker would have gone home.
He decided he would contact Walker first thing in the
morning to see if he had been able to connect the bomb
components to Max, "The Bomber" Carlson.*

*The remaining reports added no useful information, at
least at the moment. Don decided it was time for him to go
home and get a fresh start in the morning. Don went to the
police garage, got in his car and drove home.*

CHAPTER TWENTY-SEVEN

When morning came, I laid in my bed and looked up at the ceiling. I wondered what might be on the cameras' digital cards. What would it show? Would it help my case or hurt it? There was no way of knowing until I actually looked at what was on the digital cards.

I got to wondering how I was going to see what was on the digital cards before anyone else. I had to make sure that the computer I purchased would accept digital cards from cameras. I knew most of them did. My first thought was to take the cards to a store that would print off the pictures, but that could prove to be a problem, especially since I didn't know what was on the cards, if anything. Going to the library and using their computers might not be a good idea, either.

Then it occurred to me that Jackie had a computer at her home. She also had a printer that could print off the pictures for me. A quick look at my watch told me that she would probably be getting ready for work. As much as I wanted to see what was on the digital cards, it could wait until tonight when I had my own computer and could see what was on them in the privacy of my office.

I did decide to call her and ask her when she would be available to shop for a computer. I picked up my cell phone and called her.

"Hello?"

"Hi, Honey."

"Frank?"

"Yes."

"Is there something wrong?" she asked with a tone of concern in her voice.

"No. I'm sorry to call you so early, but I was wondering when you are going to be able to find time to help me find a computer? If you can tell me, I would schedule my day around that time."

"I have a pretty full day. I doubt that I will have time to do anything but grab a quick sandwich at noon. Would it be okay if we meet at Office Depot a few minutes after four-thirty? We could get you a computer and a printer and take them to your office. It won't take long to set it up, then I'll show you how to use it. How does that sound?"

"Okay."

"Maybe, I'll stay overnight, that is if you want me," Jackie said.

"That would be nice," I said.

"I've got to run. Talk to you later?"

"Sure. Love you," I said then hung up.

I was a little disappointed, but I had other things I could do this morning. I left for my office, stopping along the way to get a roll. As soon as I arrived at my office, I put a pot of coffee on. When it was ready, I sat down and ate the roll and drank the coffee while thinking about what I should do next.

Don arrived at his office at his usual time. He was hoping to have a report on the bomb fragments from the café. He thought he might have a little leverage with Max Carlson if he could prove the bomb used at the café could be connected to him. It might prove to be enough to get Max to talk to him.

It was only eight o'clock when Don's phone began to ring. He reached over and picked it up.

"Detective Wright."

"Detective Wright, this is Doctor Armstrong."

"Yes, Doc. I hope you have some good news for me."

"Yes and no. The good news is one of the women has regained consciousness and is able to talk. The bad news is the old man didn't make it."

"Is there an officer around?"

"Yes. He is talking to the woman now."

"Good. I'll be there as soon as I can," Don said, then hung up the phone.

Don hurried out of the office and down to the garage to get to his car. He got into his car and left the garage in a hurry. It didn't take him very long to get to the hospital.

He didn't bother to stop at the check-in desk because he was sure the woman was still in ICU. He went directly to the unit and asked the nurse for Doctor Armstrong. Instead of calling Doctor Armstrong, she took him into the ICU to the cubical where the injured woman was located.

As he came into the cubical, he saw a police officer calmly asking the woman questions. Standing on the other side of the bed was Doctor Armstrong. Don stopped at the foot of the woman's bed and listened.

"Can you describe the men who came into the café for me?" the officer asked, his voice calm and soft.

"They were both wearing long black coats and had black hair and black beards. The beards were not real," she said.

"How is it you know that?"

"I work in a beauty salon. The beards were fake. The smaller man's beard didn't fit his face very well. He was the one who came in first and sat down near the door with an attaché case," she said then turned away for a minute to take a breath.

The officer looked over at Don. Don motioned for him to continue his questioning.

"Is there anything else you can tell us about the two men?" the office asked.

"Yes. They were wearing wigs."

"Is there anything else you can tell us that might help us find them?" Don asked.

"No, I don't think so. I'm kind of tired."

"I think we should let her rest, gentlemen," Doctor Armstrong said.

Don nodded and followed the officer out of ICU. As soon as they were out of ICU, Don turned to the officer.

"That was a good job you did in there. I want you to sit down with me and tell me everything she said."

As soon as they were seated, the young officer began, "She described the two men who came into the café. One was about six-one and was maybe two hundred pounds. He had dark brown hair and she thinks his eyes were brown. He didn't have a beard. She said the beard was fake and he wasn't used to having it on. The second one was about five-nine, maybe five-ten and weighed about two hundred pounds. He had light colored hair and possibly blue eyes, but she wasn't sure about the color of his eyes. He also was wearing a fake beard and wig."

"Wow. She was very observant," Don said. "How did she know all that?"

"She said that she got a good look at them when they came in. She works in a beauty salon and deals with hair all the time. She said she can spot fake hair, especially when it's cheap," the officer said with a slight grin.

"So we have one suspect who is six-one, brown hair, brown eyes and no beard. We have a second suspect that is five-nine or ten with light colored hair, possibly blue eyes and no beard, right?"

"Yes, sir."

"I want you to stick around for a little while. When she wakes up, talk to her again and see if she remembers anything else."

Yes, sir."

"That was an excellent job," Don said, then turned and left the hospital.

When Don got to his car, he headed back to the office to regroup.

CHAPTER TWENTY-EIGHT

As I sat in my office thinking about what might be on the cameras' digital cards, my mind went to other things in Weatherby's chamber. I had looked around the room, but I had focused my search on what I had seen in the pictures Don had showed me. I was sure there was more. Closing my eyes, I began to visualize the pictures from Weatherby's chamber in my mind's eye.

The chamber showed no signs that the judge had put up a fight. I couldn't picture him just sitting in his chair and letting someone shoot him without resisting in some way. From what I knew about him, he was a pretty tough man for his age. He would have known that if he put up a fight, there was a better chance he could cause the person who shot him to leave some kind of evidence. They would have left evidence that he did not commit suicide.

Then it hit me like a sledge hammer. I couldn't believe I was having this conversation with myself. He did leave proof that he didn't commit suicide. He also left pictures of who had killed him. He left it on the cameras. Judge Weatherby had to have known someone would find the hidden cameras sooner or later. The cameras would be found when the box of cigars was removed from the chamber, if not before.

Now I couldn't wait to find out what was on the cameras' digital cards. But I knew I would have to wait until Jackie could go with me to buy a computer. She would know what I would need to go with it. If I went by myself, I wouldn't know what to get and what extras I would need, which would make it take longer for me to find out what was on the digital cards.

My thoughts were suddenly disturbed by the ringing of my phone. I reached over and answered the phone.

"Tidsdale Investigations."

"Franky, I've got a flash for you. It seems that two guys were sent to Las Vegas for a two week vacation, but they were called back after just a couple of days."

"How does that affect me?"

"The word is out that they were called back to take care of a small, but annoying problem."

"I take it from your comment that I might be that 'small, but annoying problem'."

"I've always said that you grasp things very quickly. I think it would be wise for you to be very careful whose toes you step on."

"Do you have some idea whose toes I have already stepped on?" I asked.

"Not yet, but I'm working on it."

"Do you know the names of the two guys that had to cut their vacation short?"

"No, but I'm working on it."

"Will you keep me posted on what you find out?"

"Of course, Franky," the voice said then the phone went dead.

I hung up the phone, then sat there for a few minutes just looking at it. The one thing I knew about my friend, he had never lied to me. When he said "be very careful", he meant every word of it. I also got the feeling he would be covering my back.

After giving it some thought, I began to wonder if I might have pictures of the two guys my friend called about. If they were responsible for the death of Judge Weatherby, I might have pictures of them on the cameras' digital cards. All I had to do was wait until I could look at the digital cards to see if they had had their picture taken by the very guy they had murdered.

Even with the description of the two men that bombed the café, Don still had little to go on. The description could have fit hundreds of men in the Denver area. He wondered if the smaller of the two men was Max "The Bomber" Carlson. He didn't think that Max was as tall as the woman had described. Don would have to see if he could get a mug shot of Carlson and show it to the woman the next time she was able to talk to them. In the meantime, he needed to get hold of Sergeant Walker to see if he had come up with anything on the bomb fragments from the café.

Don returned to the precinct. He no more than entered his office when the phone began to ring. He reached over and grabbed it.

"Detective Wright."

"Don, Walker here. I've some news for you.

"I sure hope its good news."

"I think you will like it. The fragments from the bomb used in the downtown café bombing and the method used to detonate it, showed it was built by either Max Carlson or Charles Goodman. We think it was Max, but we can't rule out Goodman. We have been trying to find out where Goodman is and if he was in this area at the time."

"One of the witnesses who was at the café when the explosion took place described for us the two men. One was tall, six-one, brown hair, brown eyes and about two hundred pounds. The other was five-nine or ten, light colored hair, blue eyes and about two hundred pounds. Does that help any?"

"I'm afraid not. The first one could be Goodman. The second one could be Carlson, but I don't think he's that tall."

"Is it possible that both of them were involved?" Don asked, thinking out loud.

"Not likely," Walker said.

"From what little we could get out of our witness, the shorter man was the one who set off the bomb. It was apparently the taller one who killed the AG agent."

"As for Max, I don't think he would shoot anyone. It's not like him to do that."

"What about Goodman? Would he be likely to shoot someone?" Don asked.

"He is known to have a temper, and he is also known to be a violent man. I guess it is possible."

"Do what you can to find Goodman or at the very least where he was when the café was bombed."

"I'll see what I can find out. What about Max?"

"Keep him on ice for now. I don't want anyone to know where he is."

"Got it. Talk to you later," Walker said, then hung up the phone.

Don wasn't sure where this left him. He had two suspects in the bombing of the café, but didn't know if either of them did it or not. He had no solid suspect in the murder of Judge Marcus Weatherby, but the two he had for the café bombing could have murdered the judge. He had one solid suspect in the bombing of Ms Hanson's apartment, there was a slight chance that he had the wrong guy in the café bombing, since the bomb squad couldn't say for sure that it wasn't done by someone else who had a very similar method of making bombs.

Suddenly, Don remembered he had a man that had seen one of the men who came out from the parking garage where Ms Hanson lived. He was currently in the hospital. He wondered if the man was able to talk to him.

Since there was nothing else he could do at the moment, he decided to go to the hospital and see if he could talk to the old man. If he remembered correctly, the old man had been taken to the Lutheran Hospital.

Don placed a call to the Lutheran Hospital and asked about Joe Miller. He was told that Mr. Miller was doing pretty well and would be able to talk. Don drove over to the hospital to visit with Mr. Miller.

CHAPTER TWENTY-NINE

Just as I was trying to decide what I should do next, I heard a knock on the door. With the warning I had from my friend, I thought it was a good idea if I was prepared for anything. I drew my gun from under my coat and held it in my lap under the desk.

"Come in," I said.

I watched as the door to my office opened. A young man stepped into my office. He had a yellow envelope in his hand and he was wearing a jacket with the logo of a local delivery company on it.

"Mr. Tidsdale?"

"Yes. Do you have something for me?"

"Yes. I do need some identification before I can give it to you."

"Sure," I said as I slipped my gun into my sport coat pocket.

I stood up and showed the young man my driver's license. It seemed to satisfy him, so he handed me the envelope. I gave him a couple of dollars for a tip and took the envelope. He thanked me, then left the office.

As soon as the young man was gone, I walked over and locked the door. I didn't want any interruptions while I looked at what was in the envelope. I opened the envelope and dumped the contents on my desk. The envelope contained the telephone reports on all the judges who worked in the criminal court division including Weatherby's.

I spread the phone reports out on my desk and began comparing calls. I started with the incoming calls to the judges. It took me awhile to go through the lists of calls, but it didn't take me very long to find several phone calls, from one particular phone number, made to three of the judges that were of interest to me. The problem I had was I didn't know who was making the calls to the judges. The report showed that the calls originated from a bar on East Colfax. I was curious as to who would be calling the judges from a bar. The problem with the calls from the bar was they could have been made by anyone if the phone was a public phone. There were still a few of them around, especially in some of the older bars.

On the list of outgoing calls, there were two numbers that had been called several times from the judges' offices. One of the numbers was to the AG's office, which I could understand. The AG might be called if he was involved in a case the judge was working on. Each of the judges had called the two numbers at least seven times in the past month. However, so many calls in such a short time to the AG's office didn't seem right to me. It seemed like a lot of calls, especially from all three judges.

The other phone number that had a high number of outgoing calls were made to an out-of-town number. It was to a phone in a restaurant in Thornton. The three judges making all the calls were Marcus Weatherby, John Wilkinson and J. Barlow Smith. Absent from the list of outgoing calls to either of the two numbers was Judge Colton. I wondered if Colton wasn't a part of the circle, in short, had nothing to do with anything.

I wondered if at least some of the calls to the AG's office might be calls to the mole in Attorney General Greene's office. This was something Greene would like to know.

I placed a call to Greene's private phone. I didn't get an answer. There was no way for me to know if he was not answering, or if he had his phone shut off because he was somewhere he didn't want people to know about the phone.

A quick look at the time told me that I should be securing the new information then get ready to meet Jackie at the Office Depot store. I locked up everything, then left to meet Jackie.

Don arrived at the Lutheran Hospital. He went directly to the admissions desk and asked where Joe Miller might be found. Don was given the floor and room number.

As he approached the room where Joe was supposed to be, he found the room empty. Don immediately turned and headed to the nurse's station. His first thought was someone had gotten to Joe.

"Where's Joe Miller," Don demanded.

The nurse just turned and looked at him as if she had no idea what he was talking about.

"Where's Joe Miller," Don demanded.

"Excuse me," the nurse said rather sharply.

"I'm sorry. I'm Detective Wright with the Denver Police Department," he said as he showed her his badge and ID. "Joe Miller is a witness in a crime."

"Oh. Mr. Miller is in the lounge at the end of the hall."

"I'm sorry if I was blunt and demanding, but we have already lost one witness."

"It's all right," the nurse said.

Don nodded, then turned and headed down the hall to the lounge. When he stepped into the lounge, he saw two people sitting next to each other. One was Joe, the other one looked like an orderly. The orderly was talking to Joe. Don took note of the orderly. He looked like he was just under six foot tall and had light brown hair. He was dressed all in white typical of what most ward orderlies would wear.

"Excuse me," Don said. "I'm Detective Wright. I need to talk to Mr. Miller. Would you be kind enough to leave us alone?"

The orderly looked from Don to Joe, then back to Don. The expression on the orderly's face gave Don the *impression that he didn't want to leave, that maybe he was even a little upset that Don had interrupted him.*

"Yeah, sure," the orderly finally said as he stood up.

Don watched the orderly as he glanced at Joe then turned and left the room. Don continued to watch him as he walked down the hall. As soon as the orderly was out of sight, Don sat down in a chair next to Joe.

"Mr. Miller, do you remember me?"

"Not really. The name seems familiar."

"I was the one who called for an ambulance."

"Oh. You're the policeman that came to see me. I want to thank you for getting my neighbor to take care of my dog."

"It was your neighbor who let me in your house and called your dog so I could get to you."

"Well, thanks anyway."

"Mr. Miller. I have a few questions for you. Do you think you could answer some questions?"

"I think so."

"First of all, who was the man who just left?"

"I'm not sure. His name tag said he was an orderly, but I have my doubts about that."

"Why's that?"

"He was asking me what I remembered about the man I'd seen at the apartment building that had the explosion."

"Really? What did you tell him?"

"I told him that I didn't remember any explosion," Joe said with a slight grin.

"I take it you remember something?"

"Yeah, but I wasn't about to tell him anything. He's not a cop. And I don't think he's an orderly, either."

"What gives you that idea?"

"Two things. The first is the stethoscope he had around his neck was not in a position to be used without having to turn it over. Secondly, there isn't a single nurse or orderly

that I have ever seen who wears expensive leather dress shoes to work in."

"You're very observant," Don said. "What were some of the questions he asked you?"

"He only asked the one about what I remembered. You came in just as he was about to ask another question."

"You're pretty smart. Would you mind answering some questions for me?"

"Not at all, Detective."

"What do you remember?"

"I had been visiting a friend just down the block in another apartment building. I had left and was walking back to my car. It's kind of hard to find a parking place in that neighborhood," Mr. Miller explained. "Well, anyway, I saw this little man come out of the parking garage with a tool box. I didn't think much of it."

"Could you identify the man if you saw him again?" Don asked.

"Sure could. He was the same man that broke into my house and hit me with a piece of pipe. I only got a glimpse of him in the mirror before he hit me, but it was the same man. By the way, my dog could recognize him, too. My dog bit him hard on the ankle," he said with a grin.

Don couldn't help but smile. He would give Walker a call and find out if Max Carlson had a dog bit on his ankle.

"Tell me what he looked like?"

"Like I said, he was short, maybe about five-five or six. He had dark wavy brown hair. He was wearing dark colored work pants, dark blue, I think, and a heavy coat. He was carrying a small black toolbox. I noticed that he sort of looked me over as I passed by him."

"Did he say anything to you?" Don asked.

"I said 'hi' to him, but he just sort of scowled at me. I thought at the time that he might not have had his prune juice that morning."

Don grinned at his comment. This old man was pretty sharp.

"Joe, I think it would be a good idea if I transfer you to a different hospital and register you under a different name for a few days. If you are right, that orderly could have been here to find out how much you know and prevent you from identifying the guy who caused the explosion. How do you feel about moving?"

"You going to put a guard on me?" he asked with a worried look on his face.

"Yes."

Don watched as Joe looked down at his feet. It was clear that he was thinking about what he had been told. It wasn't long before Joe looked up at Don.

"I guess that would be all right."

"Good. I'll make all the necessary arrangements. In the meantime, I'll have you moved to a private room and have a policeman at the door."

Joe nodded that he understood, then Don stood up and walked Joe to the nurse's station. He made arrangements for Joe to be protected in a private room until he could be moved. Don waited until an officer arrived to watch over Joe before he returned to the office.

CHAPTER THIRTY

It didn't take long to get to Office Depot. When I arrived, I looked around the parking lot for Jackie's car, but didn't see it. A quick look at my watch showed that I was a little early. I walked into the store and quickly found the display of computers. I began looking at them, there seemed to be hundreds of them. With my limited knowledge of computers, I really had little idea what I was looking at. As I began to think about what I wanted in a computer, I was interrupted by a salesman.

"Is there anything I can help you with?" he said with a smile.

"Not really. I have someone who knows a lot more about computers than I do coming to help me find what I need."

"Oh. Well, if there is anything I can help you with, please let me know."

"I will," I said with a smile.

The salesman no more than walked away when Jackie came into the store. She looked around for a moment then smiled when she saw me. I watched as she crossed the room toward me. It was hard not to watch her as she was a very beautiful and sexy looking woman.

"Hi," she said as she walked up to me and gave me a light kiss on the cheek. "Are you ready to look for a computer?"

"I've been looking at them but I have no idea which one I should get."

"Let me help you."

We spent almost the next hour looking at the different computers and talking about what I wanted my computer to do. I didn't understand half of what she told me. It was like she was speaking in a foreign language, but I answered her questions about some of the uses I would need including making photos from a camera's digital card. Finally, she recommended a desk top computer. I thought it was rather expensive, but she said anything less would not do what I wanted in a computer.

After we selected the computer, we looked at printers. We got one that would print, copy, and reproduce photos. She made sure that I would be able to print pictures from digital cards. We also spent a good deal of time picking out the software that she thought I would need for my line of work. We also picked out some of the supplies that I would need, such as paper, photo paper, ink cartridges, etc.

When we finished, I paid for everything we had picked out and loaded it into my car. Since she had driven to the store in her car, she followed me to my office. We took it all up to my office and began unpacking it. It wasn't long and we had the computer setting on a table behind my desk. We adjusted the height of the table to make it comfortable to sit at when I used the computer.

"Before we start hooking everything up, I would like to get something to eat," Jackie said.

I took a quick look at my watch. It was already after seven o'clock.

"You've worked hard. Where would you like to go for dinner? You name it."

"Why don't you get a couple of hamburgers and malts? We can eat here while we get everything hooked up and running."

"Won't that take awhile?"

"Not really. I'll get it set up so you can play with it a little before I start teaching you how to do different things with it."

"Okay."

I left Jackie in my office while I went to a local restaurant that had great hamburgers and some of the thickest malts anywhere. By the time I got back, Jackie had the computer, printer and all the hardware hooked up.

"It's all ready for you to get started," she said with a grin.

"I think you sent me off to get the hamburgers to get me out of the way," I said.

"Yes, I did," she said with a big grin.

"So now what?"

"Now we go to your apartment for the night."

"Is that it?"

"It is for now. I took tomorrow off so I will have time to show you how to add software, and have time to teach you how to use them."

"Sounds good."

I gave Jackie a kiss on the cheek, then closed my office. We rode the elevator down to the underground parking garage. I walked her to her car and gave her a kiss. As she drove out of the garage, I got in my car and followed her to my place.

Once we were in my apartment, we took a shower together then got into bed. We curled up together. It wasn't long and we were making love to each other. When our desire and our need for each other finally dwindled, we fell asleep in each other's arms.

When Don got back to his office, he made a call to Sergeant Walker. He asked him to check Max Carlson's ankle and see if he had marks from a dog bite. At first Walker laughed, then asked Don to wait and he would check. It didn't take Walker long to get back to the phone.

"Don?"

"Yeah, I'm still here."

"Max has bite marks from a small dog on his right ankle. Looks pretty new. How did you know about them?"

"I had a talk with Joe Miller. He was the guy that was hit on the head and had seen Max come out of the garage at Ms Hanson's apartment building. Joe told me that his dog bit the guy that slugged him from behind. He also said that he saw the man in a mirror just before he was struck. He described Max to a T. I want you to take a couple of pictures of the bite marks in case we need them for court."

"Sure thing. I guess we can hold Max for assault if nothing else," Walker said.

"Yes, we can, but don't file charges just yet. We don't want anyone to know we have him."

"Okay. I'll keep him hidden away for now. It will give us a couple of days before we have to do something with him."

"Good. Keep me posted on anything new," Don said.

"Will do," Walker said then hung up.

Don leaned back in his chair to think. He had Max for assault, but that was all he could prove at the moment. Someone had hired Max, but who? He began to wonder if Tidsdale was telling him everything he knew. Don knew from experience that he couldn't get anything out of Tidsdale unless Tidsdale wanted him to know it. It would be a waste of his time to try.

A quick glance at his watch told him that it was getting late. Don decided that he would go home and get some rest. Maybe tomorrow things would start to look up. He shut off the lights in his office and left for the day.

CHAPTER THIRTY-ONE

It was still dark when I woke. Jackie was lying on her side with her back toward me. She looked so at peace that I didn't want to wake her. I decided that there was no need to wake her since she didn't have to go to work today. As much as I wanted to find out what was on the digital cards I had taken from the cameras, a few hours more would not make any difference.

I rolled over on my back and began to let my mind wonder. For some reason that I could not explain, it took me to the warning I received from my friend. I had stepped on someone's toes, but I had no idea whose toes they might be. I could think of several people along the Front Range that might be involved, but I had no idea which one. There was always the possibility that there was more than one.

My mind sort of shifted to thoughts of the sexy woman who was lying beside me. I began to think that I might have put her in danger by simply having her with me. From what had happened at the café, there was little doubt that whoever was involved in the deaths of Martin and Weatherby had little concern about anyone else. Eight people had already died, and four others were in the hospital. That was enough proof that someone didn't care about innocent bystanders.

I would have to figure out a way to protect her. The best way to do that was to find out who was involved in the deaths of Robert Martin and Judge Marcus Weatherby. The question was how was I going to find out who was involved?

Suddenly, my thoughts turned to the digital cards again. Those two digital cards could be the answer. If the judge had been able to trigger the cameras, he might have gotten pictures of who killed him. Just knowing who the hit men were could go a long way toward finding out who was behind the assassinations.

Just then, I felt Jackie move. I turned my head and looked over at her. She was looking back at me.

"Good morning," she said with a sexy smile.

"Good morning. You ready to get up?"

"Not really," she said as she rolled over to me. "I would like a morning kiss first."

"Oh, I think that can be arranged," I said.

I rolled over to her, took her in my arms then rolled over on my back taking her with me. She stretched out over me as we kissed. The feel of her body against me sent feelings of desire through me. As we kissed, I ran my hands up and down the smooth curves of her back. She rose up a little, looked down at me and smiled.

"I like the way you touch me," she said softly, "but I can tell there is something on your mind other than me. Are you worried about something, maybe something you haven't told me?"

I thought for a moment or two before I answered her. I could tell by the look in her eyes that she was concerned, probably about what she thought I might say.

"Yes, I am worried about something. I'm worried about you."

"About me?"

"Yes. I'm afraid that I may have drawn you into something that could – ah – be dangerous."

She smile quickly vanished from her face as she just looked at me for a moment. I wasn't sure what she was thinking.

"What have you gotten into?" she finally asked with a hint of sharpness in her voice.

"I'm not sure, but the fact that you are with me could put you in danger," I said.

She looked at me for a moment more, then quickly rolled off me and sat up on the side of the bed. She reached down and grabbed her clothes off the floor then ran into the bathroom.

I watched her as she left me. I didn't know what to say to her, but I couldn't let her just walk out. I got up and quickly put on my shirt and pants.

When she came out of the bathroom, she was dressed. I tried to talk to her, but she walked right by me without looking at me. It was clear that she was crying. I couldn't let her leave while she was so upset with me. I grabbed her by the arm and turned her to face me.

"Honey, wait, please. Give me a chance to explain," I said.

She looked at me with tears running down her face.

"Wait for what? I know what you do for a living. Until now, it has had nothing to do with me. I was able to shut it out, but now you have me involved. I'm not going to wait around for you to get yourself killed."

She quickly jerked her arm free, turned and ran out of my apartment. I started after her but stopped at the door. I watched her as she got into her car then drove out of the parking lot.

As soon as she was out of sight, I closed the door and walked back to my bedroom. I couldn't really blame her for leaving. I had known for a long time that she didn't like what I did for a living, but she had not said much about it lately. I thought about going after her, but I was sure she would not even want to talk to me. I decided that I would give her a chance to cool down. I also needed to take some time to think about what my next move was going to be.

The one thing I knew for sure was that I had made a commitment to Attorney General Greene. When I make a commitment, I have to carry it out if at all possible. It is just the way I am.

As I finished getting dressed, I couldn't help thinking about Jackie. We had been close for a long time, but I had to make a decision. With all that was running through my mind, I decided that I would finish what I had started for the AG. The fact that I was already in up to my neck and to get out now could cause a lot of problems for both Greene and Don, played a part in my decision to continue.

The next thing was to decide where to go from here. With the decision made to finish what I had started, I finished getting dressed, then left my apartment and headed for my office.

Two men walked into the local bar and grill on East
Colfax. They didn't stop at the bar, but went to the rear of
the bar and entered a small backroom. Sitting at a table was
a rather large man eating his breakfast. The man's face
gave the impression that he was not very happy about
something, but it didn't seem to affect his appetite as he
didn't stop eating. He looked up at the men for a few
seconds before he spoke.

"It seems that we have a little problem."

"What kind of a problem?" the taller of the two men
asked.

"We have a local PI nosing around. The boss thinks he
might be a problem and wants him shut up, for good."

"What's his name?"

"Frank Tidsdale."

"Never heard of him. What makes the boss think he's a
problem?"

"He's been doing a lot of talking to Don Wright, the
detective handling the investigation of Judge Weatherby's
murder. We know that Tidsdale has Judge Weatherby's
secretary hiding out somewhere, and Wright has had a
chance to talk to her."

"She doesn't know anything," the tall man said.

"I'm not so sure. More importantly, the boss is not so
sure. You know how the boss don't like loose ends.

"What's the boss want us to do?"

"He wants you to get rid of Tidsdale, and the judge's
secretary."

"Okay."

"Don't get in touch with me until the job is done. If you
can't do it, we'll get someone who can," the fat man said in

a threatening tone, then shoveled another forkful of food into his mouth.

"We'll get it done," the tall man assured him.

The fat man nodded then continued to eat. The tall man turned and left the backroom with the smaller man following right behind him.

CHAPTER THIRTY-TWO

I arrived at my office about eight-fifteen with a small bag containing an egg and sausage roll from a local restaurant. Once inside my office, I locked the door. I set the bag on the table next to the coffee machine, then got the coffee started. While I waited for the coffee, I placed a call to my friend. It didn't take but a couple of rings for it to be answered.

"Hello," a male voice said.

"Frank Tidsdale."

"I'll get him," the voice said.

It didn't take but a moment before the phone was answered.

"What's up, Franky?"

"I need someone watched without them knowing it."

"Okay. Who is it?"

"Actually, I want her protected without her knowing."

"Jackie?"

"Yes. She stormed out of my apartment this morning when I suggested that she might be in danger just because she was with me."

"Say no more. I'll make sure she's safe."

"Thanks," I said, then hung up.

I leaned back feeling a little better. At least I would not have to worry about Jackie. She would have a bodyguard to protect her, and she probably wouldn't even know it.

I leaned back in my chair and looked at the computer. There were several small boxes alongside the computer which contained some of the software that Jackie was going to install for me.

I had no idea if I could install them myself, but I could read and understand most instructions. There was a good chance that I could install them if I took my time and read the instructions, then followed them very carefully. I opened the first one and began reading the instructions. It seemed to be complicated, but I thought I could handle it, so I booted up the computer. When it was ready, I inserted the disk and pressed the enter button. It began to run. I ate my roll and drank coffee while following the instructions as they came up on the screen. Once the first one was done, I followed the same general procedure for each piece of software that I installed. I found that it went smoothly, but it took a lot of time. It seemed that after each software item was installed, I had to reboot the computer.

It was well past noon when I had finished loading all the software onto the computer. It was time for me to see if I could retrieve any pictures from the digital cards I had taken from the cameras in Judge Weatherby's chamber.

It took me only a couple of seconds to find the right slot on the front of the computer that the digital card would fit in. As soon as it snapped in, a light came on and an array of options came up on the screen asking me what I wanted to do. I selected the one that said "open folder to review files". I suddenly found several other files. I clicked on the first one.

It brought up a photo of two men. One of the men was standing behind Judge Weatherby. It was hard to tell who he was since his back was to the camera. The other one was standing in front of Weatherby's desk. It was easy to see his face. It looked like the one in front of the desk was talking to the judge.

I moved on to the second photo. It was a picture of the same two men, only this time I could see the faces of both men. The taller of the two men was still standing in front of the desk, but the other man had moved so he was beside the judge. He was holding what looked like a small .38 caliber revolver to the side of the judge's head.

It didn't take me but a minute or so to figure out how to print off pictures of the two photos on the camera. As soon as I had them, I took the digital card out of my computer and put it in a secure place. I set the photos aside to give them a chance to dry.

While they were drying, I slipped the other digital card into the computer. It was blank. I pulled it out of the computer and set it on the desk.

I turned my attention to the photos I had made. I studied them very carefully. It was obvious that I had some very incriminating evidence. It was important that I get it to Greene and a copy to Don. I made a copy of the photos and had no more than set them aside when I heard someone trying my door.

"I know he's in there," a voice said.

I slipped one set of the photos under my desk, but I hardly had time for anything else before someone kicked open my door. Two men came busting into my office with guns in their hands. I grabbed for my gun as I dove for cover. There were at least three shots fired before I hit the floor, one of them hitting me. I knew I had been hit. I felt a sharp pain as I rolled over to return fire. It took the wind out of me, but I managed to get off one round toward my attackers. I heard a groan just before I passed out on the floor.

Don Wright arrived at his office at a little after eight. He sat down and began going over the forensic report. Things had not been going very well, but he had hoped that the information in front of him would provide him with a clue.

After he finished going over the forensic reports, he started going over all the names and addresses he had gathered with the help of Officer Williams, and the information that Sergeant Walker had provided him. He was looking for anything that might help him figure out who had paid Max Carlson to murder Ms Hanson, who killed those in the bombing of the café, and who might have ordered the assassination of Judge Weatherby.

He had been so absorbed in the paper work that he lost all track of time. It was almost noon when Officer Williams knocked on his door.

"Come in."

"I hope you don't mind my disturbing you, but I have a question I would like to ask you, sir," she said as she shut the door behind her.

"Not at all. Come in and sit down," Don said then watched her as she walked to a chair in front of his desk and sat down.

"What is your question?"

"First of all, I would like to say I'm sorry if I sounded like I didn't think you were right in trusting Mr. Tidsdale."

"That's all right. I know a lot of officers don't trust PIs."

"My question is, do you think it is a good idea to have someone outside the department to be the only one who knows where a valuable witness is being hidden?"

"I know where the witness is being held. But to answer your question, it all depends on who you trust and who you don't. What's your interest in this?"

"None really, but I thought you might be interested in what I was thinking about."

"Okay. Let me hear what's on your mind."

"Well, you know where the witness was held, but do you know where she is being held now? It is possible that Mr. Tidsdale has moved the witness since you visited with her."

"Do you think she might have been moved?" Don asked wondering why she was asking.

"No. No. It was just something I thought about last night," she said, but there was a hint of nervousness in her voice. "If she was moved, only Tidsdale would know where she is."

"I see. I guess when you put it that way, no. I'm not one hundred percent sure that I know where the witness is located at this moment," Don said as he looked at her.

Don was wondering why she seemed to be so interested in where Ms Hanson was located. Was her question just a simple straight forward question, or was there something else behind it. Did she know that Ms Hanson had been moved to another location and if so, how did she know? He suddenly had a feeling that he should be very careful what he told her, at least until he could get some idea of what she was really interested in knowing.

"Just what are you getting at?" Don asked.

"I was just wondering how you would find your witness if something happened to Mr. Tidsdale so that he couldn't tell you."

"Do you think something might happen to him?"

"No. No. Not at all," she said rather quickly. "It was just something that came to mind while I was thinking about what we had talked about the other day. I thought it was something I wasn't sure you had thought about, that's all."

"Well, you are right. I hadn't thought about it," Don said. "Thank you for sharing that thought with me."

"You're welcome. I guess I should get back to my regular duties," she said then she stood up.

She looked at Don for a moment as if hoping that he would say something. When he didn't say anything, she left his office.

Don watched her as she walked out the door. She hadn't really asked him any questions that should make him suspicious of her, yet it struck him as a little strange. She had obviously thought a great deal about where Ms Hanson might be. Why? Was she trying to get him to tell her, or was she just bringing up the question to get him to think about it?

A quick look at his watch told him it was time for him to get something to eat. Don got up and headed for the garage to get his car. As soon as he pulled out of the garage onto the street, he noticed a black Cadillac pull away from the curb about two cars behind him.

After what had happened in his office, it might not be a bad idea to go have a talk with Tidsdale. He let the car follow him. When he arrived at the building where Tidsdale had his office, he pulled over to the curb and stopped.

As the Cadillac drove past, he tried to get a look at the driver, but the side windows were tinted over. He was unable to see who was driving, but he did get the license plate number. He would run it after he had a talk with Tidsdale.

Don called dispatch and told the dispatcher where he was, then shut off the engine. He left his car and went on up to Tidsdale's office.

As he stepped off the elevator and looked down the hall toward Tidsdale's office, he noticed the door was open. It was not like Tidsdale to leave the door open. He walked a little faster as it crossed his mind that there might be something wrong.

When he got to the door, he looked inside. He could smell burnt gunpowder. It was clear that there had been a gun fired in the office within the past few minutes. As Don drew his gun, he noticed that there was blood on the door and door frame. He carefully entered the office.

Don immediately found Tidsdale lying on the floor behind his desk. There was a gun lying near Tidsdale, and there was blood on his shirt at his left shoulder and on the floor.

Don quickly checked to make sure Tidsdale was alive. Putting his fingers on Tidsdale's throat, he found a good pulse. Don immediately called for an ambulance and a black-and white unit. He then sat down on the floor next to Tidsdale to wait. People started to appear at the door to Tidsdale's office and were looking in.

"Please go back to your offices and wait there. There will be officers here any minute to talk to you," Don said as he held up his badge to identify himself.

The people glanced around, then turned and left. While Don waited, he took his handkerchief from his pocket and pressed it against the wound to help reduce the bleeding.

CHAPTER THIRTY-THREE

I could feel something pressing on my shoulder. It seemed to be making my shoulder feel very painful. As the fog in my head started to clear, I could remember what had happened. I wasn't sure how badly I was hurt, but I needed to find out. I slowly opened my eyes, turned my head to the side and saw Don kneeling on the floor beside me. He was pressing something against my shoulder.

"Don't move. I've called for an ambulance. Can you tell me what happened?"

"Yes. A couple of guys kicked in my door and started shooting at me. I took one round to the shoulder. I'm sure I hit one of them, but I don't know how badly he was hurt."

"Where were you when they started shooting?"

"At my desk. Actually, behind my desk."

"You weren't near the door?" he asked.

"No."

"I found blood on the door and door frame," Don said. "It looks like you got one of them."

"That would be the smaller of the two."

"Any idea who they were?"

"No, but I might have a picture of them," I said with a slight grin.

Just then the EMTs came rushing into my office. Don quickly moved out of the way so the EMTs could do their job. It didn't take them long to get a surgical dressing on my shoulder and to start an IV. They put an oxygen mask over my face, then put me on a gurney. After strapping me down, I was rushed out of the building and into an ambulance. Don stayed behind.

When I arrived at the hospital, they put me in a treatment room and went to work on my shoulder. It didn't take them long to stop the bleeding and stitch up the wound.

"You were lucky. The bullet missed the main arteries and bones. I don't think your wound is too serious," one of the doctors said. "It will be uncomfortable, and you'll need to take it easy for awhile. You will need to keep it in a sling for about a week before you can start exercising it."

Don stood by the door to Tidsdale's office and watched as the EMTs rolled Tidsdale out. He was concerned about his friend, but he didn't want to leave the crime scene until the forensic team could get there. The last thing he wanted was to have the crime scene compromised.

As soon as Tidsdale was gone, Don stood at the door and looked around the office. He noticed that from his position he could see at least three bullet holes. One of them had hit the back of the chair behind the desk, one had hit the wall behind the desk, and the third one had gone through the computer monitor on the table behind the desk. It was obvious that they had all been fired from the doorway or near it. Don was not sure if any of them actually hit Tidsdale. That would be something that the forensic team would have to find out. If none of them hit Tidsdale, they would be looking for a fourth bullet. From the look of Tidsdale's wound, the bullet would not be in him. They would also be looking for a slug fired by Tidsdale.

Don walked around the room looking for anything that might help him figure out what had really taken place there. He was being very careful not to disturb any evidence. As he walked around the end of the desk, he noticed what looked like a piece of paper lying under the desk. Don bent down to get a better look at it. The edge of the paper looked like it might be photo paper. It was glossy in appearance and seemed to be a little heavier than regular copy paper. Don wanted to pick it up, but decided to wait until the forensic team had photographed the entire crime scene.

Just as he stood up, two uniformed officers arrived. Don stopped them at the door.

"What took you so long to get here?" Don asked.

"We got trapped in traffic about three blocks from here. It was a hit and run," the senior officer explained.

"I want you to start interviewing everyone on this floor to find out what they saw and what they heard. I'll wait here for the forensic team."

"Yes, sir."

The officers started down the hall as Don turned around and looked into Tidsdale's office. He wasn't looking at anything special.

Don's thoughts turned to Tidsdale as he looked around his office. He remembered the question Officer Williams had asked him just a short time before leaving his office. Did she know someone had put a hit out on Tidsdale? Was she trying to get him to tell her where Ms Hanson was staying?

It angered him to think he might have a bad cop working right under his nose. He had no proof that she was a bad cop, but he would be very careful what he said to her and to anyone who might have contact with her.

CHAPTER THIRTY-FOUR

As soon as the doctors were finished patching me up, I walked out to the waiting room and sat down. I hadn't been sitting there very long when a nurse dressed in ugly green scrubs came up to me.

"How are you feeling, Mr. Tidsdale?" she asked, a pleasant smile on her face.

"A little tired, but not too bad, considering."

"That's to be expected. I'm Marilyn Norton. I have some pills for you in case your shoulder starts to hurt, and it will when the pain med wears off. Take them with a full glass of water, and no more than one table every four hours. Feel free to call me if you experience a problem."

"Thanks," I said as I took the small bottle, then watched her walk away.

As I sat in the waiting room, I began to wonder if Don had seen the photographs and the digital card that was on my desk. I wondered if he would recognize the men in the photos. I would have to wait to talk to him about it.

It wasn't long before a woman with several papers came across the room toward me. She had a smile on her face as she sat down beside me.

"Mr. Tidsdale, I have some papers for you to sign. They're your release papers."

I smiled and took the papers. After she pointed out where I was to sign, I signed the papers and gave them back to her. She thanked me then went back to her office. I was now free to leave.

I walked out the front door of the hospital and grabbed a cab. It wasn't long and I was home.

I decided to have a little something to eat, then relax before I went to bed. I found it a little difficult to make a bowl of soup and a sandwich with one hand, but I did manage, sort of. After I ate, I watched the news, then went to bed.

Don was still standing at the door to Tidsdale's office when Mel Street arrived.

"What's up? Isn't this Frank Tidsdale's office?"

"Yeah. He was attacked by two shooters. He was hit, but I think he will be okay. He was talking to me before he was taken to the hospital.

"Good. What do we have here?" Mel asked as he pointed to the blood splatter on the door and door frame.

"Tidsdale said he fired one shot from behind the desk toward the door. It looks like he might have hit one of the shooters. The blood on the door and door frame are probably from one of the shooters.

"According to Tidsdale, there were three shots fired at him, one of them hitting him in the shoulder. From here you can see three bullet holes. There's one in the desk chair, one in the wall and one went through the computer monitor and is in the wall behind the monitor."

"Yeah, I see them."

"By the way, there are two photos under the desk. I would like you to take pictures of them where they are, then I want them."

"Okay. Anything else?"

"Just see what you can find that will tell us what happened here," Don said.

"I'll do my best. Do you think Tidsdale took one of the bullets with him when he was taken out of here?"

"No. His wound looked like the bullet went through his shoulder."

"Okay, I'll get busy. I'll try to find the bullet Tidsdale fired. If I don't find it, the guy he hit might still have it in him."

"That's what I figured," Don said.

Mel had pictures taken around and under the desk, then picked up the pictures Don had pointed out to him. Don took the pictures, then left for his office.

When Don arrived back at his office, he sat down to place the call to the hospital to find out how Tidsdale was doing. He was told that he had been released and had gone home. Since it was getting late, he decided to go home. He could stop by and see how Tidsdale was getting along in the morning. Before he left the office, he locked up the two photos in his safe.

CHAPTER THIRTY-FIVE

I woke up several times during the night, but for the most part I was able to go right back to sleep. My shoulder was uncomfortable and there was some pain, but not so bad that I had to take medication for it.

When morning finally arrived, I didn't get up right away. Instead, I laid in bed and thought about my investigation. So far things had not been going well. There had to be something in the evidence I had that would get me headed in the right direction, I just hadn't found it yet.

My thoughts turned to my office. I wondered what the forensic team would find. I knew that they would find three bullets in my office, but I wasn't so sure about the one I fired. If they didn't find my 9mm slug, there was someone running around with it in him, well, maybe not running around in the literal sense of the word because I had no idea how much damage my bullet had done to him.

I closed my eyes and tried to picture the two men who had attacked me. It took a while for me to concentrate enough to bring a picture of the two men to mind. I was able to recognize one of them. He was the taller of the two men in the photos, and I had photos of him, and so did Don if he picked them up. I wasn't sure about the second man who attacked me, but I would have put money on the second man being the other one in the photos. Now all I needed were names to go with the men in the photos.

It was getting close to nine when I decided that it was time for me to get up and fix myself something for breakfast. It was not easy for me to get dressed with the lack of range of motion in my left shoulder, and the discomfort caused by moving my shoulder around.

By the time I got dressed and had my breakfast it was nine-thirty. I walked into the living room and laid down on my sofa.

Don arrived back at his office at his usual time. Once again he thought about the pictures that he had taken from Tidsdale's office. He again thought about calling Greene, but did not want to compromise Greene's investigation. He would wait until he could talk to Tidsdale. He was sure that Tidsdale would have a way to get in touch with Greene without anyone in Greene's office knowing about it.

Don knew that he had very valuable pieces of evidence in his possession. The problem was he needed to have verification as to the source of the evidence and how it had been obtained. Without that information, he knew it would not be allowed as evidence in a court of law.

It was still a little early to call Tidsdale. With all that had happened, he would probably sleep in and take it easy, at least for today.

Don got up from his desk and walked down the hall to the lounge to get himself a cup of coffee. After getting a cup of coffee, he started back toward his office. Don noticed Officer Williams talking on the phone at a desk off in the corner. He knew that the phone was not on her desk. She was some distance from him, but he could see by the expression on her face that she was having a serous conversation with someone. He couldn't hear what she was saying, but it didn't look like it was a pleasant phone conversation. It looked like she might be having an argument with someone.

As she talked on the phone, Officer Williams turned to look around, apparently in an effort to see if anyone was watching her. When she saw Don watching her, she quickly turned her back to him and hung up the phone, then quickly walked away.

Don wondered what was going on, but decided that it was none of his business. Even though he had decided it was none of his business, he could not help but think about it. It was the first time she had shown any sign that she didn't want to talk to him.

He wondered if she was upset with him for the way he talked to her about Tidsdale. Then Don remembered the question she had asked him just yesterday morning, only a short time before he discovered that Tidsdale had been shot. He thought it might be a coincidence, but was it? He was having his doubts.

As he thought back a bit, he remembered that she had suddenly appeared when his investigation into the death of Judge Weatherby was just starting. He also wondered if she knew Weatherby better than she had indicated.

Then there was the morning he caught her going over some of the forensic evidence in his office. She had no experience as a detective. She appeared to try to be very helpful, but was she? Was she just being nosey, or was she trying to find out what evidence the forensic team had uncovered at the crime scene?

That thought made him think about her collecting all the reports from the officers at Ms Hanson's apartment building. Had she destroyed some of the reports so that he wouldn't see them? Had she really visited the woman she said she had talked to? Did she know that something was going to happen to Tidsdale? Don had a lot of questions going through his mind. It was time to find some answers before he trusted her too much. One way was to interview the woman he had sent her to re-interview.

Don left his office and headed for the apartment building where Mrs. Hartman lived. Since it was almost on his way, he would make a slight detour and stop to visit with Tidsdale.

CHAPTER THIRTY-SIX

It was about ten o'clock in the morning, I was laying down on the sofa when I heard the doorbell. I got up and walked toward the door, but made a quick stop to pick up my gun from the end table. When I got to the door, I looked through the peep hole and saw Don. I reached out and opened the door.

"Hi. What brings you here?"

"I just stopped by to see how you are doing," Don said.

"Not too bad. Come on in," I said as I stepped back and let Don in. "I'm a little sore, but I think I should be all right."

"You feel like talking?"

"Sure. Have a seat."

I walked over to the sofa and sat down, while Don sat down on a chair.

"I want to talk to you about a couple of things. First of all, I found two photos under your desk. Where did you get them?"

"I got them off one of the digital cards from cameras in Judge Weatherby's chamber."

"Do you have any idea who took the pictures?"

"Yeah. I'm sure they were taken by Judge Marcus Weatherby."

The look on Don's face was priceless. It was clear that he wasn't sure I was telling him the truth.

"It's simple. The judge had two cameras set up in the bookshelves behind his desk. The cameras were aimed so that they would take pictures of anyone who was in front or close to his desk. He had them rigged so he could activate them while sitting at his desk."

I went on to explain how I had found the cameras, and the fact that I had removed the digital cards from the cameras. I wasn't sure that he believed me. I had a feeling that once he left me, he would be going to Judge Weatherby's chamber to have a look around.

"It was pretty obvious that the attack on you was a hit," Don said. "We think that you got one of them. From the looks of all the blood, if he didn't get help soon after he was shot, he was not likely to live long. We have the word out to as many doctors as we can contact and to all the hospitals in the area."

"You and I both know there are doctors that would fix him up without notifying the authorities," I said.

"You're right about that, but we have to try," Don said.

"When you were in my office, did you happen to look around?"

"Sure. I looked around while I waited for the forensic team."

"Did you get the set of pictures off my desk?"

"No. I found them under your desk. Why? Are there more pictures?"

"There was a set of pictures on my desk along with a digital card for a camera."

"They were not there," Don said looking disappointed.

"Did it look like my place had been searched? I don't have any idea how long I was out."

"No. I don't think they had time for that. You think they got the digital card?"

"If they took the pictures and digital card off my desk, they have nothing. The only thing they have is a set of pictures like the ones you have, and a digital card which was blank," I said with a slight grin.

"Do you still have the digital card that had the pictures on it?"

"I do. By the way, what brought you to my office?"

Don told me about the young female officer who had wondered if he still knew where Ms Hanson was located. I found what he had to say very interesting especially when he told me about her concern for my well-being. It was clear to me why Don was concerned about her.

"I can understand why you would come to see me," I said.

"I'll have to be very careful with any evidence I get from Mel Street and his forensic team when she's around. At least until I know for sure what she is up to," Don said. "By the way, is Ms Hanson still in the same location?"

"No. She is still in the same motel, but in a different room under a different name." I said. "The only reason I'm telling you is because of what happened yesterday. I will keep you informed as to where she is, but I would appreciate it if you didn't go see her without me."

"No problem there. I don't want to have a run-in with her bodyguard."

"Thanks. She is registered under the name Campbell."

"I've got a couple of things to do. I'll stop by tomorrow," Don said as he stood up.

"Thanks," I said as I started to get up.

"Don't get up. I can find my way out," he said as he turned to leave.

I watched him as he closed the door behind him. As soon as he was gone, I closed my eyes and thought about what he had told me. It was looking like he had a snitch in his office, too.

It was morning when a black Lincoln slowly moved down the deserted alley and came to a stop behind a bar and grill on East Colfax. Two men got out of the car and looked around. When they were sure that it was all clear, they opened the backdoor of the car nearest the backdoor of the bar. They helped a man out of the backseat and in the backdoor of the bar.

"Where have you been?" a rather large fat man said sharply. "What the hell happened to him?

"We ran into a little trouble yesterday. He was shot when we went after Tidsdale. That woman didn't tell us that Tidsdale was expecting us. She also didn't tell us that he had pictures of us in that judge's chamber. We found them on his desk."

"Why did you bring him here?"

"We need a place to hide him for awhile," the tall man said. "It's not safe at his apartment or mine. It certainly isn't safe to take him to a hospital. If Tidsdale had pictures of us, he will be telling his detective friend about us."

"You can't keep him here."

"Listen you, he's hurt bad. I'm surprised he's lasted this long," the tall man said. "If you don't like him here, then you can leave. He stays with me."

"Put him on the cot over there," the fat man said as he pointed to a cot in the corner of the room. "You will have to stay with him. I want nothing to do with him."

"I'll stay with him until midnight," the tall man said, then turned to the driver.

"Bill, you best get the car out of here and get it cleaned up. Bring back some plastic sheets when you're done."

"Okay," Bill said, then went out the back of the bar.

"What are you going to need the plastic sheets for," the fat man asked.

The tall man looked at his partner, then turned and looked at the fat man. He spoke in a whisper.

"To wrap his body in. I doubt he will make it until dark."

"Is he still alive?" the fat man asked with a surprised look on his face.

"He is now, but he doesn't look good."

"What's going to happen after midnight?"

"I'll dump his body where he can be found. Then I'm going to go settle a score with that PI, Tidsdale. He's the one who shot Harry."

"I take it you didn't get Tidsdale."

"No, we didn't, but we got the photos of the two of us and the digital card. Now he's the only one who can ID us."

"The boss isn't going to like this one bit," the fat man said.

"Now ain't that just too damn bad."

Nothing more was said. The tall man sat down in a chair next to the cot to wait. The fat man sat across the room and avoided looking toward the cot. He didn't like the idea of sitting in the same room with a man that was dying.

* * * *

Don drove to the courthouse and went directly to Judge Marcus Weatherby's chamber. It didn't take him but a few minutes to find the cameras where Tidsdale had told him they would be. He checked for the digital cards and found no digital cards in either of the cameras, but that was what he had expected.

He took a few minutes to check the angle of the cameras to see which one of them matched up with the photos. It didn't take but a minute to figure it out. He had what information he needed for the moment. He could see no reason to remove the cameras. It might be best if they were *left where they were. Don turned and left the courthouse without talking to anyone.*

Don arrived back at his office after stopping for lunch. When he walked into Precinct One, he saw Officer Williams talking to an old lady. He had no idea what they were talking about, but she looked up at him, then quickly turned away when she saw him look at her.

Her actions did nothing to relieve his suspicions of her. He would have to keep the pictures he had taken from Tidsdale's office to himself for now. Don didn't want anyone to see or even know about them, at least for now. The AG should see them first.

It was that thought which caused Don to remember that he had failed to ask Tidsdale for the AG's private phone number. He would have to contact Tidsdale again to get the AG's number.

When Don entered his office, he found an envelope on his desk. It was from Mel Street. He quickly checked to see if had been opened. It had not been. He opened it and dumped the contents out on his desk.

CHAPTER THIRTY-SEVEN

The afternoon passed slowly. It gave me a good deal of time to think about Jackie. If I really thought about it, I should have seen the day was coming when she could no longer hold back her feelings about what I do. We had been good friends and lovers for a long time. She knew what I did for a living when we started dating.

I knew that I would miss her, but maybe it was just as well that we ended it. I couldn't think of anything that I would like to do more than what I was doing. Sure, it was dangerous at times, but that came with the territory. Working with, and dealing with, some of the lowlifes of the city was all part of the job. The one thing I knew was, she didn't like the fact that I had to carry a gun. I knew that it would be one step short of suicide if I didn't.

I also knew she wanted me to get a different job. She even suggested that I get a job working in a bank or for some large company, or even for the state. Based on her comments over the years, it would have to be a position where I would be stuck behind a desk, breathing filtered air, and not having a window to look out. In other words, some place where it would be a lot safer. She hadn't said anything about it recently, but she had often told me in the past that I could get a good paying desk job because I had a degree in business and accounting.

The last thing I wanted was a desk job. I did enough of that after I got out of college. I would be bored to death if I had to do it every day, day in and day out. Going back to being a policeman would not satisfy her either, nor would it satisfy me.

While I was thinking about her, I wondered if she would come and see me. There was little doubt that the shooting in my office would be in every newspaper and on every television news broadcast in the city. The more I thought about it, the more I felt it was unlikely she would stop by to see me. It would be just something more to remind her just how dangerous my job can be.

As I laid there thinking about her, my shoulder began to throb a little. Looking at the clock showed me it had been several hours since I had had anything for pain. I got up and started toward the kitchen to get a glass of water. It was at that moment, I heard something at the backdoor. It sounded like someone was trying to get in. I picked up my gun, then looked around the corner into the kitchen.

Whoever it was, he was so intent on picking the lock that he didn't see me. Just as he got the lock to open, he looked around. His face turned a little pale when he saw me standing in the doorway to the kitchen with a gun in my hand, and it was pointed at him. He seemed to freeze for a second, then suddenly, he turned and ran away.

By the time I got to the backdoor, he was jumping over a low hedge and heading for a car. I couldn't see enough of the car to get a good look at it. I went back inside and locked the door, then sat down at the kitchen table. What Don had told me about having a hit put out on me came to life. I would need a little protection, at least for a while.

Don began sorting through the evidence that Mel Street had sent to him. It was mostly preliminary information. Checking out the reports on the blood found at the scene showed that the blood at and near the door to Tidsdale's office was not Tidsdale's. There was only one blood type which indicated that there had been only one person shot near the door. All the blood found behind Tidsdale's desk and around his computer and computer desk was the same type as Tidsdale's. From what Don had seen in Tidsdale's office, and had been told by Tidsdale, it all made sense.

Don did note in one of the reports that there were two or three drops of blood on the top of the desk, near the front, that were not Tidsdale's. Don thought about it for a moment. He knew from talking to Tidsdale there had been two photographs and a digital card on the desk. The blood drops probably got on the desk when one of the attackers saw the photos and leaned over the front of the desk to pick up the photos and digital card before fleeing the scene.

The report stated that they were running DNA tests on all the blood. Don hoped the DNA tests would tell him who the attackers were or at least one of them.

Don leaned back in his chair and looked up at the ceiling. He had a lot of things going through his mind. Who had discovered that Tidsdale had the photos and digital cards was just one of the many questions that ran through his mind.

His thoughts were suddenly disturbed by a knock on his door. He reached out and gathered the reports on his desk and began putting them in the envelope.

"Come in," he said as he closed the envelope.

Don looked up as Officer Williams came into his office. He slipped the envelope in the top drawer of his desk and closed the drawer. It was clear that she had seen the envelope and where he had put it.

"Excuse me for interrupting you, but I would like to talk to you if you have a few minutes to spare."

"What is it, Officer Williams?" Don said without emotion.

"I was wondering if you might share some of your information with me."

"I don't think that is appropriate."

"Why? All I want is to learn how you decide what is important and what is unimportant when you are looking at evidence."

"A lot of it is gut feeling and a lot of it is experience. There is no cut and dried system or rules. Certainly there are some things that are clear cut evidence that tells the investigator what happened and how it happened. In most cases, why it happened and who did it is not so clear. In other words, it is at that point you have to start using your experience. It's hard to teach someone experience. It is something you have to learn for yourself."

"I understand that, but - - - ."

"I'm sorry, Officer Williams, I have a very important interview. I have to leave now," Don said as he started to stand up.

"I'm sorry to have bothered you, sir," Officer Williams said as she started to leave.

Don noticed that she briefly glanced at the top of his desk before she turned to leave   He watched her as she left his office. Her question puzzled him. Was she searching for a way to find out what evidence he had, or was she just trying to learn more about police work?

Don couldn't take the chance since she might be a snitch. He reached into his desk and took out the envelope from Mel Street. Don set the envelope on his desk while he *opened his safe. He put the envelope in the safe, closed it, then headed for the police garage.*

CHAPTER THIRTY-EIGHT

After the attack on my life and an attempt to enter my home, there was little doubt that I would need the help of a bodyguard. It was something I couldn't expect the police to do for me. I needed someone who I could trust to be with me and not tell anyone what I was doing.

I reached over and placed a call to my friend. It didn't take but a minute for the phone to be answered.

"Hello," a male voice said.

"Frank Tidsdale," was all I had to say.

"I'll get him. It might be a moment or so. He's on another line."

"No problem," I said.

I could hear him set the phone down. I couldn't hear anything, but then I didn't expect I would. It took about five minutes before my friend came on the line.

"What's up, Franky?"

"I don't know if you've heard, but I took a bullet to my shoulder."

"Yeah, we heard. We don't know who it was that shot you, but we're working on it."

"I'm going to be a little limited in what I can do because of my injury. I was wondering if you could spare a body-guard for me. I just want someone to cover my back."

"Sure. No problem. You already have one."

"I hoped you would be around."

"The guy that tried to break-in your backdoor is with a couple of my guys. They caught him at the end of the alley. They are asking him who he works for. So far no comment, but we haven't had him very long."

"I should have figured you would be right on it. Thanks, but that one was about to get shot. I had a gun on him just as he was thinking about coming into my apartment."

"I know," he said with a slight chuckle in his voice.

I didn't see any reason to ask him anything more. He was covering by back, and that was all I needed to know.

"How's it going with Jackie?"

"We're keeping a close eye on her. You don't need to worry about her."

"Thanks. I'll talk to you later," I said, then the phone went dead.

I no more than hung up the phone when it began to ring. I picked it up.

"Hello."

"How are you doing?"

I immediately recognized the voice. It was that of Attorney General Robert Greene.

"I'm doing okay."

"Are you going to be able to continue?"

"Yes. I'm currently going over what evidence I have. I have two photographs that were taken in Judge Weatherby's chamber of the two men that shot him," I said.

There was dead silence on the phone. It was clear that I had caught Greene by surprise with that statement.

"It's little hard to believe, isn't it?"

"Yes. I sure as hell hope you have them in a safe place," he said.

"They can't be in any place safer. I have the camera's digital card and Detective Wright has the photos. I was going to call you and tell you about them, but things happened."

"I heard. I want you to keep the digital card safe. Is Wright looking for the men in the picture?"

"Yes, but not so anyone would know. He's been keeping the photos to himself, at least for the moment."

"Good. Would you pass the word on to Wright that I appreciate the fact that he is keeping the photos to himself?"

"Sure."

"I want you to see if you can find anyone else in the criminal court system that might be involved in corruption before you go after those in the photos. If it gets out that he has the photos of them, it could ruin my investigation. Evidence could be destroyed, and some of those involved could end up dead."

"I understand. I'm sure that Wright understands that as well, but I'll talk to him about it."

"Good. Take care of yourself out there, and keep in touch."

"Will do," I said, then hung up.

Don left his office and drove to the home of Mrs. Jill Hartman. She lived in the same apartment building where Ms Hanson had lived. When he drove up to the building, he noticed there was plywood over the windows to Ms Hanson's apartment. He parked his car and walked to the entrance. Don checked the mailboxes to find the apartment number for Mrs. Hartman. The number was 307 and it was on the same floor as Ms Hanson's.

Don took the stairs to the third floor and walked down the hall. Apartment 307 was located just a few doors down the hall from Ms Hanson's. When Don arrived at the apartment, he knocked on the door. He took a minute to look down the hall to where Ms Hanson's apartment was located. His attention returned to the door in front of him when he heard the door being unlocked.

"May I help you?" the woman asked.

"I'm Detective Donald Wright," he said as he showed her his badge and ID. "Are you Mrs. Hartman?"

"Yes."

"I would like to talk to you about the explosion in apartment 302."

"Certainly. Please come in. I've been expecting you."

"You have?"

"Yes. With what I told the woman officer the other day, I really expected you to come see me right away."

"That is why I'm here."

"Please have a seat. Would you like something, maybe a cup of coffee?"

"That would be nice," Don said without sitting down.

She turned and walked to the kitchen. Don followed her. He sat down on a bar stool at the breakfast counter while she fixed the coffee.

"*Would you mind telling me what you told the officer?*"
Don asked.

"*Well, when the officer came up to me, she asked me where I lived. I told her. She then asked me if I had seen anything strange, and I told her about the man I saw in the hall.*"

"*Excuse me, but would you tell me a little about the man?*"

"*Yes. He was short, maybe five-five or six, probably about two hundred pounds, but don't hold me to that. It could have been the heavy coat he was wearing. I'm not a good judge of people's weights.*"

"*Please go on,*" *Don said.*

"*Well, he had brown wavy hair, but I couldn't tell what color his eyes were because I didn't see his face. He was wearing work pants, you know, the dark blue heavy cotton pants like a lot of repairmen wear.*"

"*Yes, I know the type.*"

"*He was carrying a small black toolbox. I figured he was in the building to repair a phone or something like that. The strangest thing was he seemed to be in a hurry.*"

"*By any chance, did he see you?*"

"*No, I don't think so. He was walking away from me when I saw him. I had just stepped out of my door to pick up my morning paper,*" *Mrs. Hartman said.*

"*Could you tell where he was coming from?*"

"*No, but I did see him leave by the back stairway.*"

"*Does the back stairway lead to the underground garage?*"

"*Yes.*"

"*What happened then?*"

"*It was only a few minutes, maybe ten or fifteen minutes, after I saw him leave that the explosion occurred in Martha's apartment. The fire alarms went off and I left the building out the front door. As I walked out of the building, I* was stopped by the woman officer. She questioned me about everything I saw and did. I told her the same thing I just told you," she said.

Don looked at her as she started to pour him a cup of coffee. When she finished pouring the coffee, she sat down at the breakfast counter next to him.

There was no doubt that he had a problem. None of what Mrs. Hartman had told him matched up with what Officer Williams had said.

"Did you see Ms Hanson anytime that morning," Don asked, then took a sip of coffee.

"No. I was told later that she had left the building before the explosion. I was so relieved. She seems like a very nice lady," Mrs. Hartman said.

"I take it you don't know her very well."

"No, I don't. We see each other from time to time and say hello, but that is about it. I told the woman officer that I didn't really know her."

Don looked at Mrs. Hartman for a few minutes while he thought about what he had been told. His thoughts were interrupted by her.

"Is there something wrong, Detective? You look a little confused."

"No. I was just thinking about what you said."

"I hope I was of some help."

"You have been. Was Mr. Hartman around at the time of the explosion?"

"Mr. Hartman passed away about three years ago. He had cancer," she said sadly.

"I'm sorry."

"Thank you,"

"Thank you for your time. And thank you for the coffee, it was excellent," Don said with a smile as he got up from the bar stool.

"You are more than welcome. I'm glad you like it. If you're in the area and in need of a good cup of coffee, please feel free to drop in. I don't get much company," she said with a nice smile.

"I will," Don said. "And thank you."

Don left the building thinking about what he had said to Mrs. Hartman. He had no idea why he had said it, but he knew he meant it. It was not like him to get involved with people who were a part of his investigation. He had taken mental note that she was a very nice looking woman. If he had to guess, they were probably very close in age. The fact that she made a great cup of coffee was a plus. Don had to mentally shake himself and get back to the investigation. It crossed his mind that he might like to call on her when his investigation was completed.

He returned to his car, got in and just sat there for a minute. As his mind turned back to the reason for talking to Mrs. Hartman, Don found he had a lot to think about. It looked like the AG was not the only one with a mole in his office. He was going to have to make sure that Officer Williams didn't see any of the evidence he had, and that she didn't find out about his connection to the AG. Don knew he was going to have to find some pretty strong proof that Officer Williams was leaking information to someone, or changing information to make it lead the investigation in a different direction.

After taking a deep breath, he reached down and started his car. He checked for traffic, then headed back toward the office to review some of the evidence he had so far. He changed his mind and decided to stop in and talk to Tidsdale again.

CHAPTER THIRTY-NINE

It was just shortly after noon when my nap was disturbed by the ringing of my doorbell. I got up, picked up my gun from the end table, then headed for the door. I looked through the peep hole and saw Don standing in front of my door. I slipped my gun into my sling, then opened the door.

"Hi. I didn't expect to see you so soon."

"I need someone to talk to, and I couldn't think of anyone who would keep our talk private, except you."

"Come in. Have you had lunch yet?"

"No."

"If you don't mind sandwiches, and don't mind helping to fix them, you can have lunch here while we talk," I suggested.

"No, I don't mind. I make a pretty good sandwich, if I do say so myself.

"Good. Let's go out to the kitchen. We can make lunch while you tell me what's on your mind."

Don followed me out to the kitchen. I gave him directions to everything he might need to make sandwiches, then I sat down at the table. Don started gathering what he needed, but didn't say anything. I got the feeling that he was also gathering his thoughts. I decided that I would see if I could get him talking.

"I know you didn't come here just to make sure I had something to eat. What's on your mind? Anything new on the mole in your office? You mentioned an interview you thought might shed some light on it. How did that go?"

"I guess you could say it went very well. It made it look like I do have a mole in my office. At this point, I'm not sure what to do about it. I think I will keep her out of the loop for now. I don't have enough evidence to charge her."

"It's a woman officer?" I asked

I was a little surprised that it was a woman officer. I don't know why I was surprised. Some women are just as nasty and mean as men, some worse.

"Yeah. She worked for Judge Weatherby in his court. She signed for him when he had a deaf person in a case."

I thought about what he said. Once I get out and about again, I should look into her activities, and what other judges she might have worked for in the courts.

Don finished making the sandwiches, then sat down at the table. I took the opportunity to tell him what Greene had asked me to tell him. Don didn't seem to be surprised.

"Have you done anything to find out who they are?" I asked.

"No. I'm a little nervous about letting anyone in my precinct even know I have the photos. I don't have any idea who Officer Williams might be getting her information from or who she is giving it to. Most of the officers would talk freely with her since she is a fellow officer," Don said.

It didn't seem that Don wanted to talk too much, but I knew that he had come by to talk to me about something.

"Don, why did you stop by? I know it wasn't to fix me lunch."

"I guess I needed someone to talk to," he said. "Or maybe it was to just be away from the office while I thought about things."

"Well, if it helps any, I understand. It's hard when you think someone is not what you expected them to be. Is there anything I can do to help?"

"No, not at the moment."

"If I can do anything for you, just let me know," I said.

"I will. Thanks for the lunch," Don said.

"Thanks for making it."

Don stood up and began taking the dishes to the sink.

"I'll take care of them. You have things to do."

"Yeah," he said softly as if he didn't like the idea of what he thought he needed to do.

I watched as Don walked out of my apartment. It was not hard for me to understand what he was thinking. It is never easy finding a dirty cop right under the same roof.

As soon as he left, I finished clearing the table and put things away. My mind was wondering what was going to happen next. Once I was finished, I went in and laid down on the sofa for a short nap. It was not easy for me to get to sleep with so much on my mind.

Don left Tidsdale's apartment and returned to his office. As he entered the police building from the parking lot, he saw Officer Williams talking to someone in a sedan. He first thought that it might be her boyfriend, but he wasn't sure if she had one. Don began to wonder who it was she was taking to. From where he was standing, he could not see who was in the car. However, he could see the license plate on the car.

He stepped inside the building, then wrote the license number down on the small evidence tablet he always carried. Don then went on into his office. He walked across the room to his safe, took out the envelope he had put there earlier, then sat down at his desk. He slowly began going over the evidence.

The ballistic reports on the slugs that had been found in Tidsdale's office showed that three rounds had been left at the scene. Two of the rounds were from a gun that had once been in the Evidence Room at the police station. The report on those two rounds showed that the gun had been reported as having been destroyed. It was obvious that the report of the gun being destroyed was false. The ballistic report of the third slug showed it was from a gun that had been used in another murder. It was the same gun that had been used to kill the AG agent, Robert Martin. If the attackers had fired three rounds as Tidsdale had said, all of them were accounted for. The only one missing was the slug that Tidsdale had fired. Don wondered if that slug was in the attacker that Tidsdale had shot. It seemed logical.

The fact that the same gun that was used to kill Martin was also used in an attempt on Tidsdale, led Don to think that Tidsdale must have touched a nerve on someone. The problem was whose nerve did he touch?

Then there was the question, how did anyone know that Tidsdale had gotten hold of the cameras digital cards, and how did they know that there were cameras in Judge Weatherby's chamber in the first place? Someone had to know about the cameras. The question that needed to be answered was who? Who knew about the cameras?

As Don sat at his desk, he tried to think of everyone who might know about the cameras. He immediately could think of one person who was the one most likely to know about the cameras and that was Ms Hanson. If anyone knew about it, it had to be her. The problem with that was he didn't know how he could get to see her without having Tidsdale with him.

Don thought about calling Tidsdale, but decided that it could wait until Tidsdale was able to get around. That way, he could take Tidsdale with him to visit Ms Hanson.

With the situation resolved for the moment, Don called the dispatch center. He requested information on the license plate of the car he had seen in the police parking lot.

"The car is a new blue Cadillac sedan owned by John Wilkinson," the dispatcher said.

"That wouldn't be Judge John B. Wilkinson would it?"

"It is if he lives in Cherry Creek," the dispatcher said.

"Thank you."

"Will there be anything else, detective?"

"Not at the moment. Thanks."

"You're welcome," the dispatcher said, then the phone went dead.

Don set the receiver down, then sat back and stared at the phone while he thought about what he had been told. He wondered what Judge Wilkinson wanted from Officer Williams. Don knew that Officer Williams could sign. He wondered if the judge was asking Officer Williams to sign for someone in a case he was working on, or was there some other reason for him to be there?

It didn't make any sense to Don that the judge would come all the way over to the police station to ask her to sign for a deaf person in his court. It would have been easier for him to just pick up a phone and call her, and easier yet to have his secretary call her.

Don had no answers, but he swore under his breath that he would find out what was going on. He would find out who she was really working for.

It was getting late and it had been a long day for Don. He decided that it was time to give it up for the day, go home and get some rest.

CHAPTER FORTY

I woke to the sound of my television with the announcement of another murder. My ears instantly picked up on it. I turned over and looked over at the television just in time to find out that the newscaster was reporting on another shooting in the five point areas of the city, and that the murder was most likely gang related. It had been a drive-by-shooting in an area where there were a number of gangs that were often taking shots at each other.

I reached out and shut off the television, then laid back and looked at the ceiling. My thoughts turned to Don and what he had said about the mole in his office. I didn't know anything about the officer other than the fact that it was a woman.

I turned my attention to the attack on me. How did they know I was investigating the death of Judge Weatherby? How did they know about the cameras and the digital cards? I had made my visit to the judge's chamber in such a way that no one would know I was there, or had been there. If they had been informed by a mole in the AG's office, they still wouldn't know about my having been in the judge's chamber.

The more I thought about it, the more I came to the conclusion that the two men that came after me didn't know I had pictures of them. That is, until they saw them on my desk along with the digital camera card that was lying on my desk next to the pictures. That still didn't explain how they knew I was investigating the murder of Judge Weatherby.

It suddenly occurred to me how they found out about my investigation. Don had told the mole in his office. At the time he didn't know she was a mole. Don must have told her that I had Ms Hanson hidden away somewhere.

I needed to talk to Don as soon as possible. I took a look at the clock next to my television. It was almost nine o'clock in the evening. I was sure that Don would have gone home for the night. I couldn't see any reason to bother him at home since there was nothing he could do about it tonight. I would contact him tomorrow.

I was wide awake after having slept all afternoon and well into the evening. Going back to bed now would be a waste of effort. Instead, I went to the kitchen and cooked up a simple hot dish of ground beef, potatoes and carrots. While it was cooking on the stove, I took some time to think about what had happened over the past few days.

The one thing that came to mind was that it was time for me to get back to work. I had several things I had left undone. One of those things was to find out who it was that had attacked me in my office. I wanted to find out who had put a hit out on me.

My thoughts were suddenly interrupted by my phone ringing. I gave my hot dish a quick stir, then answered the phone.

"Hello."

I waited for an answer, but didn't get one.

"Is anyone there?" I asked.

I could hear someone breathing into the phone. Several thoughts came to mind. My first was that it was Jackie calling to find out how I was doing, but she couldn't bring herself around to say anything. Just as I was about to ask if it was Jackie, the phone went dead. I hung up the receiver and just looked at the phone. I reached out and picked up the spoon and stirred the hot dish, but my mind was not on the meal.

I knew there was nothing I could do about the call, but there was a chance that I could at least get a phone number from my caller ID. I checked the caller ID, but all it showed was a message that said it was a wireless call. It didn't give a number.

I returned to my meal. As soon as it was ready to eat, I dished up a large portion, then sat down to eat. It was pretty good and there was plenty leftover for another meal.

When I was finished, I cleaned up the kitchen, went into the living room and sat down on the sofa. I leaned back and watched a little television before I drifted off to sleep.

It was about eight-thirty in the morning when Don arrived at his office. He had no more than sat down when his phone began to ring. He reached over and picked up the receiver.

"Detective Wright."

"Don, this is Mel. I have some news for you."

"What is it?"

"It seems that we have found the body of the man Tidsdale shot at his office."

"Are you sure?"

"Not a hundred percent sure, but it certainly could be."

"Where did you find him?"

"His body was dumped in Cheesman Park. He was discovered this morning by a runner in the park who called the police. The body was sitting on a park bench near the duck pond."

"What do you mean he was 'sitting on a park bench'?"

"I can tell you this much. He did not die there. He was put on the park bench after he was dead."

"Any idea how long he had been dead?"

"My best guess is he died sometime between eight and ten yesterday evening. It may have been a little later, but not much. It looks like he lasted quite a while after he was shot. We know that he was shot shortly after noon."

"Any sign that he had received treatment for the gunshot wound?"

"None by a professional. He does look like someone tried to stop the bleeding, but I doubt he had much luck. The guy was gut shot."

"Have you identified him?" Don asked.

"Not yet. We just got him. "One other thing, he had no ID on him and it looks like someone went through his pockets after he was set on the bench," Mel said.

"You think that some homeless person might have searched him for anything they could use?"

"Possible, but it's hard to tell. I'll let you know if we find anything."

"Thanks," Don said before he hung up.

Don leaned back in his chair and thought about what Mel had told him. It was clear that whoever had put the dead man in the park wanted him found quickly. The only question was why? Don didn't have an answer.

It was at that moment Don remembered the pictures he had of the two men who had murdered Judge Weatherby. Was it possible that Mel actually had one of the men on his examining table who had murdered Weatherby? Don thought it was very unlikely, but it was worth the effort to find out. Don got the pictures of the two men from his safe, then headed for the garage.

Don got in his car and headed out of the Police Garage. He hadn't gone very far when he thought he saw a Lincoln following him. He wasn't a hundred percent sure, but it seemed to be tailing him. There was no reason to be concerned about the Lincoln at the moment, but it might be a good idea to try to get a license plate number just in case it became a concern.

Don pulled into the parking lot where the Morgue was located, then stopped quickly. The Lincoln drove on by. As it passed, Don got the license number. He quickly wrote it down, then parked his car and walked into the building.

CHAPTER FORTY-ONE

I woke while the sun was just starting to come up over the ridge behind my apartment. My shoulder was hurting a little bit. I got up, went to the bathroom and got a glass of water. I took one of the pain pills that the doctor had given me, then returned to my bedroom and laid down again.

It wasn't long before the pain in my shoulder had subsided to a point where it was just a little uncomfortable. I got up and went into the bathroom, ran a tub of warm water, then sat down in it. The warm water helped me to relax and cleared my mind. I would have preferred a shower, but the dressing on my shoulder sort of prevented that.

After spending sometime in a warm tub, I began to feel a little better. I washed, being careful to wash around the wound in my shoulder to prevent getting the dressing wet. I got out of the tub, then got dressed, which was not very easy to do without help, and with a stiff and somewhat painful shoulder.

Once that was done, I put my sling back on, then went out to the kitchen. I fixed a breakfast of cold cereal, fruit and coffee. I had just finished my breakfast when my phone began to ring. I got up and walked to the counter and picked up the phone.

"Hello," I said.

"I just called to see how you are doing?"

"Jackie?"

"Were you expecting someone else?" she asked.

"Well, no, not really. But after the way you left, I didn't really expect to hear from you again. It is nice to hear your voice."

"It's nice to hear yours," Jackie said, but didn't say anything more.

"I guess the question I have is will I be seeing you again?" I asked.

There were several moments of silence.

"I just called to find out how you are doing. I read in the paper that you had been shot. I called the hospital to see how you were doing and they told me you had been discharged."

"I'm doing okay. My shoulder is a little stiff and a little painful at times, but I'm doing okay. You still haven't answered my question."

"I'm sorry," she said softly followed by silence.

"It's okay. I understand. I really do, but I can't change what I do or who I am."

"You can't, or you won't?" she asked with a hint of sharpness in her voice.

"I guess to be honest, I won't. I can't be a desk jockey. It's just not in me. I'm sorry," I said.

"Well, I guess there is nothing more to say, except - - - goodbye, and - I wish you well," she said, then the phone went dead before I could respond.

I hung up the receiver, then just stood there for a minute looking at it. It was over and that was it. I had known for a long time that she didn't like what I do. When I took a minute or so to think about it, I think I knew the day would come when she would end our relationship. There was no sense trying to talk to her about it. She had made up her mind and she was not about to change her mind. But then, neither was I.

I sat back down at the table after pouring another cup of coffee. When I was done, I went into the living room and laid down on the sofa. There was nothing to be gained by thinking about Jackie and our relationship anymore. It was time to turn my mind to the case I had been working on. It was time to go back to my office and get busy trying to find out who ordered the killing of Judge Weatherby, and finding out who was involved.

Don arrived at the morgue and found Mel in the examining room with a body laid out on a table. He took the picture out of the envelope and looked at it. He studied the picture for a couple of minutes before he put it away. Don knocked on the window looking into the examining room to get Mel's attention.

Mel looked up and saw Don standing at the window. He motioned for Don to come in. Don walked into the examining room and looked down at the body on the table. He recognized the man as the shorter of the two men in the picture. He looked up at Mel.

"I don't know the man's name, but he is one of the men I've been looking for," Don said.

"You're working on two cases as I recall," Mel said. "One involving the bombing of the café downtown, the other, the death of Judge Weatherby. Am I right?"

"That's right," Don replied, not wanting to say anything more about it.

"What's Tidsdale got to do with it? After all, the slug I took out of this guy was from Tidsdale's gun."

"Nothing that I know of, but I would appreciate it if you didn't say anything about it to anyone, at least for now."

Mel looked at Don as if he was thinking about Don's request. He had known Don for a long time and respected him, both as a person and as a detective.

"I don't know what is going on, but I will keep quiet for now. I would like to know what it is all about when you feel it is safe to tell me. I take it you want it kept quiet for a very good reason."

"Yes. I know that I'm asking a lot, but it is important that you keep quiet about what you find, at least for now."

"Okay," Mel said. "I'll let you know what this guy's name is as soon as I can."

"Thanks. I owe you one."

"You owe me nothing. Just catch the person or persons who killed the judge and those people in the café," Mel said.

"You got it," Don said, then turned around and left the examining room.

Mel watched as Don left. As soon as he was gone, Mel turned back and looked at the body.

"Well, let's see what you can tell me," he said as he continued his examination of the body.

Don left the building and got in his car. He started back toward the precinct. He had just turned onto the street when he noticed a black Lincoln about three cars behind him. He wasn't sure if it was the same Lincoln that had followed him to the morgue or not, but it looked like it.

Don returned to the precinct. As he turned into the parking lot, he waited to see what the person in the Lincoln was going to do. To his surprise, the Lincoln turned into the parking lot and parked in the visitor parking area. Whoever was driving the car did not get out.

Don was a little confused, but it was time to find out who was in the Lincoln, and why they were following him. Don walked up to the Lincoln with his hand on his gun. As he approached the car, the driver's side window rolled down. He could see the man in the car. The man had both hands on the top of the steering wheel where Don could see them. Don walked up to the door.

"Can I help you," Don asked, being very cautious.

"I have a message for you, Detective Wright," the man said.

"Who are you?"

"That's not important. What is important is the other man you are looking for can be found in The Colfax Bar and Grill on East Colfax.

"Who are you? I want a name."

"Let's just say my boss is a very good friend of Mr. Tidsdale's. The guy you're looking for hangs out there. I don't know if he's there now, but he uses the backdoor a lot. It's a hard place to watch because there is no place close where he can't see you when he's coming or going, but it can be done."

"I could arrest you and find out who you are."

"I don't think that Mr. Tidsdale would like that."

Don looked at the man. He knew Tidsdale had friends in some interesting places. He also knew that to arrest this guy would accomplish nothing, and would probably turn out to be a waste of his time.

"Okay. I got the message. Thank your boss for me," Don said.

The driver of the car smiled at Don and nodded slightly. Don stepped back as he watched the Lincoln back out of the parking space and leave the parking lot. Don wondered if what he had been told was true. The only way he might be able to find out was to call Tidsdale.

Don turned, walked into the precinct and went directly to his office. He put the envelope back in the safe, then sat down at his desk. He placed a call to Tidsdale at his home.

CHAPTER FORTY-TWO

Just as I was getting up, my phone began ringing. I reached over and pick up the receiver.

"Hello."

"Tidsdale, this is Don."

"Hi, what's up?"

"One of the men that attacked you in your office has been found."

"No kidding."

"No kidding. The only problem is he's dead."

"You want to fill me in?" I asked.

"He was found sitting on a park bench in Cheesman Park. He didn't die there. The guy is one of those in the photos I found in your office. You know, the photos I found under your desk."

"Yes, I know. From what you're saying, the guys that attacked me were the same ones that killed Judge Weatherby."

"That sounds about right."

"It looks like I was getting a little too close for someone."

"Any idea who you were getting close to?" Don asked.

"No idea."

"We know it's one of those who shot at you because the ME took a slug out of him that matches your gun, the one we found on the floor next to you in your office."

"Well, that means that there is still one of them out there."

"It does," Don said.

"So I still have someone who wants me dead."

"I would say so. I have some other information for you. It has to do with a guy I met in the police parking lot this morning."

"Someone you met in the police parking lot?"

"Yeah. It seems he saw fit to follow me right into the parking lot. When I confronted him, he said he had an important message for me. He said that I could find the man I was looking for at The Colfax Bar and Grill on East Colfax. He even warned me about how easy it would be for him to spot someone watching the alley."

"You're kidding, right?" I said somewhat surprised at what I was hearing.

"No, I'm not kidding. He even told me that you wouldn't like it if I arrested him because he refused to give me his name."

I thought about what Don had said for a minute and began to smile to myself. I didn't know who the guy was Don had met, but I had a pretty good idea who he worked for and why he was sent to talk to Don.

"Are you still there?" Don asked.

"Yes, I'm still here. The message you got was probably from a friend of mine. Let's just say he prefers that you not know who he is. I can tell you this, you can count on the message being true. He knows what he's talking about," I said.

"I'll take your word for it. Is he working for you?"

"No, not really. I call on his boss from time to time. He can get information that is almost impossible to get anywhere else. He has a lot of connections in the Denver area."

"I won't ask you any more questions about this source of yours. In fact, I'll pretend that I never heard it," Don said.

"Thanks," I said, then took a deep breath as I began to think about what Don had told me.

"Are you about ready to get to work or are you going to sit around all day?" Don asked.

"I was just about to get out of the house and go to my office. I will probably be there most of the day."

"Okay. Well, I best be getting on my way. I want to take a drive by the bar on Colfax. Maybe I'll see a place where we can watch it without worrying about being seen," Don said.

"That might be a good idea. Just make sure you don't hang around there very long and make the guy nervous."

"I'll do my best. Talk to you later," Don said, then the phone went dead.

Don got up from his desk, walked out of his office and went to the police garage. He took a car and drove out onto the street. As he drove across town to East Colfax, he kept an eye out for anyone following him. He didn't see anyone.

It wasn't long before he found The Colfax Bar and Grill. He didn't stop, but drove on by. He went down the street a few blocks before turning a corner, then turned into the alley that ran parallel to Colfax. He had just turned into the alley when he stopped. He was at least two and a half blocks from the bar.

Don studied the area and could see why it would be hard to cover the area without being seen. There were lots of trees and bushes, tall fences and tall houses that had second story windows overlooking the alley. Don decided to leave the area.

As Don drove back to the precinct, he kept a lookout for anyone who might be following him, but didn't see anyone. He arrived back at the precinct with a lot on his mind. He was mostly thinking about how he was going to keep an eye on the bar. He went directly to his office.

Entering his office, he was surprised to find Officer Williams. She looked as if she was surprised to see him. After all, he had not been gone very long. The surprised look on her face quickly turned to a pleasant smile. For her, that kind of an innocent smile seemed to come easy. It was the kind of smile that probably fooled many men, but not Don. He didn't trust her.

"What are you doing in here?" Don asked rather sharply.

"I was looking for you. Since you were not here, I thought I would leave you a note. I was looking for a piece

of paper to write the note on when you came in," she said calmly and with an innocent childlike smile.

It was clear by the look on Don's face that he didn't believe her. He glanced at the small pad of paper in the middle of his desk that he used to make notes of things he wanted to remember, or calls he received. Beside the pad was a pen, but there was nothing written on the paper.

"If you needed to leave me a note, there's a pen and paper right there," he said as he pointed at it.

"I see it now," she said softly.

"What is it you needed to tell me?"

"Have I done something to upset you? I get the feeling that you have been ignoring me."

Don just looked at her a minute. He wasn't sure how to answer her question.

"Let's just say that I made a mistake."

"I don't understand. What kind of a mistake?" she asked as if she was hurt by what he said.

Don didn't buy it. She was not one who he wanted to confide in.

"Let's just say that having you work with me for a couple of days was not a good idea. You lack the experience and the necessary skills to be a detective. In short, you lack the knowledge of what and how to ask questions to get good solid information."

"What?" she said sharply. "How did you come up with that?"

"You need more experience as a police officer. You are fresh out of the academy. You haven't even had a full month on the streets. In fact, you haven't even been on the streets."

"My supervisor had me working with deaf people. It's not my fault that I don't have street experience."

"I understand that. The reason you don't have any street experience doesn't change the fact that you lack the

experience," Don said. "Now, I suggest that you return to the duties that you were assigned. I have work to do."

Officer Williams looked at him for a couple of seconds. She didn't like the fact that he had simply dismissed her. She turned to leave, but on her way to his door she glanced at his safe before she left his office.

Don didn't miss the fact that she glanced at his safe. He wondered what she had hoped to find in his office. He had made sure that he locked everything up on his current case.

It took Don a minute or so before he turned his attention back to the case at hand. He needed to find out who the two men were that were in the pictures. Just knowing who they were would go a long way in finding out what was going on.

Don took all the information he had on the death of Judge Weatherby as well as the information on the bombing of the downtown café. The one thing he had not found out was what the connection between the two was, but he was sure there was one.

CHAPTER FORTY-THREE

It was time for me to get off my butt and get to work. I was going to go to my office to do some research on my computer, but I remembered that the monitor had been shot. I decided that I would need to get a new one before I could use the computer. I started for the front door of my apartment to go get a new monitor when the phone began to ring. I turned around and picked up the phone.

"Hello," I said.

"Frank Tidsdale?"

"Yes," I replied recognizing the strong male voice.

"I'll get him," the voice said.

It only took a couple of minutes before my friend came on the phone.

"Franky, how are you doing?"

"I'm doing fine. What's up? Do you have something for me?" I asked.

"Are you done with the case?"

"Not hardly. I want the man who shot me."

"I can understand that, but if I know you, you want him for more than shooting you."

"Yes, I do. Since I have you on the phone, I have a couple of questions for you."

"Shoot. Excuse the pun," he said with a slight chuckle.

"Okay. Are you still watching Jackie?"

"Yes. Do you want us to stop?"

"No. I think she might still be in danger," I said. "Are you watching my back?"

"Yes. There is still a contract out on you. Someone wants you dead, and I still don't know who, yet."

"I had a feeling there was a contract on me. The attempt on me was pulled off by the same people that killed Judge Weatherby."

"I heard."

"Do you think if I can get you a picture of a couple of shooters, you might be able to ID them for me?" I asked.

I didn't know if he could or even if he would, but it was all I could think of at the moment.

"I might. Let me ask you something. How would you like to have a woman come visit you?"

"I hope you're not trying to fix me up with someone."

"No," he said with a chuckle in his voice. "One of my people will be stopping by with my friend. She has something I think you might like to have."

"Sure. When can I expect her?"

"Shortly after dark, at your apartment. Talk to you later," he said, then the phone went dead.

I wondered what he could have for me. I would just have to wait and see.

I decided that without the new monitor, there wasn't much I could do in my office, besides it was probably still a mess from the shooting. Instead, I spent the afternoon cleaning up my apartment, and wondering what it was that my friend had for me. Cleaning was hard with only one good arm, but I managed even if it did take most of the afternoon.

It was almost dinner time before I was done cleaning. I was getting a little hungry so I fixed my dinner. After I finished eating, I cleaned up the kitchen. Since it was still light outside, I went into the living room and laid down on the sofa to wait.

As Don went through the information he had, his mind kept going back to the alley behind the bar on Colfax. If there was a chance he could grab the other shooter, he really thought that he should take it. There was a pretty good chance that the shooter had already left the Denver area.

Don decided that it was time to take a chance. He made a call to Sergeant Walker and asked for his help. He decided not to use people from his own precinct to make sure that Officer Williams didn't find out what he was doing.

"Bomb Squad. Sergeant Walker. How may I help you?"

"This is Detective Wright, have you got a minute?"

"Sure. What's on your mind?"

"I would like you and a couple of your men to help me."

"Sure. What's it all about?"

"Can you get two or three men you can trust and meet me at Cheesman Park near the Pavilion? I'll tell you what it's about when you get there," Don said.

"Sure."

"Come prepared."

"Got it," Walker said, then hung up.

Don smiled to himself. He was going to attack the bar from all sides at once with little chance that anyone would suspect anything until it happened. Don left his office and walked to the elevator to the police garage. He signed out a car and headed for Cheeseman Park.

CHAPTER FORTY-FOUR

It was shortly after dark when I was awakened by the ringing of the doorbell. I got up from the sofa, slipped my gun into my sling and went to the door. I looked out the peek hole in the door and saw Betty, my friend's girlfriend, standing there. She looked around as if she was making sure that no one else was around.

I opened the door for her, and she quickly stepped inside.

"Hi, Betty. It's nice to see you," I said as I closed the door.

"I thought I saw someone sitting in a car across the street," she said nervously.

"It's probably someone watching over me. What is it you have for me?"

"I was told to give you this," she said as she handed me an envelope. "He said you would probably like what's in it."

"I'm sure I will. Is someone waiting for you?"

"Yes, but he said to wait until he toots his horn. I'm to stay inside until he does."

"Okay."

"Franky, why would he do that?"

"I'm sure he just wants to make sure you are safe."

Just then a car horn tooted. She looked at me and smiled.

"Have to go."

"Thank him for me," I said as I opened the door for her.

Betty quickly left my apartment and hurried out to a car parked in front. I watched her to make sure that she got into the car safely. As soon as the car was gone, I took a quick look around. I didn't see anything or anyone so I stepped back inside, closed the door and locked it.

As I took the envelope to the kitchen, I thought about what Betty had said. I smiled to myself as I thought about the fact that she had not once mentioned my friend's name. It had been agreed on some time ago, by my friend and me, that I would never mention his name. He went by the belief that every room was bugged and every phone was tapped. And as he often told me in the past, it is what has kept him alive for so long. I was not about to go back on our agreement.

I dumped the material from the envelope out on the table. There were several sheets of paper that at first glance appeared to be reports on the person whose name was on the top. I took the first report and began to look it over.

The name at the top of the first sheet of paper was that of Judge John Wilkinson. It showed that he had been selected to fill the shoes of Judge Weatherby as the senior judge on the bench. That didn't come as any real surprise. Based on information that I already had, he seemed the one most likely to get the position. However, it was the rest of the report that would interest me.

The report showed some of the cases that Judge Wilkinson had worked on. I quickly noticed that most of his cases involved bodyguards, enforcers, and other lowlifes in the city. I had heard of, or at least known about, most of them. However, there were a couple of names that I didn't recognize.

The report on Wilkinson also gave me some information on his income. There was a section in the report that was like a mini-balance sheet. It made it clear that Wilkinson was spending a bit more than he was making. The report didn't indicate he had any other source of income than that of a judge. It was clear that I needed to take a closer look at him. He was definitely one that I should consider as someone to check out for the AG.

The second report was on Judge J. Barlow Smith. It showed that Judge Smith had also appeared to have had a number of cases over the past five years involving a few of the local lowlifes in the area. There was some financial information on Smith indicating he was living on the edge of spending more than he was earning in the only job he appeared to have. Since the information was inconclusive, it let Smith off the hook, for now. It would require a bit more investigation into his finances before any conclusion could be reached.

The third and final report was on Judge David R. Colton. From information I got from Ms Hanson, I knew that Colton had been on the bench for a long time. A look at the cases he had presided over in the past five years showed he had handled only two or three cases that involved any of the local lowlifes. Those few cases had been relatively minor with most of them being misdemeanor charges. The financial part of the report showed that Judge Smith seemed to be living well within his means. It looked like he was the only one that I could scratch off my list of possible dirty judges. However, it might be a good idea if I looked into his background a little closer. He might have been sending all the money he earned on the side to an off shore account, like Weatherby had been doing.

This information was something I was sure that AG Greene would want. It would be a good idea if I let Don in on it, too. Although the information was interesting, none of it proved anything. I needed something that would prove one way or the other which judge or judges were dirty. It would be nice to have something that would lead me to the one who was paying them.

I leaned back in my chair and looked at the reports that were on the table. What I had in front of me was nothing but circumstantial evidence. There was no absolute proof of wrong doing by any of them.

I decided that it was time to hide the information I had received in a safe place. I went into my bathroom and very carefully put the envelope in a cabinet that contained a stack of towels. I put the envelope back behind the towels where it could not be seen.

As soon as I felt the envelope was secure for tonight, I got ready for bed. It wasn't very long and I was curled up in my bed. I found it was not easy for me to go to sleep. I had a lot on my mind, but I finally did drift off to sleep.

Don arrived at Cheesman Park only a few minutes before Sergeant Walker and three of his officers. They gathered at the rear of Don's car to go over their plan of attack. It was a simple plan that required a three point attack to prevent anyone from getting out of the bar.

Once the plan was explained, all the officers got in their cars and moved into position. One car was to come up the alley from one end while a second car came up from the other direction. When they met at the backdoor of the bar, they were to go in and grab everyone they found. Don and one of Walker's officers would pull up in front of the bar and enter while Walker and his other two officers were coming in the back.

As soon as everything was ready and in position, Don gave the order and they all started to move in. Just as Don, and the officer with him, entered the front door with guns drawn, Walker and the two officers with him entered the backdoor of the bar. Everyone in the bar looked at Don when he yelled out.

"This is the police. Everybody put your hands on top of the tables where we can see them. You at the bar, put your hands on the bar and don't anybody make a move."

There were eight patrons in the bar. Everyone did as they were told.

It was only a few seconds before a fat man came out of the back of the bar with his hands in the air. He was immediately followed by Walker and his men.

"All of you put your hands on your heads and move over there against the wall," Don ordered.

"What the hell do you think you're doing?" the fat man yelled.

"Shut up and stand next to the wall," Walker said.

"Check everyone's ID. Let those go that you can immediately clear," Don said to Walker.

While the other officers watched the patrons, the bartender and the fat man, Don went into the backroom to look around. There was a table with a plate of half eaten food on it. It was where the fat man had been sitting. There were also several beer barrels and a couple of stacks of cases of beer along one wall. It was obviously the storage room.

The fact that the fat man had been eating in the backroom, caused Don to wonder who he was and what he was doing there. Don turned around to go back to the front of the bar, but stopped suddenly when he saw a rag lying on the floor. It had been hidden from sight behind the door. Don turned on a light next to a cot so he could get a better look at it. The rag was covered with blood. It seemed to him that it was too much blood to be from a simple cut. The thought that this was where one of the men who shot Tidsdale had been hiding came to mind. Don returned to the front of the bar.

"How's it going," Don asked Walker.

"We got statements from them, names and addresses from everyone, and let all of them go except for the fat man and the bartender. We kept them."

"Good. Who is the fat guy?"

"I don't know. He's not talking to us other than to complain about our raid on the bar, and demanding a lawyer."

"Does the fat guy own the bar?"

"No. Not according to the bartender, he just eats a lot of meals here and meets with guys in the backroom. He did say that the fat guy doesn't own the bar."

"Did he tell you who does own the bar?"

"He says he doesn't know who owns the bar. He was hired by an employment agency and has never met the *owner. According to him, he is paid regularly with checks from the employment agency."*

"Did he tell you what agency?"

"Yeah. I have it here in my notes."

"I found a bloody rag in the back," Don said. "Close the bar. I'll call in the forensic team to check this place out. Place the fat guy and the bartender under arrest and take them to your precinct. Hold them there. I'll come by in the morning."

"What about a lawyer for the fat guy?"

"Process him first, but don't question him or let him call a lawyer until I get there in the morning."

"Okay." Walker said.

Don watched for a moment while Walker gave his officers instructions. Once the two men that were arrested had been cuffed and taken to patrol cars, Don went out to his car and called for a forensic team. When he returned to the bar, he looked around. There was nothing else he could do until the forensic team finished their work. He was disappointed that the man he was looking for was not there.

"You mind waiting for the forensic team?" Don asked Walker.

"No. Why don't you go home and get some rest. There's nothing you can do here until the forensic team gets done."

"I think I'll do that. It's been a long day."

"See you in the morning," Walker said.

Don stepped outside the bar and looked around. It was dark and quiet on the street. It was time for him to go home and get some rest. He wouldn't get a forensic report until sometime tomorrow anyway.

Don went to his car and returned to the police garage where he turned in the police car. He then went right to his own car and drove home in the hope of getting a good night's sleep.

CHAPTER FORTY-FIVE

I woke rather early, well before I had intended. My mind was still going over the material that I had received from my friend. Some of it was clear, but most of it left me trying to figure out what was really going on. What I really needed was something that would give me a direction. Something that would point me to the person or persons who were behind what was going on at the courthouse.

The more I thought about it, the more I felt there had to be someone who worked in the courthouse who was able to organize everything. Someone who could direct cases to one of the judges after the case was filed by the Attorney General's Office.

The problem I had with what I was thinking was what Ms Hanson had told me. She had indicated that the file clerk for the criminal court division didn't assign the cases to a judge. She had said that Judge Weatherby assigned the cases. If that was the case, the file clerk would have had nothing to do with who got what cases. I was beginning to think that another visit with Ms Hanson was in order.

I looked at the clock and decided to get up. After all, I wasn't likely to get any more sleep. It was still a little early to make a call to Jake and find out where he was keeping Ms Hanson. I needed to know where he was and if everything was okay, since I had not heard from him for several days.

I took a bath, shaved and got dressed, but not without some pain and discomfort in my shoulder. I also noticed that the dressing on my shoulder had gotten wet. It had been a couple of days since it had been changed. I thought that it might be a good idea if I stopped by the hospital and had a fresh dressing put on.

I didn't feel much like making my own breakfast. There was a little café not very far from my apartment. I could stop there and get something to eat, then go on to my office.

As I drove out onto the street, I noticed a car pull away from the curb about a block away. There wasn't anything special about the car except for the fact that it remained well behind me. I continued on down the street keeping a close eye on it. After going several blocks, I turned off on a side street and continued on. As I watched the car through my rearview mirror, I saw it continue on down the street. It did not turn and follow me. I pulled over and parked between a couple of cars and waited to see if it might double back thinking that I would turn again in the same direction that I had been going.

After waiting for almost ten minutes, I decided that the car had not been following me. I would head for the little café, but would still keep an eye out for anyone who might try to follow me.

I arrived at the café and parked alongside the building. It was a space where it would be difficult to see my car from the street. I went inside and found a place to sit where I could see the traffic as it went by. I didn't see the car again.

After I finished my breakfast, I drove over to the receiving room of the hospital and asked the woman at the desk if I could get my bandage changed since I had gotten it wet. I gave her my name and told her who my doctor was. She called someone, then told me to wait.

It wasn't very long and a nurse showed up. I saw her walking toward me. She smiled when she saw me. She looked a little familiar.

"Good morning, Mr. Tidsdale. I'm told that you need a new dressing on your shoulder."

"Yes. I got it wet and thought it should be changed."

"Come this way," she said as she turned and started down the hall.

I immediately walked up beside her.

"In here, please," she said as she pushed a door open to a small treatment room.

I went into the room and sat down on the examining table. I watched her while she got out a clean dressing and medical tape from a drawer. She was a very nice looking woman. It was obvious that she had a nice figure under the scrubs she was wearing. She also had a pretty face.

"Let's get your shirt off," she said as she set the dressing and tape on a table next to the examining table.

After she helped me take my shirt off, she carefully removed the old dressing. She used some alcohol to clean the area around the wound.

"It looks like it is healing well. You will have a small scar, but it won't look bad."

"That's good to know," I said.

She just smiled at me as she started to put a new dressing on my shoulder. I watched her as she worked. She seemed to know what she was doing. I also noticed her name tag.

"Do you mind if I call you, Marilyn?" I asked.

"No, not at all," she said with a smile.

"When I was discharged from the hospital, you took me to the waiting room for discharge."

"Yes, I did," she said.

"If I recall, you told me that I could call you if I needed anything. Did you mean that?"

"Yes. I did tell you that, and yes, I meant it," she said with a smile.

"Would you think it unprofessional if I was to call on you, say for a dinner date?"

She just looked at me for a minute as if wondering what I was thinking. A smile slowly came over her face.

"Not at all."

"I have to ask you a personal question. Do you have a problem with someone who carries a gun as part of his job? By the way, it is legal, and what I do is also legal," I said.

"I know that you are a private investigator, and that you were shot while working on a case, so the answer to your question is, no. I don't have a problem with you carrying a gun. I would think someone in your line of work would be a fool not to carry a gun. By the way, my father and brother are policemen."

"Great. Are they policemen in this city?"

"No," she replied. "They are policemen in Dallas."

When Marilyn was finished dressing my wound, she gave me her phone number. As I left the examining room, I told her that I would call her at her home.

I left the hospital and drove across town to a small café I knew about. Once inside, I ordered a cup of coffee and sat there just thinking. I didn't really want to go back to my office just yet. I was sure that it would be a mess and I didn't want to face that today, but I knew I would have to face it sooner or later. Sooner seemed to be the thing to do.

Don returned to his office a little before eight in the morning. He sat down at his desk as he thought about what had happened last evening at The Colfax Bar and Grill. He was anxious to find out if the blood he found in the back of the bar was that of the dead man found in the park. He glanced at his watch. Don was not sure if Mel was in his office yet. He was pretty sure that he had a late night.

Don decided to give Mel a call just the same. He picked up his phone and placed a call to him.

"Crime Lab. How may I direct your call?" a woman said.

"Mel Street. This is Detective Wright calling."

"Doctor Street just came in. I'll transfer your call to his office."

"Thank you."

It didn't take but a couple of minutes before Mel came on the line.

"Good morning, Don. What can I do for you?"

"I was just calling to find out if you have had a chance to look at anything from the bar on Colfax."

"Yeah. You have to remember that I have not had a chance to do the DNA test on the blood we found in the backroom, but everything points to it being the same guy that was found in the park. I take it that is what you want to know."

"Yes, it is. What makes you so sure that it is from the same guy without the DNA results?"

"Well, the blood we found on the rag was the same type as the dead guy's in the park. It also had traces of the same drug in it that was found in the dead guy's blood."

"What drug did you find?" Don asked.

"*The dead man was taking a prescription cold medicine we don't often see around here. The blood on the rag contained traces of the same cold medicine and in the same strength.*"

"*That confirms my belief that the guy held up in that backroom of the bar.*"

"*There's also a pretty good indication that he died in that backroom.*"

"*Have you ID'd the guy?*" *Don asked.*

"*No, not yet. I hope to have fingerprint results later today.*"

"*If you find out who he is, keep it to yourself. I'll call you later,*" *Don said.*

"*Okay. If you say so.*"

"*Thanks,*" *Don said, then hung up.*

Don thought about what he had been told. There was not much else he could do but go to the precinct where the two that were arrested last night were being held. He might be able to get something out of them.

Don went to the police garage and checked out a car. He then drove to Precinct Two.

CHAPTER FORTY-SIX

As I sat in the coffee shop sipping on a latte, I looked around. There were only a couple of customers in the shop. Since I was sitting back in a corner by myself, I decided to give Jake a call and find out where he was. He should still be at the same motel, but in a different part. I took my cell phone and called Jake's number. The phone was answered in a matter of seconds.

"Hello,"

"Is this Mr. Hubble?" I asked.

"No. This is Mr. Guardian, Jake Guardian."

"How are things going there? Is all secure?"

"We had a little problem the day after your last visit, but all is well now."

"What happened?"

"A woman who claimed to be a police officer came to the motel. She talked to the owner. She was asking about Ms Hanson. She described Ms Hanson and insisted the owner tell him where she was. He told her that the person she had described to him went by the name of Mrs. Hubble and was registered with her husband, but they had checked out. She insisted on seeing the room Ms Hanson had been staying in."

"Did he show her the room?"

"Yes. According to the owner of the motel, she looked the room over very carefully."

"Good."

"I didn't think she was safe in the motel. I took a risk and moved her to a private home just outside of Bennett, just off I-70. I am staying with her, and have a couple of guys I trust keeping watch over the house from a house across the road. She is very safe here."

"Good. How is she doing?"

"She's scared, but she is holding up well. She wants to talk to you," he said.

"Put her on," I said, then waited while Jake gave her his phone.

"Mr. Tidsdale, are you sure this is necessary? I feel like I'm a prisoner."

"I'm sorry about that, but I think it is necessary. I'm working very hard to resolve the murder of Judge Weatherby, and so are the police. Until we find who killed him and who put them up to it, I think it is necessary for your well-being."

"Okay," she said, but sounded a little disappointed.

"Can you tell me who the person is who the AG files the charges of a criminal case with? I'm talking about the person who registers the case for the record, then sends it on to the senior Judge."

"That would James Dieter. He is the one who registers the files from the AG for the records before they are scheduled for trial."

"Thank you," I said. "Are they treating you okay?"

"Yes. They have been very nice and very understanding of my feelings."

"Good. Put Jake back on, please."

She didn't respond, but simply gave the phone back to Jake.

"Anything else?" Jake asked.

"No, but thank you for looking out for her."

"No problem. I hope you find out who the woman was who said she was a cop."

"I think I know who she is, at least where she works. And by the way, she is a cop."

"Oh. Does Detective Wright know about her?"

"I believe he does. He is keeping an eye on her, at least until he has proof she's dirty."

"Good."

"I'll talk to you later," I said, then hung up.

I leaned back to think about what Ms Hanson had told me. I didn't know who Dieter was, but I was sure that I would find out. For now, I needed to pay a visit to the courthouse. I wanted to meet this James Dieter. I finished my coffee and left the coffee shop for the courthouse.

Don arrived at the Second Precinct. It only took him a few minutes to get to Sergeant Walker's office. Bill was in.

"Hi, Don. What can I do for you?"

"I would like to have a little talk with the fat guy you brought in last night."

"Sure thing. Right this way," Bill said as he got up and left his office.

Don followed him down a long hall to a steel door. Bill opened the door and closed it again once Don had entered the room.

The room was a fairly large room with two cells on each side. Bill started toward the back of the room.

"We have him over here," Bill said over his shoulder.

"Is he still screaming for a lawyer?"

"Not so much. He's quieted down a lot since last night."

"Any idea why?"

"Yeah. I told him that the minute we booked him, it became public record. Any newsman in town could come in and get the list of those booked and publish it in the paper. He suddenly shut up. Now he wants to talk to you. By the way, his name is Marco Galvani."

"You're kidding?"

"No. Do you know him?"

"His old man was one of the crime bosses down in Pueblo some years back. His old man was killed trying to shoot it out with some FBI agents."

"I've never heard of Galvani before."

"I was just a kid when I heard about it."

"You think he's hooked up with one of the crime bosses around here?"

"*Could be. He would have been a teenager about the time his father was killed.*"

"*Well, he's all yours,*" Bill said as he stopped at the cell door.

Bill unlocked the cell door and opened it up. Marco was sitting on the bunk in the cell. He slowly turned his head and looked at me.

"*I understand that you would like to talk to me. Is that right?*"

"*Yeah, but not with him here.*"

"*What could you possibly want to say to me that you don't want Officer Walker to hear?*"

"*I know things. Things you would like to know,*" Marco said with a grin.

"*Well, I know that you harbored a criminal in the backroom of the bar. I know that you are an accessory after the fact to an attempted murder, and there may be other charges. I know that it looks pretty good for you to do some serious jail time.*"

"*I know who killed that judge,*" Marco said.

"*That is one thing that I don't know,*" Don said, then paused for a moment.

Marco began to grin. He was sure that he had something that Don wanted bad enough to deal with him.

"*But, I have a picture of him and it won't be very long and I will have him in custody.*"

The look on Marco's face went from one of someone who was sure of himself to someone who was scared to death.

"*You see, you have only one thing I want. I want to know who gave the order to assassinate Judge Marcus Weatherby.*"

"*I can't tell you that,*" Marco said softly.

"*You can't or you won't?*"

Marco simply sat on the bunk looking at the floor in front of him. Slowly, he turned his head and looked at Don and Bill. He took a deep breath and let it out slowly.

"I want a lawyer. My lawyer."

Don looked at Bill, then back at Marco.

"Lock the door, then call him a lawyer," Don said, then turned and walked out of the cell block.

Don had a pretty good idea that he was not going to get anything out of Marco once he lawyered up. It was time to see if Mel had any new evidence he could use. He left the Second Precinct and returned to his office.

CHAPTER FORTY-SEVEN

I arrived at the courthouse after stopping at a cafe for lunch. It was around one o'clock when I walked into the office where criminal records were filed before being assigned to a judge for trial. There was an older woman sitting at a desk in front of several offices.

"May I help you?" she asked.

"I'm looking for Mr. Dieter. Is he in?"

"Yes," she said as she picked up the phone. "Your name, sir?"

"Tidsdale, Frank Tidsdale,"

"There is a Mr. Frank Tidsdale here to see you." she said, then listened.

"He says that he is very busy right now. He would like you to make an appointment for tomorrow or the next day."

"Tell him that it would be in his best interest to talk to me now," I said with a strong hint of authority.

She relayed my message, then looked at me while listening. I had no idea what she was thinking, but I was reasonably sure she was thinking about calling security.

"He said that he could give you five minutes," she said.

From the look on her face, I got the feeling that she was also told that if I wasn't out of his office in five minutes she was to call security.

"Thank you," I said with a slight grin, then went into Dieter's office.

Sitting at a rather large desk was a fairly skinny man with a long narrow face who wore horn rimmed glasses that hung close to the end of his long nose. He was almost completely bald. His desk was littered with papers and file folders.

"What is it you find so important that you have to see me right now. I'm a very busy man," he said rather sharply.

"Relax. All I want is a little information."

"What is it you want that can't wait until tomorrow?"

"I have a deadline to meet. I need some background information on Judge Weatherby. I want to hear from someone who knew him, not the general information that anyone can get off a computer or at the library. I figured that you might have known him pretty well since you had almost daily contact with him."

"Oh. Well, I did know him fairly well. I suppose I could take a few minutes to talk to you."

"Good," I said.

The phone rang just as I took out a small spiral notebook and a pen from my inside coat pocket. I was sure it was the woman out front, but I couldn't hear what she was saying.

"That won't be necessary," he said, then hung up the phone.

I didn't bother to comment on his phone call. I simply began with a question.

"Please just tell me what you know about him. I'll just make a few notes."

Mr. Dieter started talking about the judge, telling me a little about him. He didn't really say too much about him that I didn't already know. After talking to me for almost thirty minutes, he seemed to run out of things to say. That's when I started asking him questions about the judge.

"I understand that Judge Weatherby had a lot of cases that involved crime bosses. I was wondering if you could comment on that."

"Well, he did handle of lot of cases over the past few years that had to do with some of the, - I guess you would call them crime bosses."

"Was it his practice to take those cases himself, or did he hand some of them off to other judges?"

"He handled most of them himself, although he did hand some of them off to other judges."

I asked him a number of questions that I already had the answers to, which supported what I already knew. Then I surprised him with a couple of questions about himself.

"Mr. Dieter, how much are you involved in assigning cases to the Judges."

That question caught him a little off guard.

"Me? I – ah – ah – I don't really have much to do with that."

"Oh. Don't be so modest. I happen to know you are a very important man around here," I said with a slight smile. "I've heard you are the man who makes this place run, who gets things done."

"Well, I do have some say in who gets what cases," he said as he straightened up and drew back his shoulders.

"I think you are being modest again. You actually assign the cases to the judges based on their workload, and possibly on their experience."

"Well, that is true," he said with a shy grin. "Experience and workload have a lot to do with who I assign a case to."

"Would you say that Judge Weatherby got a higher percentage of the mob related cases, then say Wilkinson or Smith?"

"Yes, but it was not unusual."

"I see. Did you work closely with Judge Weatherby?" I asked.

"Yes. I would say that I did."

"Did you have a personal relationship with him? By that, I mean did you – say – have a beer with him after work, or play golf with him on weekends, things like that."

"Not really. However, we would have lunch together about once or twice a month. We seemed to enjoy each other's company," he said with a hint of pride in his voice.

"Did you have these lunches with others from the office?"

"Well, yes. Sometimes Judge Wilkinson and Judge Smith would join us."

"Well, I think I have everything I need. Thank you for your time and insight into Judge Weatherby," I said as I got up.

"You're welcome."

I reached across his desk and shook his hand, then left his office. I returned to my car and left the courthouse parking lot. I had gotten some useable information from him. The one thing that was clear was he had met with Judge Weatherby fairly often and on a fairly regular basis. I had a pretty good idea what the conversations were about.

I drove directly to my office. I needed to find out more about Mr. Dieter.

When Don returned to his office, he found a note on his desk that he had received a phone call from a woman named Jill Hartman. He smiled at the thought of her calling him. The note asked him to call her, but gave no reason.

Don reached out, picked up the phone and placed a call to the number. The phone rang just a couple of times before it was answered.

"Hello?" a woman's voice said.

"This is Detective Wright. Is this Mrs. Hartman?"

"No. Just one moment."

It was only a few seconds before a woman spoke.

"Detective, this is Jill Hartman. Thank you for returning my call so quickly."

"Is there something the matter?"

"Yes. I believe there is. My neighbor told me that there was a policewoman looking for me while I was out. She said that the policewoman was very insistent, to the point of being rude. She even threatened my friend with arrest if she didn't tell her where I was. It kind of scared me. I've been staying with my friend until I could get hold of you."

"You did the right thing. What can you tell me about the policewoman? What did she look like?"

"From what I am told, she was probably the same woman that interviewed me before."

"Stay where you are. Don't answer the door until I get there. What is the apartment number where you are now?" Don asked.

"314, I'll wait here for you," she said, then hung up.

Don left the office for the police garage. He took one of the plain police cars and drove to the apartment building where Mrs. Hartman lived.

CHAPTER FORTY-EIGHT

I returned to my office expecting to find blood on the door frame and on the floor. To my surprise, I found that someone had cleaned up the place. There was still a bullet hole in the back of my chair, but my computer monitor had been replaced with one just like I had before the shooting. I had no idea who had replaced it, or who had cleaned up the place. It really didn't matter at the moment. I needed to get some information on James Dieter.

I immediately turned on my computer. As soon as it booted up, I started a search for James Dieter. It came up with two James Dieters. One with a middle initial of 'J', and other with a middle initial of 'K'. I took them one at a time and quickly found that the one with middle initial of 'K' was the one I wanted.

I scanned through all the information I could find on him. It contained things like where he was born, past addresses, relatives, siblings, etc. It wasn't until I got into his past jobs that I came up with anything of interest. I found that he had held a job in Scranton, Pennsylvania very much like the one he now held at the Denver Courthouse. I noticed that the day he left his employment in Scranton was in the middle of the month and in the middle of the week. That was unusual for most people, and I wondered why.

I decided that I would look up newspapers from Scranton, Pennsylvania around the time he left his position at the court system there. Once I found the major newspaper, The Scranton Times, I put in a couple of key words, one was his last name. Bang, up pops a story about some corruption that had been discovered in the court system in which Mr.

Dieter's name was mentioned. It didn't indicate that he had done anything wrong, but it was clear that he resigned before an investigation into his activities was complete. To me, that meant that he was guilty of something, but they probably couldn't prove it. The problem I had was there was no indication of what they thought he might have been involved in.

I read several of the articles related to the corruption case, both before and after he resigned. I leaned back in my chair to think about what I had read in the newspapers. The article pointed toward several people in the courthouse that might be involved in some kind of scheme to keep certain people out of jail, or at least get them reduced jail sentences. I couldn't help but think that the same thing was going on here.

As I thought about what I had read and what little I knew about Mr. Dieter, it began to appear that he had been hired to work in the Denver Court System. I was sure that they would have done a background check on him, but if he had resigned his former position before any charges, it would be difficult for his former employer to say anything negative about him for fear of a lawsuit. They were probably glad to get rid of him and avoid the publicity.

Now that I had all this information, how was I going to use it to get the information I wanted? One way would be to get Dieter off somewhere private where I could make him talk, but that wouldn't help in court. I needed to scare him enough to get him to talk freely. I was sure that was not going to be easy with the kind of people he was probably working for. If he talked, they would not hesitate to kill him.

There was also another problem. I had no idea what or how much he really knew. He might be taking his orders from some lowlife and didn't really know who the boss was. It was the boss I wanted.

It had been a long day and I was beginning to feel tired. I decided that I would go home, get something to eat and then hit it again in the morning. It might be a good idea if I tailed Dieter for a couple of days. I shut down my computer, locked the office and headed for home.

As I drove out of the underground parking garage and pulled out onto the street, I noticed a gray sedan pull away from the curb behind me. Since I had a good idea that it was one of my friend's bodyguards, I didn't think much of it. The further I drove with the gray sedan behind me, the more I got to thinking. I was pretty sure that my friend's bodyguard would be more discreet. In fact, he had been so discreet that I had never seen him before, even though I knew he was there.

I didn't like the idea that I was being followed. It was time to do something about it. I made a quick turn at the next corner and hit the gas. I turned into the next alley and raced down the alley. I had no more than turned out onto the next street when I got a glimpse of the gray sedan turning into the alley.

I slowed down a bit as I approached the next alley. I wanted my tail to get a glimpse of me going into the next alley. I turned in and quickly stopped the car about fifty feet from the end of the alley. I stepped out of the car, closed the door, then quickly hid behind a Dumpster. I had no more than crouched down when I heard a car screech to a stop. I knew I was in no condition to get into a physical confrontation with anyone. However, having my gun firmly gripped in my hand did tend to even things up a bit. Nothing seemed to be happening. It was quiet. I had a feeling that he was just sitting there wondering if I was still in the car.

Suddenly, I heard what sounded like a car door being opened. It was clear that the person in the car was being very cautious. It was easy to understand because he couldn't see me, and he had no idea where I was.

"You might as well get out of the car," a strong male voice said. "There's no one here to help you, and there's no place to go."

I waited and watched. I thought I could hear his shoes on the ground as he moved closer to my car. As he stepped up closer, I could see that he was concentrating on the car. I was very close to him. I rose up and pointed my gun at him.

"Don't even move a muscle," I said. "Drop the gun."

He hesitated for a second, but dropped his gun. It was clear to him that I had the drop on him, and he had no real choice.

"Put your hands on the top of the car and lean against it," I ordered.

He did as he was told. Now I had a problem. With my one arm in a sling, it made patting him down a little difficult. It was at that moment I heard something move behind me. I quickly glanced toward the sound. Standing close to the car behind mine was a guy big enough to be a linebacker for a major football team. He had his hands held up in front of his body so I could see he didn't have a weapon in his hands.

"Need a little help, Mr. Tidsdale?" he said with a grin.

I immediately recognized the man's voice. He was the guy who usually answered the phone when I called my friend. Since my friend never wanted me to mention names, I didn't bother to ask my bodyguard his name, not that I would know it, anyway.

"You are a welcome sight," I said.

"What do you want me to do with him?"

"Do you know who he is?"

"No, but I know who he works for. The man he works for is not a nice man. He will not be very happy that one of his best men got caught by a PI," he said with a grin.

"He may be his best man, but he can't follow anyone worth a damn."

"I'll agree with that. I've been on his tail even before he started following you."

"Is there somewhere you can keep him for a while?" I asked.

"Yeah. I know just the place for a guy like him."

"Okay. He's all yours. I'll call my friend when I'm ready to talk to him."

My bodyguard simply nodded while I held a gun on the man until he could pat him down, then put handcuffs on him. My bodyguard took him to his car and shoved him into the backseat. He then turned and waved as he got in his car. I watched him as he backed out of the alley.

I walked over to the car behind mine, reached inside and shut off the engine. I removed the keys and tossed them into the Dumpster. I figured the police would find the car and have it towed to the impound lot. I'd call Don in the morning and let him know about it.

I returned to my car and drove away. It didn't take me long to get home and into bed. I was tired and had no difficulty getting to sleep.

Don arrived at Mrs. Hartman's apartment building. He went right to apartment 314 and knocked on the door.

"Who is it?" a female voice asked.

"Detective Wright," Don said as he stood right in front of the peep hole in the door.

The door opened and Don stepped inside closing the door behind him.

"Are you okay, Mrs. Hartman?" he said when he saw her sitting on the couch.

"Yes," Mrs. Hartman said with a smile. "But please call me Jill."

Don walked over to her and sat down on the couch next to her. The other woman sat down on a chair in front of them. Don turned and looked at the other woman.

"This is Mrs. Bonny Brian. She is a friend of mine."

"Nice to meet you. Now, Jill, tell me what happened," Don said.

"I wasn't here when the officer came by," Jill said. "Bonny was here."

"Mrs. Brian, tell me what happened. How is it you know that the woman officer had interviewed Jill, and how is it you know it was the same officer?"

"I was outside the apartment building shortly after the explosion. I saw Jill being interviewed by a tall blond woman police officer. I was interviewed by a male officer. When she showed up here earlier today, I recognized her."

"Where did you first see her today?"

"I was coming down the hall and saw her knocking rather hard on Jill's door. I asked her what she wanted. She said that she needed to talk to Mrs. Hartman as soon as possible. I told her that Jill was not home, but I guess she didn't believe me.

"Why do you think she didn't believe you?" Don asked.

"I'm not sure, but it might have been that Jill had left her television on when she came to visit me. She might have heard the television."

"You said that you were coming down the hall, where had you been?"

"I went to borrow some sugar from one of our neighbors. I had run out and I like sugar in my tea," Bonny said with a smile.

"What gave you the idea that you shouldn't tell the officer that Jill was in your apartment?"

"I guess it was really two things. One was the way she had been pounding on her door, and the other was that she looked angry. She seemed to be in a hurry, or maybe she was frustrated over something."

"You did the right thing," Don said, then he looked at Jill.

Jill looked concerned about what had happened. It was beginning to look like Officer Williams was getting a little careless. Maybe it was time to confront her.

"Bonny, would it be asking too much to have Jill stay here with you for a few days?"

"Do you think that is necessary, Don?" Jill asked.

Don looked at her. It was the first time she had called him Don.

"Yes. I think it would be a good idea."

"Detective, I would be glad to have her stay with me. I think it is a good idea."

"Well, I guess it would be okay," Jill said.

"I don't want you to go out of this apartment without letting me know. If you have to go somewhere, you call me. Should anyone ask, you went to stay with a sick a relative."

"If anyone asks me, I will tell them she went to stay with her son for a few days in California," Bonny said.

"Very good," Don said with a grin. "Don't answer the phone, and don't answer the door no matter who it is. Let Bonny do all that, and you stay out of sight."

"Okay," Jill agreed.

"I have to be going. Call if you need me," Don said as he gave Jill his card.

"Thank you for coming so quickly," Jill said as Don stood up to leave.

"I'll be in touch," Don said, then left the apartment.

Don returned to his car and left for his office. He had a lot to think about, and some of that was how was he going to find out what was going on with Williams. One thing was to put a tail on her. He needed to know who she was talking to, and who was she really working for. It didn't look like she was working for the police.

Don decided that it was time for him to call it a day. Instead of returning to the police station, he went on home. He would have dinner, then call it a night. A little sleep might give him a chance to see things in a new light.

CHAPTER FORTY-NINE

It was early when I woke. My shoulder was hurting a little, probably from the strain of yesterday's activity. As I rolled out of bed, my thoughts turned to the man who had been following me. My bodyguard told me that he knew who the guy worked for, but didn't tell me.

It took me a few minutes to get dressed. My shoulder was still stiff and it hurt to put a shirt on. Once I was dressed, I decided to go to a restaurant since I didn't feel much like fixing my own breakfast.

Just as I was about to leave my apartment, the phone began to ring. It only rang a couple of times before I picked it up.

"Hello?"

"Franky, how's it going this morning?"

"Pretty good. I was just going out for breakfast."

"We have the guy that was following you hidden away. We thought you might like to talk to him."

"Yes, I would."

"Okay. Meet me in the alley behind Downing Street between Virginia and Center. Watch for the bodyguard you met last night. I'll have breakfast for you here." he said with a chuckle.

"Okay. I'm on my way," I said as I hung up the phone.

I didn't hesitate for a second. I slipped my gun into my sling and headed out the door. It didn't take me very long to get to Washington Park. I knew that Virginia Street went across the north end of Washington Park. I had been very careful to make sure that I had not been followed before I turned into the alley.

I slowly drove down the alley keeping a watch out for anyone that I didn't know, and for the bodyguard. I drove all the way through the alley, but didn't see anyone. I figured that since I had not seen the bodyguard, something might have gone wrong, or they were watching to see if I had been followed. I drove slowly south down the alley for a couple of more blocks, but didn't see anyone. I even watched in my rearview mirror to make sure there was no one behind me.

I drove out of the alley, then went down the street for several blocks. Being in a residential neighborhood, it would be harder for someone to be following me without being seen. Since I didn't see anyone, I drove all the way around the park before I drove into the alley again. Only this time, I entered into the alley from the opposite end. I had only gone about two hundred feet when I saw the bodyguard step out into the alley and motioned for me to turn into a garage.

I pulled into the garage and stopped. As I was getting out of my car, the bodyguard was closing the garage door.

"Had to make sure you were not being followed," he said. "Right this way."

I followed the bodyguard to a set of stairs that went down into a tunnel. After I was in the tunnel, he secured the door behind us, then led the way along the tunnel. At the end was another door. He opened the door and I found myself in what appeared to be the basement of a house. In the basement was a table, a couple of chairs, and a lamp. There was a ceiling light in the center of the room.

Sitting at the table was my friend, another bodyguard, and a man with his hands cuffed behind his back and a pillowcase over his head. I figured the guy with the pillowcase was the man who had been tailing me last night.

"How's it going," my friend asked. "I understand that you would like to talk to our guest."

"Yes, I would," I said.

"He's not very cooperative at the moment, but I think he might be willing to talk with the right incentive."

"What's your name?" I asked the man with the pillowcase over his head.

"Go to hell. I'm not telling you anything," he said. "If it wasn't for your bodyguard, I'd have killed you."

"I seriously doubt that. You see, I had a problem last night. If I tried to search you for weapons while you were leaning against the car, you might have been able to get to me. I had already decided that I was going to lay my gun across the back of your head. Once you were lying on the ground out cold, I would then search you for weapons. So you see, you didn't have a chance. In fact, my bodyguard saved you from getting your head cracked open."

I noticed that he didn't comment on what I had told him. Even with the pillowcase over his head, I could tell he was scared, as well he should be.

"Okay, I have a question for you. How you answer it depends on what happens to you next. Do you understand?"

"Yeah," he said. "But if I tell you anything, you won't be able to use it in court."

"Oh, didn't I tell you? I'm not one bit interested in presenting anything you say in court. I'm assuming you are referring to a court of law. That never entered my mind. Now if you're referring to this court, right here and right now, that's a different matter. In this court, we are the judge, jury and executioners."

He didn't seem to have anything more to say. I smiled at my friend.

"Okay. With that out of the way, I want to know the name of the two men who attacked me in my office. I want no discussion, no stalling. You have two minutes to tell me their names starting right now."

It was as quiet as a tomb in that basement. I wondered what he was thinking about. I was sure that he knew the names of the two men, but he was probably thinking about what was going to happen to him if he didn't tell me.

"One minute," I said.

I could see the pillowcase was getting wet where it touched his forehead. He was really nervous.

"Thirty seconds."

"Ten Seconds," I said.

"Okay, okay. The two guys were Joe Berger and Harry Cartel."

"Now that wasn't so hard. Which one was found dead in the park?"

"Harry Cartel. Joe promised to get you for killing his friend."

"There's a contract out for me. Who put it out?" I asked.

"I don't know, but it was probably Marco, Marco Galvani."

"I doubt that. We have him in jail."

"Who is your boss?"

"God, you want me dead," he said.

"I want your boss. Frankly, I don't give a damn about you."

"What's the difference if I die here or as soon as you let me go? I'm not going to tell you."

I looked over at my friend. He was smiling. He motioned for one of his men to take the prisoner to another room. As soon as he was out of the room and the door closed, I sat down at the table with my friend.

"What do you want to do with him?"

"Can you keep him out of circulation for a while?"

"Sure."

"I know that Detective Wright has Marco Galvani hidden away. He might let me talk to him."

"What are you thinking?"

"Maybe, I can get Wright to help me get to Marco Galvani by using this guy as bait. By the way, what's this guy's name?"

"His name is Bill Taylor. He's a driver for Marco."

"Good. Keep him out of circulation for a while. I'll get back to you."

"You're not staying for breakfast?"

"No. I need to get hold of Wright as soon as I can."

"Okay."

I nodded, then turned and followed the bodyguard back to the garage. I got in my car and waited for the bodyguard to check and make sure it was clear for me to leave. As soon as it was clear, he opened the garage door, and I backed out. I immediately headed for Precinct One and Don's office.

It had been a long night for Don. He had a lot on his mind, the most pressing to him was what he should do about Officer Williams. He had evidence that she had lied to him about her interview with Mrs. Hartman, she had tried very hard to find out where Ms Hanson was located without Don knowing about it, and she had had a couple of phone calls that appeared to be less than friendly. She had also been snooping around in Don's office, and tried to get him to tell her what evidence he had in the Weatherby murder case.

Don felt he had reason enough not to trust her, and to think that she was trying to get information to pass on to someone else. He didn't know who she was trying to get the information for, but with what he knew about Tidsdale's investigation it looked like it might have been for Judge Wilkinson. He remembered seeing her talking to someone in the judge's car in the police parking lot.

He had thought last night that it might be a good idea if he put a tail on her to see if he could find out who she was talking to. The problem he had was, who could he get to tail her? If it was another policeman, she might recognize him, or he would know her well enough to tell her. Just the thought that he had a dirty cop right under his nose made him angry.

Suddenly, a thought came to him. Tidsdale was working on the same case. Maybe it would be a good idea if Tidsdale tailed her for a while. He might do it, if he thought that it would help his case, Don thought. He could do it without anybody in the police department knowing about it.

Don took a look at his watch. It was a little early to be calling Tidsdale. Don got up, took a shower, shaved, and got dressed. It wasn't long before he was ready to go to the office. He arrived at the police station at the usual time.

Just as he was pulling into the parking lot, he saw that same Cadillac, the one that belonged to Judge Wilkinson, leaving the lot. Don wondered what Judge Wilkinson was doing at the police station at this hour of the morning.

Don returned the car to the police garage, then went to his office. As he entered the squad room on his way to his office, he saw Officer Williams sitting at her desk. It looked like she was going over some papers.

She looked up and saw Don looking at her. She smiled at him, then returned to the papers on her desk.

Don wondered what she was looking at, but the fact she smiled at him set him back a bit. The last couple of times they had talked, she seemed to be upset with him. He thought that maybe something had changed, but he had no idea what it might be. Don nodded slightly, then went on into his office.

CHAPTER FIFTY

I arrived at Precinct One just a little after ten and went directly to Don's office. As I walked through the squad room, I noticed a tall, slender, blond officer walking toward a desk. I took a moment to watch her before I turned and knocked on Don's office door.

"Come in," he said.

As I walked in, I noticed that Don closed a file he had sitting on his desk in front of him. He looked like he might have been expecting someone else.

"What are you doing here?" he said as I closed the door behind me.

"I came to talk. I think we can help each other."

"How so?"

"Do you still have Marco Galvani in jail?" I asked.

"Yes. What's your interest in him?"

"Let me put it this way, I know a man who has already told me that Marco was the one who put a contract on me, at least, he thinks it was Marco."

"What's this guy's connection to Marco?"

"He's Marco's driver and possibly his bodyguard. He might also know where we can find Joe Berger," I said.

"What's your interest in Joe Berger?"

"He is the second man in the pictures I gave you, the tall one. He is also looking for me."

"I take it you still have this guy, or at least know where he is," Don said.

"Yes, I do, but I can't take you to him."

"I won't ask you anything more about him."

"How are you coming on finding your snitch?"

"Did you see the blond officer in the squad room?" Don asked.

"You mean the tall, sexy looking woman in uniform," I said with a slight chuckle.

"That's her."

"She's your snitch?" I asked.

"Yeah, and she's good at it, but she made one mistake. It's a little complicated. She interviewed a woman that lived in the same apartment building as Ms Hanson. I went and interviewed the same woman. What Officer Williams told me was nothing like what Mrs. Hartman told me."

"And I'll bet that Mrs. Hartman told you some very interesting information," I said.

"You got that right."

"What are you going to do about it?" I asked.

"I was getting ready to call you. I was wondering if you might find some time to follow her. I'd like to know who she is seeing and where she goes."

I thought about what he had to say. It was easy for me to see why he wouldn't want to put anyone on her tail from his precinct.

"I could do that for a day or so," I said.

"That might be enough."

"Okay. When does she get off?"

"About five."

"I'll be here at four-thirty and see where she goes tonight," I said.

"Good. I'll make sure she is on duty until then," he said as he wrote down her home address, the make and model of her car, and the license plate number.

"Have you gotten anything out of Marco?"

"No. He wanted to bargain with me, but he had nothing to offer me. He wants to lawyer up. I'll have to let him talk to his lawyer tomorrow."

"You might let him know that his driver is interested in talking to save his ass. He isn't, but he doesn't know that," I said with a grin. "You might want to give it a try."

"I'll think about it. If I need his driver, can you produce him?"

"Yes. And you might want to put out an APB on Joe Berger for assault and attempted murder."

"I'll to that," Don said.

"I'll talk to you later."

Don simply nodded as I stood up, then left his office. I didn't see the blond officer as I left the Precinct, but then I didn't really want to see her. I left the police parking lot and drove home. It could prove to be a long night. A little nap this afternoon might make it a little easier for me to follow the blond if it turned out to be a long night.

Don watched as Tidsdale left his office. He had decided not to ask Tidsdale where he was hiding Marco's driver, he didn't really want to know. If he did, he might have to arrest one of Tidsdale's friends that lived on the edge of the law, and that wouldn't do his relationship with Tidsdale any good. Don knew that their relationship was built on trust and a past history of helping one another.

Don picked up the phone and called dispatch to put an APB out on Joe Berger. When he was done, he sat back to think.

Don's thoughts turned to Officer Williams. He decided that it might be a good idea to find out as much as he could about Officer Williams. He went over to personnel and asked to see her file. Don knew he was taking a risk that someone might tell Williams he was looking into her background. He made it a point of not signing out her personnel record.

Don sat down at a table in the personnel office and began looking over her record. The first thing he noticed was that she had scored very high on the test to get into the police academy. She also had a degree in criminology from a local college.

On further examination of her work history, he found that she had worked in the criminal court system as an assistant to Judge Wilkinson for four years before taking the police exam.

Don remembered seeing her talking to someone in Judge Wilkinson's car. Since it was such a nice car, he assumed that the judge was in the car. He knew that some assistants get very close to their bosses. He wondered what kind of a relationship Officer Williams might have with the judge. Don also knew that she had worked with other judges because of her ability to sign.

When Don finished examining her personnel record, he returned to his own office. The only thing he found out was that she probably worked, at least to some extent, with all the judges in the criminal court system. He had no idea what that meant to him, but if there was corruption in the criminal court system, she might know something about it.

For now, Don was going to just keep an eye on her with the help of Tidsdale. He had to know if she was dirty or not. Until he knew one way or the other, he would continue to keep all evidence from her.

There was nothing Don could do now to get the answers he wanted. A quick look at his watch told him it was time to call it a day. He would be interested in what Tidsdale found out after following her but that would have to wait until tomorrow. Don left the office and went home.

CHAPTER FIFTY-ONE

It was three-thirty in the afternoon when I woke from my nap. I quickly made some coffee and filled my thermos, then made a sandwich. As soon as I was ready, I headed for the Precinct One police station where I was to begin following Officer Williams. I waited outside the precinct almost a block away. From my position I could see the parking lot and the entrance that was used by the police officers who were leaving or going to work. I knew what kind of car Officer Williams drove, and I could see it from where I was parked.

I tipped back in my car seat so it would be hard for anyone to see me. The last thing I wanted was to have some policeman come up to see what I was doing and give my position away.

Time passed slowly. For the first half hour or so, there were very few officers coming or leaving. A glance at my watch showed that it would not be much longer before the routine shift change took place.

After a while, there was a lot of activity. Officers were coming to work. It wasn't long and other officers were leaving the building. The flow of officers leaving seemed to be slowing when I saw Officer Williams walk out of the building, get in her car and leave the parking lot.

As soon as she pulled out of the parking lot and turned down the street, I pulled away from the curb and began following her. I had followed her for some distance before she drove into an apartment building's parking lot. It was the same address that Don had given me as her home address.

I parked at the curb behind some bushes that would make it hard to see my car. I watched her as she went into the apartment building. There was nothing for me to do but wait and watch.

It was about an hour later when I saw a dark blue Cadillac enter the parking lot and stop in front of the entrance to the building. Within a couple of minutes, Officer Williams came out of the building and got into the Cadillac. Officer Williams was dressed up as if she was going to a party, or to a fine restaurant.

As soon as the Cadillac pulled out onto the street, I began following it. I followed the car to a rather expensive restaurant. Judge Wilkinson and Williams went into the restaurant. It was close to two hours before they came out and left the parking lot.

I continued to follow them to Cherry Creek where the judge pulled into the drive and stopped in front of a very nice, and rather large home, which I knew to be his home. Judge Wilkinson got out of the car, then walked around to the passenger's side and opened the door for Officer Williams. She wrapped her arm around behind him and he slipped his arm around her as they walked up to the front door. Judge Wilkinson unlocked the door, then they went inside, closing the door behind them. I had a feeling that it was going to be a very long night.

I had been there about an hour and a half when a patrol car rolled by me. I had seen it coming and was able to duck down as it drove by. There was a good chance that the patrol car would make another pass by the house to check on my car. It was time for me to leave. The last thing I wanted was to get caught nosing around outside Judge Wilkinson's house, besides it didn't look like they were going to be leaving anytime soon. I left after having made the decision to make a pass by the house in a couple of hours.

* * * *

It was dark when I returned to Cherry Creek about three hours later. The Cadillac was still parked in front of the house in the very same spot it had been when I left the area, and the house was dark. I got the impression that Officer Williams was spending the night with the judge.

Just as I was about to leave, I noticed a black Lincoln turn into the drive and pull up in front of the house. Two men got out of the car, went up to the front door and walked into the house without a problem. I had no idea what was going on, but for two big guys to walk into the house at this hour without so much as waiting for someone to come to the door, made me wonder what was going on. I left my car and found a place in some shrubbery where I could not be seen by anyone in the house or by a patrol car going by. I decided to watch and see what happened next.

I no more than settled in when a light came on in a second story window. My best guess was it was the window in one of the bedrooms. With the curtains covering the window, I couldn't see what was going on. Unable to hear anything, I just watched the house.

Don arrived at the office earlier than usual. He was anxious to find out what Tidsdale might have discovered. He didn't like the idea that one of the officers in his division might be dirty. With nothing to do but wait, Don turned to the reports that he received from Mel.

Don quickly found out that it was hard for him to concentrate on the reports in front of him. Even though he was having difficulty concentrating, something in the back of his mind grabbed his attention. He remembered that he had seen Judge Wilkinson's car in the police parking lot a couple of days ago, and whoever was in the car was talking to Officer Williams. It was only fair to assume that it was Judge Wilkinson in the car.

Don tipped back in his chair and closed his eyes while he thought about Judge Wilkinson and Officer Williams. The judge was a nice looking older man. He seemed to have money. He dressed well, drove a very nice car, and had a very likeable personality.

Officer Williams was a very nice looking woman. In fact, some would consider her to be sexy. She carried herself well, and when not in uniform dressed very nicely. Nothing about her clothes was cheap. Even in uniform, she turned the head of many a man.

When Don began to put his thoughts of Officer Williams and Judge Wilkinson together, along with the fact that they had worked together for several years, he was beginning to form a picture of the two of them in his mind. He began to think that there might be something between them, something more than a working relationship.

It occurred to him that with Tidsdale following Officer Williams, he might be able to confirm what he suspected. He knew that Tidsdale was investigating the judges in the *criminal court system. If Officer Williams was involved with Judge Wilkinson, and if he was dirty, then there was a chance that she was dirty, too. That thought didn't set well with Don.*

CHAPTER FIFTY-TWO

I don't know how long I was hiding in the bushes, but the dark sky was starting to get a little lighter. It was still dark, but it would not be long before it would be light enough to make out the features of individuals. I was beginning to think that it might be time for me to get out of there before it got light enough for someone to see me.

Just as I was getting ready to move, I noticed some movement at the front door of the house. The door suddenly opened and the two big guys that had gone into the house in the wee hours of the morning were coming out. As soon as they were outside, I could see that they had Officer Williams between them. They appeared to be supporting her, and she didn't look like she could stand up very straight. Her hair was a mess and she was not wearing the same clothes she had on last night. Although it was hard to tell in the dim light of morning, I got the impression that she might have been worked over, or possibly drugged.

I glanced back at the door, but didn't see the judge. I wondered if they had worked him over as well, or did he have her worked over for some reason.

The thugs pushed Officer Williams into the back of the car. One of the guys got in the back while the other one got in behind the wheel. I pulled back a bit as they drove down the driveway. As soon as they started down the street, I ran to my car and began following them.

At first, I had no idea where they were going, but it didn't take long before I had it figured out. If they continued on the way they were going, it would not be long before they would be at Officer Williams's apartment.

Sure enough, they pulled into her apartment building's parking lot and drove up to the door. It was still pretty early in the morning and there was no activity in the parking lot.

The car stopped in front of the entrance to the apartment building. Both of the men got out of the car, then helped Officer Williams out. They took her into the building. It was only a few minutes later when they returned to the car and drove away.

I waited until I was sure that they were gone before I drove into the parking lot. I parked my car, then went into the building. It only took a couple of seconds to find out which apartment she lived in, and only another minute to get to her front door. I reached for the doorknob and slowly turned it. The door wasn't locked. I slowly pushed the door open and peeked inside. I could not see anyone, but thought I could hear someone sobbing. I followed the sound to a bedroom.

I found Officer Williams lying on her side and curled up in the fetal position on her bed. She had her arms over her stomach, clutching herself as if her stomach hurt. Her back was to me, but it was clear that she had been worked over pretty good.

I went up to her, leaned down and touched her shoulder. My touch startled her causing her to call out and say, "Please don't hurt me."

"I'm not here to hurt you," I said softly.

Sharon turned her head and looked at me. She had the look of someone who was scared to death, and her makeup was a mess from crying. She had a cut on her lower lip, a bruise on her left cheek, an apparent broken nose and some blood on her face. The way she was holding herself there was little doubt that she had been beaten pretty badly. The way she was breathing with short painful breaths was a good sign that she might have a few broken ribs.

"I think you need a doctor," I said.

"Get out," she said, but it was painful for her to talk.

"I'm going to call for an ambulance."

"No," she said painfully.

"Fine," I said. "I'll just call Detective Wright and see what he as to say,"

"Please don't - - call him," she begged.

"Do you really think you can keep this from him?"

"I have - - a couple - - of days off," she said as she cringed with pain.

"Would you rather talk to me?"

She just looked at me for a couple of minutes, before she started to cry again. I reached over to the bedside table, picked up the phone and called for an ambulance. I then called Don at his office. I told him about what was going on and that I would meet him at the hospital later and fill him in.

I waited until the ambulance arrived then left for the hospital with Officer Williams on a gurney. As soon as they were gone, I left her apartment for Judge Wilkinson's home in Cherry Creek.

Don hung up the phone and immediately headed for the hospital. When he arrived, he found Office Williams in the receiving ward. Since she was in a treatment room, he was unable to talk to her, but the ambulance attendant was still there. He pulled the attendant to one side, identified himself, then started to question him.

"What's her condition?" Don asked.

"She probably has a few broken ribs, which is the most serious problem for her at the moment. She also has a cut lip, and several bruises, mostly on her abdomen with a couple on her face."

"Did she tell you how she got them?"

"No, sir. She didn't want to talk to us."

"Did she identify herself to you?" Don asked.

"No. We didn't know she was a police officer until one of the nurses recognized her. She didn't say a word to us. She wouldn't give us any of her medical history. She wouldn't even tell us where she hurt, but it wasn't very hard to figure it out."

"Thanks," Don said.

There was nothing Don could do until the doctors were finished with her immediate treatment. She would probably have to have some x-rays to see if she had broken ribs.

Don stopped at the nurse's station and identified himself. He then requested that they let him know as soon as she was able to talk to him, whether she wanted to talk to him or not. He then took a seat where he could keep an eye on the door to the treatment room where she was located. He didn't want anyone to get to her before he could talk to her.

As he waited, he wondered what Tidsdale was doing. He was a little surprised that he had not come to the hospital.

CHAPTER FIFTY-THREE

Since I had not seen Judge Wilkinson at the time the thugs had taken Officer Williams from the house, I had to wonder if he might have been killed just like Judge Weatherby, and for the same reason. There was only one way to find out, and that was to go to Wilkinson's home and see what I might find there. I was hoping that I wouldn't find him dead.

I arrived at Judge Wilkinson's home in Cherry Creek just shortly after eight. As I pulled up to the driveway, I didn't see any police cars, or any other cars except Wilkinson's Cadillac. I turned into the drive and drove up to the house, parking behind Wilkinson's car.

As I got out of my car, I looked around. I didn't see anything that I thought should concern me. I walked up to the front door and found it unlocked. Not knowing what I could expect, I drew my gun and held it down at my side as I pushed the door open. I stepped inside, then closed the door behind me while I looked around.

The foyer was fairly large and had a light colored tile floor. I noticed that there were a few drops of blood on the floor. From what I saw of Officer Williams, the blood could have been from her broken nose.

Since it looked like Williams and Wilkinson had spent the night together, and neither of them had opened the door for the two thugs, there was a good chance that all the action took place upstairs in the bedroom, assuming they had slept together. I went up the spiral staircase to the second floor. I noticed that there were a few drops of blood on the stairs.

The droplets of blood led me to a door I found closed. I stood off to the side, turned the knob then slowly pushed the door open. When it was open enough to see inside the room, I could see a king sized bed that looked like there had been a wrestling match on it, a bloody wrestling match.

I entered the bedroom and began to look around. I hadn't been in the room for more than a few seconds when I heard what sounded like a soft moan as if someone was in pain. After going around to the far side of the bed, I found Wilkinson lying on the floor. He had been beaten pretty severely. There was blood all over the place.

"John, can you hear me?" I asked as I knelt down beside him.

When I got no response, I reached out and placed two fingers on the side of his neck. He seemed to have a pretty good pulse, but he was still unresponsive. I placed a call to Don on my cell phone to his cell phone. It rang only a couple of times before it was answered.

"Yeah."

"Tidsdale here. I'm at Judge Wilkinson's home in Cherry Creek. It looks like someone worked him over pretty good. He's alive, but unresponsive. You might want to get an ambulance over here as quickly as possible."

"I'll call in for one. What's the situation there?"

"I'll tell you later. I think you should stay with Officer Williams. I'll hang around here until Wilkinson is picked up. I'll try to stay with him."

"Okay. If he comes around, see what you can get out of him."

"Will do. Talk to you later," I said then hung up.

I sat on the floor next to Wilkinson and just looked at him for a moment before I reached out and touched him on the cheek. He responded.

"John, can you hear me?"

"Yeah, - - who are you?"

"I'm Frank Tidsdale, a private investigator."

"I've - - -heard - - - of you." he said, his pain showing in his speech and on his face.

"I've called for an ambulance."

"I doubt - - I will - - make it," he said as he gasped for breath.

"Is there anything you want to tell me?"

"Is - - Sharon - - okay?"

"I don't know, but she is in the hospital. From the last I saw of her, I think she will pull through."

"Good. I'll - - give you - - a dying - - declaration," he said, then stopped to catch his breath. "I was - - beaten by a - - couple of - - Marco Galvani - - thugs. I've been - - helping to - - keep them out of jail."

Wilkinson coughed. From the look on his face, it was very painful. I also noticed that there was some blood coming out of his mouth. There was little doubt in my mind that he had some internal injuries.

"Who else is in involved?" I asked.

"He - - had - - Weatherby - - killed. He was - - afraid - - he would - - talk if he was - - questioned."

"Marco had Weatherby killed?" I asked.

I took down what he said on a small pad I carried in my jacket so I would have a written record of what I was told.

"Yes. Dieter, Judge - - Smith, and - - Sharon were all involved."

"Was anyone else involved?"

"There's - - a little book - - in my chamber - - behind a picture - - of the court room. Find it," he struggled to say.

"Was Colton involved?

"No. - - Colton - - didn't - - know anythi- - - -."

He stopped talking, looked up at me, then closed his eyes and exhaled a long slow breath. He was gone. He had no more than died when I heard the ambulance. He had no need for an ambulance now.

I heard the EMTs coming into the house.

"Up here," I called out as I moved over to a chair in the corner and sat down.

I watched as the EMTs came into the room. They looked at me, and I pointed to the body on the floor.

"Just check and make sure he is dead. If he is, do not move him. You'll want to standby until the police get here," I said.

They checked the judge to make sure he was dead.

"He's dead," one of the EMTs said as he looked at me.

I heard the sound of a black-and-white as it was coming toward the judge's home. It wasn't long before two uniformed officers came into the bedroom.

"Don't touch anything," I said. "Secure the area and make sure no one comes in this house."

"Yes, sir."

"I'll call Detective Don Wright." I said as I picked up my phone.

Don was in the waiting room watching the door to the treatment room where Officer Williams had been taken. Time was going by slowly. He watched as one member of the medical staff after another went in and out of the room. He had no idea what her condition might be.

He started to put together a list of questions in his pocket notebook that he wanted to ask her. He wasn't sure if he would be taking a dying declaration or not, as no one would tell him her condition.

It was getting on close to mid-morning when the doctor came out of the treatment room. Don could not tell by the expression on his face what kind of news he brought.

"How's she doing, Doc?" Don asked.

"She will live, but it will be a long time before she can return to work. She has several broken ribs, a cracked jaw, her cheek bone is broken, her nose is broken, and she had a number of bruises on her abdomen. Whoever worked her over did a good job on her. She looks like she was used as a punching bag," the doctor explained.

"Is she able to talk to me?"

"I would think so, but it might be a little hard to understand her. She is pretty well out of it. She may not make much sense. It would probably be a waste of your time. She should be able to talk to you in the morning."

"I'm going to put a guard on her."

"I would think that would be a good idea. I'll make sure that she is moved to ICU. You can put a policeman just outside the door."

"Thanks, Doc. I'll call for one right now," Don said as he reached for his phone.

Don placed a call to the Watch Captain and requested a guard to be placed outside ICU. Don explained that Officer

Williams might have information on the murder of Judge Weatherby. He agreed.

After Don finished with his call to the Watch Captain, he pulled up a chair to wait for the guard to show up.

CHAPTER FIFTY-FOUR

I placed a call to Don, I knew he was at the hospital. The phone rang only twice before it was answered.

"Yeah."

"Tidsdale here. I'm still at Judge Wilkinson's home. He died before the ambulance could get here."

"Damn!"

"Not so fast. He came around long enough that I got at least a partial dying declaration."

"Is it going to help any?"

"Yes. He named names of a couple of others who he claims are involved in corruption in the criminal court."

"So there is corruption in the criminal court?"

"That's what he said."

"He mentioned Smith, Dieter, and Sharon as being involved in it. I have a couple of bits of information that might help show Dieter was a major player. The one thing I think you should do is arrest Smith and Dieter before they have a chance to find out that Wilkinson is dead. They find that out, they may try to run."

"I'll get on it."

"You might want to get a homicide detective over here along with a forensic team. I'll have the police wait here until they get here."

"Okay. Where are you going?"

"I have a little something to do then I'll meet you at your office."

"Okay," Don said then hung up.

I told the policemen to wait for a detective and the forensic team, and to keep everyone else out. I then left the judge's home and headed downtown to the courthouse.

Don placed a call to Sergeant Walker.

"Walker, I want you to call AG Greene. Don't talk to anyone else, that's important. Tell Greene to issue arrest warrants on James Dieter, Sharon Williams, and Judge Smith. Have him meet you at the courthouse. After you call him, go to the courthouse and detain them until he gets there with the warrants."

"Okay. If I arrest them, where do you want me to take them?"

"You might as well take them to your precinct. We have proof that Marco is involved in the murder of Judge Weatherby and Judge Wilkinson.

"I didn't know Wilkinson was dead." Walker said.

"According to Tidsdale, he died just a few minutes ago, but he talked first," Don said. "Get on it before they find out Wilkinson is dead."

"I'm on it," Walker said then hung up.

Don continued to wait for a guard to protect Sharon Williams. It wasn't very long before a uniformed officer showed up.

"You are here to do two things," Don told the officer. "You are here to protect Officer Williams from anyone who might want to kill her. You are also here to make damn sure she stays here. She is under arrest. Do you understand?"

"Yes, sir."

"It's your ass if anything happens to her,"

"Yes, sir," the officer said.

Don turned and left the hospital. As he was about to get into his car, his phone began to ring. He quickly answered it.

"Don Wright."

"*Don, Walker here. We have the warrants for the three you mentioned, but Dieter isn't here.*"

"*Any idea where he might have gone?*"

"*The office secretary said he was here a moment ago, but he just disappeared.*"

"*Close off the building and keep looking for him. I'll be there shortly.*"

Don hung up and got in his car. He immediately headed for the courthouse.

CHAPTER FIFTY- FIVE

When I arrived downtown, I found several police cars with flashing lights in front of the courthouse. I didn't want to try to go barging in. It was at that moment, I remembered the secret entrances to the judges' chambers.

I parked in the street on the back side of the courthouse, then hurried to the back of the courthouse. I entered the backdoor that would take me to the basement. I wanted to get to Judge Wilkinson's chamber before the police were swarming all over it. I wanted to make sure that I got to the book Wilkinson had told me about before anyone else could find it.

I knew how to get to Judge Weatherby's chamber by going through the secret passages. I wasn't sure which one of the doors would lead to Judge Wilkinson's chamber. When I got to the door that would take me into Weatherby's chamber, I stopped and looked at the other doors. Since none of them had names on them, I would be guessing. I tried to think of where Wilkinson's chamber might be. I figured it might be close to Weatherby's, which would put it the next door down the hall.

I knew it was a guess, but it was the best I could come up with. I went to the next door, put my hand on the knob and turned it very slowly. I pushed the door open very slowly and peeked around it. There was no one in the office. I could see the desk, and I could see the nameplate. The nameplate made it clear that I had picked the right office.

I stepped into the room and looked around. It only took a couple of seconds to find the picture of the courtroom. I went directly to the picture and took it off the wall.

Tucked neatly behind the picture was a small dark brown book. It was at that moment I heard the sounds of someone in the outer office.

I slipped the book into my pocket, quickly hung the picture back on the wall, then scrambled to the secret door. I ducked into the hallway, closing the secret door behind me as quickly and quietly as possible. I then moved down the hall and ducked into the shadows of a shallow alcove to hide.

It wasn't but a couple of minutes before I heard the secret door open. I waited in the hope of seeing who was using the secret passages to get out of Wilkinson's chamber. I drew my gun, just in case. With policemen all over the building, I was pretty sure that Don was starting to arrest people.

I could hear someone move into the passage. The figure of a thin man was about all I could make out in the darkness. He moved quietly with the hope that no one would hear him.

As he moved by me, I could see him well enough to know that it was Dieter. Once he had gone by me, I stepped out into the passageway.

"Going somewhere, Mr. Dieter?" I asked.

He froze in his tracks.

"Don't do anything that will make me put a very large whole in you. I have a gun, and I will use it to stop you," I said.

"Well, if it isn't Mr. Tidsdale," he said without turning around.

"Yes it is, and you are under arrest."

"You can't arrest me, you're not even a cop," he said.

"This gun says I can. Now turn around, put your hands on top of your head, and don't do anything stupid."

Dieter turned around and put his hands on top of his head. I started marching him back the way he had come. Just as he entered back into Judge Wilkinson's chamber, he made a sudden move. He slammed the door into the chamber into me. The sudden pain of the door hitting my already injured arm caused me to cringe. I lost my balance and dropped to me knees. Dieter took advantage of the situation and began to run toward the door.

"Halt or I'll shoot," I called out.

Dieter chose to stop. He turned around and looked at me. I guess he thought that I wouldn't shoot since I was on my knees, and probably looked like I was in pain. Not having my gun pointed directly at him might have had something to do with his decision to run.

He turned back around then reached for the door. I pulled my gun up and pulled the trigger. My gun went off and the slug hit him in his right thigh, causing him to go crashing to the floor in pain.

It was only a matter of seconds before Don and three of his fellow police officers came charging into the room with guns in their hands. Don looked at the man lying on the floor close to the door, then looked at me.

"I take it this is Mr. Dieter," Don said.

"Yes," I said while holding my injured shoulder.

"You hurt?" Don asked.

"I think so."

"You need an ambulance?"

"No, but I could use a ride to the hospital to get my shoulder checked."

"You got it."

One of the officers helped me to his car, then took me to the hospital. When I arrived at the hospital, Attorney General Robert Greene was waiting to talk to me. I was taken into a treatment room to wait for a doctor to come and check my shoulder. I sat down on the treatment table while Greene sat down on a stool.

"Don called me and told me that you might have reinjured your shoulder, so I came here to see you. Don also told me that we got all those working in the criminal court system who were involved in the corruption. It seems that Dieter can't talk enough. It turns out that Marco Galvani was in fact the headman."

"I'm glad you got them all."

"Dieter even told us who the snitch is in my office. He has been arrested and taken to jail."

"I have something that I think you might like. It could help in your prosecution of those involved," I said as I took the little brown book out of my pocket.

Greene took the book and began thumbing through it. I could see by the look on his face that he was very pleased.

"This should come in very handy during the trial. It tells me everyone involved, what they did, and what they got paid. Very nice work, Frank," Greene said with a big grin.

"I'm glad you like it, but I think I'll take a few days off to heal up a bit."

Just then Greene's phone rang. He answered it, then listened.

"Thanks, I'm sure Frank will be glad to hear that," he said then hung up.

"That was Don. Joe Berger was just arrested in Thorton."

"Great. Now I know I will take a few days off.

"Let me know if I owe you anything. Send me a complete report as soon as you can," Greene said.

"I'll get my notes together and get the report to you in a couple of days," I said.

"That will be fine. It looks like someone is here to check you out," Greene said as Marilyn Norton came into the treatment room.

"I'll get out of here," Greene said as he acknowledged Nurse Norton's presence with a slight nod.

Greene turned and left the treatment room.

"Nice to see you again," I said.

"I hope this isn't going to be the only way I see you. You did say you were going to call me at home," she said.

"Yes, I did. My investigation is now finished and I have some free time. How would you like to go out for dinner tomorrow?"

"Do you think you will be ready to go out for dinner?"

"Yes, but I'm open to suggestions."

"Why don't you come over to my place tomorrow and I'll fix you dinner?"

"What time."

"About six. I have the weekend off."

"That would be nice," I said with a smile.

I watched her as she checked my shoulder and put a new dressing on it. When she was done, she smiled.

"You can go now. I'll see you at six at my place tomorrow," she said after she gave me her address.

"I'll be there," I said then left the hospital and got a cab.

I had the cabby take me to where I had left my car. After paying the cabby, I got in my car and drove home.

My shoulder was hurting when I arrived home. I took one of the pain pills, then went right to bed. It wasn't very long before I was sound asleep.

.